A Practical Potions Mystery

Practical Potions
and
Premeditated Murder

Wren Jones

WOOPS

To the giants who lifted us up
so that we could dream bigger.

May we one day return the favor.

ONE

Inquire Within for Daily Offerings

"THIS IS GETTING DEPRESSING," Sella said. She stared out the large bay window of her shop, but her gaze was empty. It was raining, and the view was mostly obscured by water droplets and fog that clung to the edges of the glass. She could make out a few figures – people busy in the morning on their way to work or the market.

"I think the sign will help," said the gray tabby cat at her side. He padded at the blue cushioned bench and curled peacefully as if he really believed it. His ear flicked, then his tail: an obvious clue that he was actually as annoyed as she. "People didn't know before that you were *certified*." He closed his eyes. "They might have thought you'd accidentally poison them."

Sella leaned forward and squinted. The large sign taped to the window read 'Certified Kitchen Witch: Inquire Within for Daily Offerings.' The sign was Beejee's idea. Of course the cat thought it would help.

It hadn't.

Sella squinted into the fog and rain as a shadow

approached the door. She stood tall, adjusting her face to a wide smile just as the bell above the shop door chimed. Beejee stood at attention as a tall, broad man entered. He had to duck through the opening so his ram's horns wouldn't bump the upper door frame. He smiled at them, though it was difficult to discern with the bushy auburn beard covering most of his face.

"Hazen, good morning!" Sella's genuine smile broke her customer-facing mask and gestured for him to come in. Relief spread through her shoulders as she moved through the shop, past the wall of wooden cubbies filled with glistening jars of premade potions and lavender honey. While she moved, little flames lit overhead at her unspoken command, illuminating the shop with a warm, welcoming glow.

"The usual?" She ducked below the counter to grab her pestle, mortar, and metal coffee maker. Another quick flick of her wrist, and calm music began to play. She popped up and placed all the ingredients and tools in a neat row.

"Please," Hazen said. He stepped deeper into the shop and gave Beejee a small nod. "Add a splash of patience, if you don't mind."

Sella dipped the tablespoon into the jar of coffee grounds. "May I ask?" She raised her brow at him.

Hazen shrugged. "My new bookkeeper is keeping me busy. Apparently, I've been doing my files all wrong, and she's reorganizing the whole system."

Sella chuckled. She poured the grounds into the metal container and lit the fire beneath with her finger. "That would be frustrating for a stubborn old man like you." She retreated under the counter again to pull premade spell jars labeled 'Keep it Together,' a focus blend with hints of chestnut, and 'Don't Strangle People,' her patience blend with rich caramel notes. She added scoops of each to the coffee grounds and mixed it with a tiny whisk. Then she closed her eyes, hands hovering over the warm steam rising from the metal pot. Her fingers tingled with magic — and as an afterthought, she added a little extra happiness to his cup today.

Beejee leapt onto the counter. "Can we get her info? Your receipts in a box would appall anyone with business sense."

All Hazen heard was meows. He cocked his head at the cat. "Talkative today, huh?"

Sella opened her eyes and flicked near Beejee's ear playfully. He swatted her hand. "He thinks I'm bad at business."

Hazen's eyes surveyed the shop. He looked from the spell jars on the wall, most of them gathering dust, to the little fires overhead. "Well…" he said cautiously. "You don't exactly have the thriving clientele your mother did."

"We've only been back less than a year." Sella rolled her eyes. She poured Hazen's cup, an extra large yellow ceramic mug, and slid it across the counter. The space between them filled with silver steam, tinged with the scent of rainy earth and nutty, sweet caramel. "And small towns are small towns. It'll take time for people to trust me after I left. I've changed a lot."

Hazen took a sip of the dark liquid. He raised the glass to her, a half grin sliding across his face with appreciation, and took another long drink before leaning back a little, letting the magic take hold slowly. "Well, you did come back with new spells and ingredients that sounded a little suspect." He fished out a few coins from his pocket. "Some of us 'stubborn old men' are stuck in our ways."

He set the gold coins on the counter and smiled at her. "My brain is still processing your bloodbane lecture. Something about it being bad for the gut?" He went on before she could interject, "And frankly, I'm still not sold on wolfseye not being an actual wolf's eye. It *looks* an awful lot like a wolf's eye."

"Bloodbane causes headaches. Wolfseye is a far superior substitute," Sella said urgently, as if she would have to explain it all over again.

Hazen raised his hands and laughed. "I know, I know. I saw the error of my ways, but it took me a while. Your mother opened this shop decades ago… kept the same spells, the same recipes… You come back from traveling about and start serving coffee and changing things up?"

"We still sell honey." Sella leaned on the counter.

"Ah yes, the retirement honey," Beejee mumbled.

"All I'm saying is, between your return home, and now my new foreign bookkeeper coming in here and changing everything I've been doing for years… It's a lot." Hazen eyed Sella with a raised brow. "You'd actually like Cali a lot. She loves numbers the way you love your potions. Maybe talk to her next time she's in here. I know she comes in on occasion." His tone made Sella bristle a little. He was being a little too obvious.

Beejee was having none of it. "We don't need new friends. And you certainly don't need a—"

"Keep the change, little guy." Hazen unwittingly cut him off. He tapped the counter and pushed the coins closer to Beejee.

Beejee half hissed, half purred at him.

The bell above the door rang again. "And we have Aadel," Sella pushed herself up from the counter and smiled at the woman. "Good morning, Aadel!"

"Oh, honey," the older woman said. "It's a dreadful day out there. Dreadful. Lohrna is checking on the bees, but should be in soon." She shook out her coat on the entryway. Droplets of rain splattered across the dark floor, where they slid into the thick cracks of the old wood. She ran her hands through wild gray hair. Some of it tangled in her antlers, but she didn't seem to notice. "Oh, hello, Hazen!" Her sharp eyes scanned him. "Good to see you in here so early."

"My new bookkeeper is keeping me busy." He shrugged.

"The human girl?" Aadel asked.

Hazen nodded. "She's a good kid. From Tollintal. Kind of an interesting background on that one… I can't quite figure her out." His voice drifted off, as if lost in a dream for a moment.

"Imagine – *you* – letting a human girl boss you about. I promise I won't tell anyone about it; you'd never hear the end of it."

Sella's eyes drifted from Hazen to Aadel. Sella knew she'd tell everyone. Immediately. As soon as they left the shop.

Aadel squeezed his arm lightly as she approached the counter, unaware of Hazen's odd moment. "Our sweet Sella…" she said. "A strong cuppa, if you don't mind, please. And a scone…" She sniffed the air. "Is that blueberry I smell?"

Sella's face brightened. It was rare enough that people bought her potions. Almost no one bought her baked goods, but she was up before dawn everyday making them anyway. She tucked a chunk of choppy black hair behind her pointed ear. Whatever had changed Aadel's mind to make her crave one now, Sella would have to try to replicate in the future. She tried to hide her excitement by blurting out, "I made them fresh early this morning."

"Infused with anything special?" Aadel asked.

"A little cinnamon," Sella said. "And courage."

"Courage!" Aadel slapped the counter with both hands.

Beejee yelped at the sudden sound. He scrambled away and up the narrow stairs behind the counter.

Aadel didn't seem to notice. She ushered Sella along. "Now some courage, I could use! One scone please."

Sella followed Beejee toward the stairs. "Coming right down," she told Aadel. "Hazen? You overpaid for the coffee anyway. No charge."

"I have an overabundance of courage!" He patted his soft stomach beneath the plain tunic. "Appreciate it, though."

Sella laughed and ascended the stairs after her familiar. It only took a moment to retrieve the trayful of blueberry scones, still warm with magic, from her cozy kitchen. Halfway down the stairs, she caught her name in a hushed tone.

She should have known Aadel would be busy gossiping. She paused so she could hear whatever the latest town drama was this time.

"Well," Aadel's voice went on, "it wasn't really her fault. You have to admit, everyone drove her out after… you know. *The Incident*."

Sella hung her head. Even years later, no one would let it go. Everything in her body felt heavy at the mention.

'The Incident' referred to a failed potion that Sella made decades ago, before she decided it was time to move to the bigger cities and learn to better her magic properly. It wasn't that big of a deal. It shouldn't even have a name, but her mother calling it "The Incident" had caught on. Sella personally thought everyone blew it out of proportion.

The spots on people's skin went away in a few days. And it wasn't like they itched or anything. They were just spots. Harmless, really.

Hazen spoke quickly. "All I'm saying is she needs a better marketing plan. Coming back after being gone for so long *and* with new potions?" There was a pause, and Sella took another step down. "How many people come in here for her coffee and pastries?"

"Lohrna," Aadel said without missing a beat.

"Besides your daughter."

If this conversation went on any longer, Beejee would overhear. He'd be insufferable if he knew Hazen agreed that her marketing was garbage. She stepped down the rest of the stairs with her boots thumping loudly.

"Blueberry scones!" she said cheerily, trying to hide the embarrassment and shame that crawled across her skin. "Hazen, I brought you a few to bring to the tavern. Maybe it'll help you endear yourself to your bookkeeper?" She set the tray on the counter and pushed them closer to the two. "You could even sample a few out to your morning drinkers?"

Hazen finished his coffee with one big gulp. He took a few scones in his large hands and smiled. "Thanks, Sella. I sure will." He gave Aadel a quick nod on his way out — and maybe it was Sella's imagination, but she swore their shared expressions were ones of pity.

HOURS PASSED and no one else entered the shop. Sella told herself it was the rain, which had steadily worsened throughout the day. Honestly, though, that was a terrible excuse. Hazen was nothing if not honest. People still didn't trust her completely. Her new recipes were subtly different enough, and no one wanted to risk another incident.

"Maybe it's time to move again," Sella mumbled. She felt as cold and low as the rain sliding down the window panes. The part of her that longed for more – to learn, to grow, to change – was growing pale.

"We can't," Beejee said with his usual brashness. "You wasted all our money moving back here, remember? Anyway, at least we have each other. We can be miserable together in this tiny town until we both die from boredom."

Sella side eyed him. "That seems a little extreme."

"It's not just The Incident that keeps people away, you know," Beejee turned from Sella to face the large bay window.

"We don't need to talk about that." Sella closed the drawer she had been rummaging through with a swift burst.

Beejee barely reacted to the sound. "In all our travels, do you remember anyone on good terms with an elemental witch? You have always been too close to fire. You shouldn't use it as much here. It makes people wary."

Sella's heart beat faster. She held the drawer's brass knob tight and felt it warm within her grasp. She took a deep breath in, counting as she did. But she was interrupted by a voice, a whisper in her mind. *They're afraid you'll burn them. Like you burned your mother.*

"I'm going to make more scones." Sella released the handle like it was a snake. It glowed red, and she pretended not to notice. Her heels clicked on the wood floor as she stormed behind the counter and up the stairs.

TWO

Rocks, Of Course

Several hours passed before the bell above the door chimed again. Wind, rain, and a tall woman blew into the shop.

Beejee scattered, leaving claw punctures in the yellow pillow he was lying on, but Sella remained still. A small smile crept across her face as the woman shook off rain from her coat and huffed loudly.

"Hello, Lohrna," Sella said as she crossed the shop to close the door behind her friend.

"Hello to you," Lohrna said, her voice a little strained. She pulled off her wide-brim hat, revealing thin dark horns that looped delicately around her ears and up into her hair. She let down a mess of black curls and fluffed them with her fingers, trying to reshape them as best she could. She was already mid-sentence as she handed Sella a heavy bag. "-- Replaced the patching on the roofs, should be good to keep the little bees dry. Good thing you have me around or they'd fly right out of here. Where's Beejee?"

"Took off when he heard Hurricane Lohrna approach."

Sella heaved the bag onto the bay window bench. "What's in here?"

Lohrna shrugged off her coat and threw it at the long counter on the far wall. She missed and it landed with a wet thud on the floor. She sighed, and went to go pick it up… but Sella managed to snatch it first.

Lohrna rolled her eyes, then continued: "Rocks, of course."

"Of course." Sella smiled.

Lohrna opened her bag and pulled out a circular, pewter rock to show Sella. "See? I'll bet there's something shiny in there!"

"Mhm," Sella glanced at the rock and stacked her friend's coat and hat on the counter.

Lohrna was Sella's childhood friend and the one person in town who never once so much as side-eyed her for being a witch who, as Beejee pointedly said, used fire a little too much. They met at the beach one day. Lohrna approached her, loudly declared that she wished *she* could start fires with her mind, and then unilaterally decided they were now friends.

Lohrna followed a reluctant Sella home, then told Sella's mother that she was a good friend and was staying for dinner. With her, she had brought a rock which she bestowed upon the witches as payment. "I read in a book that it could have gems inside it," Lohrna had said proudly. "You'll have to crack it open to be sure, though."

The gesture charmed Sella and her mother. And luckily, Lohrna's own mother, Aadel, found the shy and odd little Sella just as endearing, though Sella could never figure out why. From then on, their friendship was solidified.

Watching Lohrna now, Sella still felt warm with satisfaction that her time away hadn't diminished their friendship.

Beejee wasn't so pleased, but he had always been crotchety about Lohrna anyway.

"Thank you for taking care of the bees." Sella changed the subject away from the rocks. As much as she loved her friend's passion, Sella wasn't in the mood for another conversation about geodes. Her friend was prone to tangents and Sella's mental energy had already been spent trying to formulate an escape plan from this town. "Coffee?" Sella asked.

"With a little something to keep my momentum, please," Lohrna said as she set the rock back into her bag.

"More than caffeine, got it." Sella ducked behind the front counter. With smooth confidence, she pulled the silver kettle from the shelf below, mixed water and grounds, and a snap of her fingers lit a tea light beneath it. She ducked below the counter again, scanning the shelf for the right mixture. Colorful glass jars, each labeled with her neatly printed handwriting, stared back at her. A thought crossed her mind. "Motivation or physical energy?"

"Motivation, please!"

Sella grabbed the yellow jar labeled 'Keep Going,' twisted the lid open with a firm grasp — always a bit stuck, that one — and inhaled deeply. The familiar scent of cinnamon, cardamom, and clove wrapped around her like a hug. Her mind cleared, her posture straightened. Yes, that would do. She used the little golden spoon within the mixture to scoop a single serving into the metal pot.

"Honey, too, please!" Lohrna called from her seat at the

window. She rubbed away the little hearts and stars she had drawn on the windows with her finger and hot breath.

"Of course." Sella added a dollop of chamomile honey to Lohrna's small pink mug as the kettle began to boil.

"Can you tell her to go away?" Beejee leapt on the counter as Sella began to swirl the coffee and honey. "I'm not in the mood for any of her half-baked ideas today."

Sella side-eyed the cat, but said nothing in return.

"Hi, Beejee," Lohrna called in a sing-song voice. Lohrna knew that Beejee might not like her — and spent her days avidly trying to change the cat's mind. Hopefully, Lohrna didn't take it personally. Beejee wasn't particularly friendly to anyone… even to Sella, sometimes.

Lohrna's determination flickered into hesitation as Beejee stared her down with his intense gold-flaked eyes. "Aren't you in a good mood today?" Lohrna teased.

He tossed his head to the side dramatically, a pointed gesture that he was not engaging.

"He's feeling salty today," Sella whispered as she approached Lohrna at the small table by the window. She handed her the steaming mug and sat with a blue cup of her own. "Motivation blend." They clinked the mugs together gently.

"Much needed, thank you." Lohrna looked back out the window and closed her eyes, inhaling the steam with a heavy sigh.

"Everything okay…? It looks like you got quite the haul today. That bag weighs more than you."

Lohrna closed her eyes a little tighter and blew into the steam carefully. "Yes, I'm alright," she said. "Just busy."

"Sure." Sella reached for Lohrna's arm. "Thank you again for visiting the bees."

Her eyes followed Lohrna's posture toward the large window. Rain still tapped against the glass, but with the morning fog dissipating as the sun rose, the street grew more alive. But while the town woke up, Lohrna's eyes stayed shut.

Sella finally closed her own. She rested her head against the wall and took a sip of coffee. Warmth spread through her, radiating from her cheeks all the way to her toes. Spicy cinnamon was the first thing she noticed, followed closely by the sweet honey that lingered in a coating on her tongue. She swallowed, and the final taste — bitter coffee grounds — shot through her mouth and jolted her system. She sat straighter, letting the magic take hold in her body and mind.

It *was* weird that Lohrna was being evasive, she decided. Concern warred with duty as Sella sipped her coffee.

Lohrna wasn't usually secretive. Maybe it would be best to let Lohrna reveal her problems naturally. The woman's many, many hobbies were all always competing for her attention. New knowledge about some strange subject or the latest town gossip was always boiling out of her. Sella doubted it'd be long.

Lohrna took a small sip, and a smile spread across Sella's face. The magic was working. Sella slipped a pinch of the 'I Love Me' confidence blend into her friend's cup. Just enough, she hoped, to encourage her to take a moment and acknowledge that it was alright to not be *totally* alright.

"Thank *you* for the extra magic," Lohrna said as she opened her eyes. "Do I detect a hint of lemon balm?"

"Just enough," Sella echoed her thoughts.

A pause.

It stretched too long.

Sella leaned forward, resting her forearms on the table carefully. "Ready for tonight?" she asked at last.

Lohrna's lips quirked up knowingly. "I am." She gave Sella's hand a quick squeeze. "Thanks for asking. I'm going down to the beach, I think. It'll be nice to be in the shallows this month."

Sella clinked her mug against Lohrna's, her voice lightened from its previous serious tone. "You'll let me know if you ever want a suppressant potion, right? I can make them."

"Yes." Lohrna winked at her. "But better to simply disappear for a night a month than have spots all over my body."

"Low blow," Beejee snickered from the countertop.

Sella inhaled in mock offense.

"I'm kidding!" Lohrna giggled. "I didn't mind the spots; I thought they looked awesome."

Sella grumbled under her breath.

Lohrna took another, deeper swig of her coffee. "Come on, I trust your potions. Actually, I need to buy one for those headaches I get after. What's it called again?"

"I call it Thimble Fix because remember–"

"You only need a little," they said in unison.

"Right," Sella continued. "No repeats of taking an entire spoonful. We don't want to end up like last time."

"My body was only numb for the morning. The feeling came back eventually."

Sella couldn't decide whether to groan or laugh. "Just a few drops when you wake up. And no charge for you."

"You're killing me!" Beejee yowled.

Lohrna leaned over to get a better look at him. "I think Beejee disagrees. You'll take my coin, Sella, or I'll whack you with a rock."

Normally, Sella would have laughed, but her friend's tone said clearly, *I'm not joking.* Sella rubbed the back of her neck, draining her own mug. "Half price, then."

Lohrna pushed off the window seat, stretching her back. "I'll let you know if I ever change my mind on the suppression potion. For now, the change is a part of me. It's freeing, in a weird way."

"I understand," Sella said. And she did, at least partially. Being a witch always made her feel different. *Other.* Maybe that might be bad to someone else, but Sella did feel it was freeing, personally. It meant she could be whoever she wanted, since she would be judged either way. Still, insecurity crept in often. She wondered if it was the same for her friend.

She smiled at Lohrna and took another sip of coffee. Despite her telling herself she didn't care at all what people thought, she was glad that Lohrna had always accepted her as she was.

There was something beautiful about the simplicity of that.

THREE

A Cat Named Koukie

No ONE else had come into the shop. By the time the sun set and they flipped the little wooden sign to 'Closed,' Sella and Beejee were both tired with the dullness of it all. They silently retreated to their one-room living space above the shop, seeking refuge from the nothingness below.

It was warmly lit, with a brightly burning fireplace and the same floating fires from downstairs that hovered over them like fairies. Small shadows flickered about as the embers drifted lazily around the room.

The smell of lavender, old books, and rain wrapped around the sleeping tabby cat. This little home was safe, away from everything in the town below. The darkness outside felt far away, though the pattering of rain on the large circle window above the wooden desk was growing more insistent. In the fireplace, a piece of wood snapped and the fire crackled around the split.

Sella was busy working at a long table in the kitchen, crushing flower petals into a gray stone mortar. Today felt off, but she couldn't place it. Between intrusive thoughts of her mother and the ominous storm brewing outside, she'd have to call this day a loss.

Except for this tea. She *needed* to get this right. If nothing else, to prove she could. It was an old recipe with a calming spell infused into the tea. But the petals she was using hadn't dried how they were supposed to with all the rain. She had to focus if she was going to make this work... Her dark eyes shifted to the quiet bubbling of boiling water beside her. She added the crushed flowers to the water and sprinkled a pinch of spice. The bubbles stilled.

Sella breathed a sigh of relief. "That was a close call," she whispered aloud.

She heard a voice seemingly respond... *not* Beejee's voice.

Sella's gaze shifted to the large round window, then flicked back to a sleeping Beejee. Her familiar was still in a tight, comfy ball, deep asleep on the rug by the fireplace. "Did you hear that, Beejee?" she asked.

The tabby's ears flicked, and he yawned. With closed eyes, he stretched out a single paw to pull at the plush fabric with his claws. "It's the rain," he said through another yawn. His voice held disinterest that only a cat could muster.

Sella rolled her eyes. He was probably right. She watched her floral tea, carefully adding fire to the base of the trivet.

She heard it again. It sounded like a high-pitched cry from the window. This time, it was unmistakably something outside... and close. A chill swept up her spine, and she turned again to Beejee. "I think there's something out there."

Beejee unfolded his second paw in front of him but made no answer.

Another whine howled past the drumming of rain.

They were on the second floor. It was unlikely, especially through the pouring rain, that she could hear anything from the square below. Something had to be *right* near the window.

Another yowl…

"I think it's a cat." She rose from her stool.

Beejee opened one eye, watching her with disinterest. "Stupid cat to be out in this rain," was all he said.

She wanted to tell him to have some compassion, but she knew he wouldn't be bothered. Beejee was as kind as any cat could be expected, when he wanted to be. Now, it seemed, he was content to lay by the fire and let her do the work.

Sella unlocked the window and propped it open a finger's width. Cold rain blew in, splattering her desk, and a soaked orange face emerged through the slit. Large ears, bright green eyes, and whiskers pushed through. Then, just as swiftly, sleek shoulders and the body of a very wet, very angry long-haired cat pushed through the opening.

Sella yelped, but it was too late. It leapt past her stacked papers, now covered in raindrops and claw marks, and landed on the floor with a violent shake.

"Beejee!" Sella closed the window, then spun towards the intruder. "A little help?"

The orange cat, with no hesitancy, raced past both of them toward the fire.

Beejee scrambled to get out of the larger cat's way. He

hissed, claws extended, and swiped at it with a few quick bats.

The other cat bared its teeth, hissed back with a deep spitting sound and then, like nothing happened, began cleaning its paws with its tongue.

Beejee retreated between Sella's legs. "That *thing* is a monster! No manners!"

"What was it doing out in this weather?" Sella wondered aloud.

"And this high up... Suspicious…" Beejee studied the cat with narrowed eyes. It had taken his spot by the fire. "Cast him out. He's clearly a villain up to no good."

Sella felt herself relaxing as the adrenaline and panic wore off. The cat didn't seem interested in her, which made her feel braver. It clearly wasn't a monster – Just a cat looking for a warm place to shelter. She took a few slow steps closer.

Beejee weaved between her legs as she moved. But he wasn't content with the slow progress.

"What are you doing here?" he scolded the other cat. He stalked to the table Sella had been working on and leapt atop to get a better vantage point. "And speak quickly; you're muddying my napping station!" As if an afterthought, he added with more force, "*And* you're in the company of a witch! So answer me or my familiar will cast a spell on you. You'll be smited before you can exhale!"

The orange cat stopped mid-lick of its paw and slowly turned to them, like it forgot where it was. It meowed, then shook its fur again.

Beejee hissed. "She tells lies." He glanced disdainfully at Sella. "She says she needs your help, but clearly, she's just a desperate stray looking for a hot meal and a warm bed." His tail flicked behind him with anger. "Kick her out immediately," he ordered.

Sella, pretending not to hear her familiar's protests, approached the visitor with an outstretched hand. "Hi there." She gathered the most soothing tone she could muster. "Are you lost, little buddy?"

The cat leaned its forehead into her hand.

"Heeeey!" Beejee stomped a paw on the table. His claws clinked hollowly against the wood. Not quite the threatening gesture he was going for, Sella figured. "You already have a cat! Don't touch that one, it could be diseased!"

The other cat meowed again, and then purred gently into Sella's hand.

"How dare you!" Beejee paced the table, looking down at the cat with wide eyes. "This is *my* witch!"

The orange cat looked up at Sella and meowed.

"What'd she say?" Sella asked, turning back to Beejee.

Beejee jumped down from the table and perched himself on the back of the high velvet loveseat facing the fire. He tilted his head at the other cat, then blinked. "She says…" he paused. His ear flicked.

"Beejee?"

Beejee's tone shifted to deep concern. "*If* she's telling the truth, we have a serious problem—"

The cat meowed at him again, this time more urgently.

Beejee's eyes flicked to the cat, and he hesitated. "Her owner was murdered tonight."

. . .

THE ORANGE CAT, Sella learned, was called Koukie. It was short for something... the cat didn't remember what. She didn't remember much of anything, in fact. She relayed the events of the evening in sparse detail, which Beejee pointed out was yet another clue to her untrustworthiness.

In response to his protest, Sella simply gave him a pat on the head. "Alright, buddy. I know. But remember what we said about *facts only* when you translate."

Beejee huffed, but got back on track. "Earlier this evening, she was resting in the cellar of her home, as she usually did during rainstorms. Which is *not* where any cat worth their claws would be caught. In the damp? Are you kidding me?"

"Beejee!" Sella shot him a stern look. She pointed to Koukie. "I feel like this is a bit more urgent..."

Beejee threw his head back indignantly. "I'm telling you what she's telling me. It's not my fault she is going into dumb details. *This* sort of thing is how you tell if someone is lying, you know. Trivial details are a clear sign."

Sella waved her hand and Koukie continued to meow beside her.

Through Beejee, Koukie explained that while she enjoyed the soft rains, the harder nighttime rains often left her feeling frightened. The cellar was cold, yes, but safe from the storms, and her owner had brought her a small bed and blankets to keep her free from the damp.

"Yeah, because cats are known for loving cold, damp basements," Beejee commented after his translation.

Koukie spit at him, a single paw reached out to swipe as if threatening him with another dose.

"Anyway," Sella prompted him, and Beejee continued Koukie's story after a quick growl in her direction.

Koukie was awakened by shouting and a loud thud. When she came up from the cellar, her owner, a woman named Cali, had already 'left her body.' She had bruises around her eyes and mouth and smelled intensely of dark, wet earth.

"Cresablatt?" Sella whispered, and the cat blinked in agreement.

It was a powerful poison, made of ingredients from Orakan and across the sea. So, as far as Sella knew, it was known throughout the world for its deadly effects. Only skilled and very careful makers could get the proportions right. It was quick, painless, and nearly impossible to detect in food or drink. The only marking that someone succumbed to the poison was the pattern of bruising around the face, something that happened postmortem. No one could determine why these markings appeared shortly after death or why the bodies always smelled of rain and mud.

There was no clue Koukie could find surrounding Cali's body other than the means for murder. No items left behind, no smells, no sounds... nothing. A few of Cali's precious stones were missing, but that was all the cat could determine was different.

Beejee mentioned to Sella that the lack of any substance or clues was awfully convenient, but she told him to leave it alone. Koukie was clearly going through a trauma. "Please keep translating," she urged him.

"She says this Cali woman is young," Beejee said begrudgingly. "They just were getting started in this town after coming from across the ocean." He sounded bored but a twitch of his nose deceived him. He'd always loved boats, and during their travels, he consistently begged her to go across the sea. Sella was ashamed that she had been too scared to ever do so. Beejee went on: "She says Cali had come to you before… She purchased a potion for… I'm not sure how to translate this…" His head tilted and finally said, "She is unable to digest milk."

"Dairy?" Sella prompted.

"Milk," he responded.

"So yes, then," she said. She scratched behind Koukie's ear. Now that the cat was warm and mostly dried off, her impressive fur expanded. She looked twice her size, but as vulnerable as she did when she first sprinted in. Sella already felt protective of her.

"Call it what you will," Beejee continued. "She says she came to see you for a variety of other ailments." He paused, descended from the couch, and eyed Koukie suspiciously as he passed her to get closer to the fireplace. "I'm not sure I buy this whole murder thing. She sounds sickly. Probably just fell down dead after eating milk."

Koukie hissed.

"Beejee!"

"What?" He curled up into a tight ball. "I feel like we'd remember a girl from across the ocean who came for potions 'all the time.' The one Hazen was clearly trying to talk up. Koukie's trying to appeal to our softer side – and it won't work. This woman is new to town, has been abroad, and is always sick. She probably brought back some weird disease. Best we leave this one to the authorities. Or even better – to the crematorium."

"The 'authorities' are…" Sella wanted to say 'inept' but

she stopped. She didn't want to encourage Beejee's cynicism. Benka, the sole detective in Marra, rarely had anything to do with his time. To stay busy, he appeared at places randomly, asking bizarre questions like he was investigating something when nothing had happened at all.

She sighed, and the fires overhead dulled as she did. "The town council and Benka do things their own way... and the king's guard won't get involved in some small-time murder."

His ear twitched as the other cat yowled indignantly. Beejee bared his teeth at her, but translated regardless, "She says Cali was in the gem business, formally. Many of her items were stolen..." He snapped his teeth at the other cat to quiet her at last. "How is this *our* problem?"

"If someone here was murdered tonight, it's everyone's problem," Sella said. She finally rose from the floor and felt her legs tingle as blood rushed back into circulation. She ran her palms down her thighs. Had it only been that she had been sitting too long, or was something else wrong? She felt a slight shiver in the air and brushed her shoulders to remove any negativity that lingered there.

"If she died from Cresablatt poisoning," Sella thought aloud, "that is incredibly bad news for us. We're probably the only ones in Orakan, or at least this far south, who can make it. And we sell a lot of the ingredients in the shop."

"Plus, no one's trusted your potions since *The Incident*," Beejee reminded her. "Probably best we leave this to the morning. The smell of Cresablatt will mix with the rain and be less detectable. Maybe they'll assume someone strangled her?"

Sella hated this. Someone just died, and Beejee wanted

them to go to sleep like it was any other night. And worse, he may have a point. If they waited until morning, it would be less noticeable that Cresablatt was involved. That *she* could be involved.

The manner of death didn't matter as much as the culprit. Right?

A lingering feeling of guilt pricked at the back of Sella's neck... *Right?*

She could go check on the body, but if Cresablatt was involved, it would be too late to save anyone. Benka may be bumbling, but he wasn't stupid. A poison victim's cat runs to the exact shop of the witch who can make the poison? At best, Sella would be thrown in jail. At worst... Well, Sella didn't want to think about that.

"We'll wait until morning," she muttered. A heaviness descended on her shoulders as she let out an exhale. Her fingers curled into fists, as though she was trying to hold on to the air around her before it all left the room. Her legs felt weak again, but this was the right choice. "The path will be clearer in the morning."

The rain outside slowed. A calm darkness settled over the loft as the fires above them dimmed. The little home chilled as the lights slowly died. With a shiver, Sella pointed two fingers at the fireplace. Sparks ignited until the fire was once again full and the long shadows in the room were banished to smaller, flickering shades. The two cats glanced at each other, made silent peace, and positioned themselves at different ends of the room — but still close to the merry flame in the large hearth.

Sella curled up on the couch, staring at the flames drifting between the rafters – close enough to burn, but never quite managing it. She sighed, her brain whirling. What could this newcomer have done to deserve a violent death? Were the gems *that* valuable?

And what of the murderer, lurking in their tiny town…? That made her shiver, even though the loft had warmed nicely. This Cali must have brought enemies here. That was the only thing Sella could tell herself for now. There was no way that anyone Sella knew could have done something like this.

Despite the feeling of uneasiness settling into her core, Sella drifted to sleep.

FOUR

Oh, Sheet

SELLA AWOKE ON THE LOVESEAT. Her back ached from the unnatural position she had fallen asleep in. A flash of panic jolted her upright – the pale morning light was already glowing through the large window, which meant she'd slept in way too late. She swore silently. Now she wouldn't have time to bake anything before they opened the shop.

She squinted, blinked, and pushed back a mess of dark hair that fell in her face. Some of it was stuck to her cheek "Beejee?" she called, pushing into a stretch.

The room came into clearer focus. The fireplace was only embers now – orange, red, and gold flickering back to life when she glanced its way.

As the fire grew, her eyes widened suddenly at Beejee and Koukie, both still curled on little pillows by the flames. She winced, remembering in a flood of images the events of the night before. She studied them for a moment, trying to decide her next move.

Koukie's fluffy orange fur caught light with every deep inhale. She shifted her head a bit but kept her body tightly curled. Beejee, on the other hand, was all wire. The gray and black tabby was still as stone, excepting for the slight indent and expansion in his shoulders as he breathed.

Everything around her felt exactly as she had left it the night before. Except for the smell. Something else filtered through the air. Something like fresh baked bread…

"Hi," a quiet voice called from the corner.

Sella's body jerked and she nearly fell out of the velvet couch. "What the–!"

"Don't be frightened!"

It was far too late for that.

Sella pushed herself up from her mangled position from the floor, squinting at the room's corner. A rush of panic swept through her. It sounded like a woman, but… a woman wasn't what Sella found herself looking at. Floating before her was a white sheet, one of hers from her linen closet, shaped into the silhouette of a person. Sella's reading glasses were perched over the sheet, right where the face would have been.

"I thought this would be… funny?" the voice from under the sheet said. "Or, at least, less scary than a ghost in your living room. I mean, right? The glasses are a good touch, at least?"

Sella rubbed her face with both hands. She blinked hard, just in case she was hallucinating. "What the–"

"Right," the figure interrupted again. "This may seem kind of odd. It's odd for me, at least. I don't know; do dead people show up often at your home? Am I doing this right?"

"Doing… Doing *what* right?" Sella stammered.

Beejee finally lifted his head from his slumber. "Can we not with all the noise…?"

Koukie, too, began to untangle herself and rise. She meowed loudly, then bounded to the corner, rubbing her face along the bottom of the sheet that hovered a few inches from the ground.

"Who are you? What are you doing in my home? I have no money, not really, if you're trying to rob me."

"Oh," the sheet said, "I'm not here for money. I don't need it. I'm… I'm pretty sure I'm dead?" She said the last part like a question. It hung in the air between them like the moment between lightning and a burst of thunder. The sheet spoke again, adjusting the glasses. "I didn't want to believe it, but… well, the evidence is fairly damning. I mean, you never expect to see yourself, you know, dead. But yes. I'm pretty sure that's what happened."

Beejee hissed and Sella snapped herself from what felt like a dense fog.

"You're Cal–uh, Cal–"

"Calisyali. I go by Cali, if that's easier." The sheet bent down to pet the fluffy orange cat. "You're Sella the witch, right? And you can see me?"

"I see a sheet in the shape of a person in the corner of my house." As soon as the words left her lips, Sella realized that might be rude. She amended, "And yes, I'm a kitchen witch." She perched on the couch. "Listen, I don't want to be insensitive or anything. But it is very difficult to take you seriously when you look like… that." She gestured at the figure broadly.

The sheet shifted as Cali laughed, a light, happy sound despite the situation. "Sorry. So far, no one in town has been able to see me. It took me most of the night to figure out how to get this over my head in the first place."

Sella glanced at her open linen closet, where clothes and sheets were scattered about the floor. She raised a brow.

"Sorry about that, by the way. But you're a heavy sleeper." The sheet shuffled forward. What looked like hands grew out to the sides, then the fabric fluttered to the floor. The glasses clattered to the wood, and Cali gasped. "Oh no! Sorry!" She paused and looked from the crumbled sheet to Sella with pleading eyes. "Can you still see me?"

Sella stared, her mouth agape. A woman stood before her, the white sheet pooled around her ankles and Sella followed it from the floor to her face slowly. The ghost wore a long dark skirt and simple white blouse, buttoned to her collarbone so her long neck was exposed despite the frill of a lace collar. Waves of auburn hair cascaded to Cali's elbows and shifted about her frame as if a light breeze had blown into the still room and only affected her. Her green eyes almost distracted from the sea of freckles that flecked her olive complexion.

The odd thing was that she seemed to shimmer. Colors were there, but she was vaguely see-through unless Sella really concentrated.

As a morbid afterthought, Sella was glad to see that any bruising from the poison hadn't made it to her ghost's image.

"Well," Cali said, arms lifting to make herself bigger. "Can you see me without the sheet, or do I need to put it back on?" She let out a heavy, defeated sigh. "It was no small feat getting it over my head. Try being dead and moving things. Not. Easy."

"No, I see you," Sella said, rubbing her eyes to make sure. The woman remained.

Beside Sella, Beejee bounded onto the couch and sat upright to get a better look. "She's pretty. For a ghost."

Sella side-eyed her cat. She wanted to scold him and remind him that it was wholly inappropriate to discuss Cali's appearance at all, let alone now, after everything the ghost had been through. But that might clue Cali into the fact that Sella's cat had just spoken to her— and that seemed like the last thing she wanted to talk about.

"Aw, she likes me!" Cali gestured at Beejee with a bright smile.

"He," Sella corrected, giving him a rough pat on the head. "His name is Beejee."

Beejee only narrowed his eyes in response.

"This is Koukie." Cali rubbed her cat's cheek with a curled finger. It was so impossible that Sella eyed the interaction with disbelief. The ghost's hand seemed tangible. But that shouldn't be possible. Not like this, not so soon after death. Sella would have to explore this magic, because she'd never heard of anything like this. "I'm so glad to see you're alright," Cali whispered to her cat. Her mouth pulled into a tight line and she leaned in closer as Koukie tried to head-butt her, but missed. Cali straightened quickly, standing to her full height. "Thanks for taking her in… She must be traumatized after the night she had."

"I know." Sella watched Cali closely, unsure of how to proceed. She went with the truth. "She told us everything last night."

"You can speak to cats?" Cali's eyes grew wide.

Sella's shoulders slumped. It seemed the conversation was happening now, time and place aside.

"Just Beejee. He translates." Sella pushed off the couch,

and the springs groaned under the release of pressure. It took a moment to realize she'd accidentally slept in her day clothes and now her long, black dress was terribly wrinkled. Pair that with her messy black hair, and it was amazing that a ghost somehow looked more put-together than Sella.

Embarrassment tinged Sella's cheeks, and she attempted to divert before Cali noticed. "Look, like I said, this all must be very traumatizing—"

But Sella hadn't gotten far before Calisyali made her way to the window. Her footsteps were silent, like she wasn't really reaching the floor.

"Traumatizing is one word for it," Cali said quietly, if not a little overly casually. She shifted her body to get a better look out the window, her face hidden from Sella. "But I must still be still in this world for a reason. Whoever did this to me, I want them brought to justice."

"Then, you don't know who—" Sella cut herself off before she voiced the word "murdered." She fumbled to course-correct: "—um, who did this?"

"All I remember is…" Cali's voice faded and her image seemed to flicker. "Ah, nothing. Hey, when do you think they'll find my body?"

The light from the window was growing. The town would start waking up soon.

Sella shook her head. "I don't know. Do you have a job to report to?"

Cali pointed to the tavern at the far corner of the town square. Sella could barely see out the window from this angle, but things still looked quiet below, so she must not have slept in *that* long. Cali sighed again, seemingly flustered with Sella's slow pace. "I did bookkeeping at the tavern.

New job. I thought it was going well enough." Doubt flickered into her tone.

"You're Hazen's new bookkeeper?"

"You make it sound weird. Everyone needs a bookkeeper." Cali's voice sounded self-conscious. It reminded Sella of her own anxious rambling when people asked her about her new recipes. Cali spun back to Sella, almost accusatory. "You run a shop. Don't you have one?"

"No…?" Sella frowned.

Cali winced. "How do you keep track of your transactions, your goods, your imports, your orders?"

Sella cleared her throat. "I, uh, I don't really." When did the conversation shift to *her* business? Fumbling for a defense, Sella blurted, "I keep track of sales. What I sold to whom, and the dates…"

"Yeah, we're probably bleeding money," Beejee chimed in. "You're terrible with the accounts. Didn't you give your throat ache drops to Bry for the promise of a basket during his apple harvest? Well, where are my fresh-baked apple crisps?"

"Hush." Sella waved at her cat.

Cali's green eyes shifted from Beejee to Sella. She raised an eyebrow as if she understood that Beejee was on her side.

"My paperwork is fine," Sella said, although whether to Beejee or Cali, she wasn't sure. The pointed tips of her ears burned.

Cali seemed to realize that Sella was embarrassed, and she cleared her throat. "Well, I'm sure it's just fine, then. You know your business." She turned back to the window, as if suddenly remembering the reason for her being there was not to make small talk or get to know one another. "So, what's the plan? Shall we alert the council and have them find my body? Being dead is somewhat undignified. It's bad enough I'll be known as 'that stranger who showed up, worked with numbers, and then died on the floor.' Last thing I want is to start decomposing before I'm found."

Meanwhile, Sella wished that she would never be found. She wanted to slip into the folds of the couch and never resurface.

Her plan of "we wait until morning" didn't allow for waking up to the dead woman's ghost. Now, every ounce of control Sella felt possessed vanished, and she was left grasping for anything left. "Well, about that. I'm not entirely sure—"

Cali gasped, snapped her fingers. Papers on Sella's writing desk fluttered as she pressed her body across the desk and her nose to the window. "Isra! The milk delivery! Today is delivery day! I always talk with Isra at the door. She'll knock. She'll notice."

Sella joined her at the window, but hesitated before moving close enough to see out into the early morning fog. Should she keep her distance, given Cali's situation? Sella stuffed her hands into her dress pockets and decided to hang back.

"Milk delivery?" Beejee had no such qualms about closeness. He leapt onto the writing desk and also pressed his pink nose to the window, leaving a little smudge. "You know you can't digest that, right?"

"She's turned the corner." Desperation tinged Cali's voice. "Come on, she's going to notice!" Cali stiffened, twisting for the staircase. "I want to be there when she does. We can look for clues as more people arrive!"

The window where her palms and nose were pressed was clean of prints as if she was never there at all. Sella's heart sank a little.

"Hold on." Sella backed a few paces away. "I think I need to stay low, at least for a bit."

"What?" Cali stopped short. She looked at Sella with narrowed eyes. "Why?"

The question was not one Sella anticipated. She felt foolish for not having a good explanation ready to go.

"Witches here… the trust we have in this region is nebulous. And I only just moved back. They don't exactly have a lot of love for me."

"You were the first recommended stop when I arrived. Why do you think I'm here?" Cali's voice lowered, and she puffed out her chest, offering quotation marks with her fingers. "'We're so glad to have her back; she's the best witch this town has seen in a decade.' That's what everyone said."

"There was *no* witch here for a decade after I left." Sella forced a smile she didn't feel. "I think that's the joke."

"It seemed sincere." Cali's brow wrinkled. She waited, but Sella's silence only grew. Cali put her hands on her hips. Her skirt and hair began to shift as though underwater. "You won't help me?"

Cali's sudden accusatory tone made Sella pause. She didn't really *owe* this woman anything. She didn't need to risk her safety for her, especially if she was already dead. … Right?

Sella didn't want to think that way, but the dark whisper of her mind was hard to ignore. Still, someone needed help, and that alone made Sella grimace.

"I can *try* to help you. I just need to go about it properly."

That seemed to be everything the ghost needed to hear. Her entire body seemed to flicker for a moment, and her shoulders hung in relief. Her clothes and hair stilled, restored to laws of gravity, if that is what it was.

"Thank you," Cali whispered. Sella thought she saw a hint of tears in the ghost's eyes. But Cali blinked and they were gone.

Worry churned in the bottom of her stomach, but Sella turned away. With a flick of her hand, she reignited all the little fires in her home so they glowed brightly, casting away the cold and shadow of the morning's pale light. Warmth filled the space in a way she hadn't felt since the thunderstorm the night before.

"Alright." Sella clapped her hands together. "It's possible going to the scene, seeing who is there and how they respond, could give us a few leads. We just have to be *very* careful." Sella slipped on a pair of heeled boots next to the staircase. "We can go under the guise of running errands, but I have a few conditions."

"Yes! What are they?" Cali said cheerfully.

"Number one," Sella cast a glance at her disarrayed wardrobe, "the sheet stays here."

FIVE

Definitely Dead

THE MORNING WAS JUST chilly enough that Sella wished she brought her cloak. Or, at least, a ceramic travel mug of hot coffee. Mind racing, she barely had the wherewithal to grab her basket, a last-second prop to make their market trip look convincing.

Koukie had ventured into the shop when they all came downstairs, and now seemed perfectly content to curl herself on the cushioned window seat. Beejee, meanwhile, strolled towards the door with his tail high.

Sella paused at the doorframe. "Beejee, maybe you should stay here."

"There's a *dead body*," he said as if that explained everything, and slipped past her.

The town was small, but it felt expansive, especially since Sella moved back. Her street, home to her little shop and apartment, Hazen's large tavern, and the huge hotel, was like an afterthought: A mix of brick and stone buildings of various sizes, each building looked like it was under threat of being overtaken by the vines that scaled its walls. The rest of the town was well-manicured, identical brick stonework buildings. Potted flowers and hanging vine leaf plants purposefully, carefully decorated the shops and homes. But Sella, Hazen, and Penya, the hotel's ancient proprietor, were too busy to tend to anything alive. They let nature do what it was prone to do to their side of town. And it was generally prone to expansive bursts of growth.

As they moved to the next street, everything became more uniform. A series of shops and homes above them all looked similar. Only the lettering in the windows gave any clue as to their differences. From here, Sella could hear the sound of the wind and smell the salt coming up from the sea. Nowhere in the town, except for a few outlier homes, was far from either the cliffs or the beach overlooking the expanse of the shimmering teal ocean.

Traveling with a ghost was… strange. Along the worn down cobblestone path toward the market near Cali's apartment, only Sella's heeled boots made any sound. Though Cali strode confidently beside them, her steps were silent; and as they passed the shops that lined the street, so close they were all nearly touching one another, only Sella's image was reflected back in their large glass windows. It was so disconcerting that Sella paused without thinking.

Cali noticed, following her gaze. "Huh. That's certainly interesting."

"Mhm…" Sella gestured toward the street. "Let's keep going."

"You look like you're talking to yourself," Beejee said.

Across the street, a few early risers, mostly vendors heading to the open air market, were beginning to come out of their homes above the shops, carrying their wares precariously or hauling loads behind them in little wagons. One man looked at Sella with a quick amused expression but continued on, arms full of bushels of some fruit that Sella couldn't quite identify. Sella nodded to him politely, then cast her feline familiar a deadpan look. "How is that different than when I'm walking with you?"

Beejee's tail flicked. "Well, people can see me."

Oblivious to his responses, Cali drifted ahead and around a corner. Sella and Beejee caught up to her just as she paused, pointing across the street. "This is my place." Cali forced a laugh. "Or it *was* my place. Well, at least I don't need to pay rent anymore, am I right?"

The corners of Sella's mouth twitched. "That's… one point in favor. And I think whatever tense you use is fine," Sella agreed at last.

"Great. Then I'll go with 'is,'" Cali said brightly. "No rent, but I like the idea of it still being mine."

"She's awfully chipper," Beejee grumbled as they rounded the corner.

Sella agreed, and it made her slightly uneasy.

This street was, thankfully, empty. A connected row of brick, single-story homes lined one side. On the other side of the pathway, a large, gray stone wall blocked the view to the market. But they could still hear a few chattering voices as booths began to open up.

Each little home had a distinct color door. Red, sapphire blue, yellow, and green… Sella's mother used to say they were painted to help out-of-towners find their way home in the thick winter mist.

But Sella was sure that was simply the origin story. Most of these homes were empty. This was where rebellious youth came when they wanted to leave their family, but were too scared or poor to leave town. Like Sella, once upon a time.

Cali broke Sella's thoughts as she paused at a large emerald door. A single glass jar of milk perched on the stoop. Cali stared at it, silent, motionless. Her image flickered.

"But I always answer the door," the ghost whispered. Her hair began to shift about her, a small wind growing turbulent. "Why didn't she call for help?"

Guilt twinged in Sella's chest, and she strode forward. They were still alone on this street, but she couldn't assume they would be for long. Yet, the bigger crisis was the agony in Cali's whispered voice.

The ghost seemed to take everything in stride. Even her death. But if something so minor had cracked her mask, even a little, her circumstance must be impossible for her to hold.

Sella reached for her instinctively – then pulled back before her fingers brushed Cali's translucent skin. "I'm so sorry, Cali," Sella murmured. "Maybe she was in a rush this morning."

"S-She was supposed to notice," Cali replied, voice trembling.

"I know. But it's okay, because I'm here, and you're here. She wasn't the only person who could help."

At Sella's ankles, Beejee sniffed the milk canister. "I'm also here. Just in case either of you care."

Sella never took her eyes off Cali. "Okay? We're okay."

"We're okay." Cali drew a slow breath, and the storm around her dissipated. "Sorry. Sorry." The ghost hung her head.

"I was more worried about you *before* that happened, honestly." Sella's half smile lingered for a moment, then she glanced at her familiar. "Beejee, keep watch. We'll be quick."

He trotted off to the middle of the street, head turning like an owl.

There were no signs of forced entry. Unless the murderer came through the back garden, or through one of the walls, Cali willingly let them inside.

Sella stood on her tiptoes to look at the windows. Unless, she thought, someone had used a window... or, "Do you lock your door?"

"Um..." The ghost shimmered for a moment, scuffing her boot along a groove in the cobblestone. "No, I don't."

"A single woman living alone and not locking the door?" Beejee scoffed.

Cali squinted at Beejee. "It sounds like he's scolding me."

Sella snorted. "He is." She looked back at the door, her brow creasing. If it was unlocked, anyone could have strolled inside and left the Cresablatt for her. Sella scratched her head. "You're really not making this easy, you know."

Cali put her hands on her hips. "I was *murdered*. I don't need to make anything easy. That's like a double snake in Tinther."

Beejee and Sella exchanged confused glances. Whatever that meant, Cali did have a point – she was allowed to complain, given the circumstances.

"Should... should we go inside?" Cali changed the subject. "Look for some more clues?"

Beejee looked at Cali with narrowed eyes. "So first we

have to put up with your ghost, and now you want to traumatize us with your dead body? Big no from me."

"Just keep watch," Sella said to the cat. She turned to Cali. "I'll go in quickly to see if I can find anything. But… maybe you should stay here with Beejee?"

Cali looked relieved. "I already saw my body once. That was enough for a lifetime."

Sella's eyes darted down the street. The coast was clear… for now. She gripped the gold doorknob with one hand and drew a deep breath. Just a body. Nothing she wasn't expecting to see. She turned the knob and ducked inside before she could talk herself out of it.

The door closed behind her with a gentle *click*. Darkness sat heavy on her shoulders as she crept through the unfamiliar space.

The home was… oddly cute.

The little kitchen reminded her of her own place once. A black stove in the corner was still producing faint heat. A yellow cast-iron teapot, slightly faded in places where it had been well worn, sat atop the stove. The place smelled of cinnamon and clove; a byproduct of the tea, no doubt.

A kitchen towel with an embroidered wyvern hung from the ledge of a wood slab counter. Sella crept closer, squinting at it. The design was intricate, with large reptile wings spreading from edge to edge, a tail coiled around its thick body like vines. Wyvern lived across the sea, and as far as she knew, couldn't make the trek across the ocean, so she'd never seen one before. The image here made them look almost sweet. Its expression was calm and playful. Sella moved on. She had a job to do, and quickly.

The rest of the kitchen was typical. A half-finished tea,

now cold in its ceramic, hand-painted mug, rested on a table. Only one chair, Sella noted. A blush pink blanket was folded neatly on the seat to make it more comfortable. Her eyes drifted to a potted plant she didn't recognize with sharp thorns by the window… and….

Right beside the odd plant was a series of small indents… like scraping. Something heavy had been moved from here. Sella touched the scratches gently. Maybe someone broke in through the window after all.

That'd be hilarious, considering the front door was unlocked.

Sella moved deeper. The floor plan was similar to her old one, and she paused at a door that she was certain led to the sole bedroom. Her heartbeat quickened in her chest. Koukie said she heard a thud before she found Cali. The house was small; if she wasn't in the kitchen or living area, that meant she was here.

Or at least, her body was, anyway.

Sella closed her eyes and opened the door. It was kind of funny how she immediately went back to her childhood tactic of squinting through her eyelashes to avoid seeing something scary.

It wasn't… scary, per se. It was rather anticlimactic, actually.

From a distance, it almost looked like Cali was sleeping. She was slumped at the foot of the bed like she'd been too tired to lay across it properly. Strands of auburn hair covered her face, revealing the distinctive bruising pattern along her throat, and under her closed eyes.

It was morbid, but Sella couldn't stop staring. Cali's skin was the wrong tinge. The lighting in here was dim, but Sella didn't want to risk touching anything– disturbing anything, so she cast a flame along her fingers and raised her hand. In the flickering light, it almost looked like Cali was still breathing.

Sella bent over the mattress. No blood. No stains. Just the bruising… and the fact that her skin was an unnatural, rotting green tinge… not pale. And near the body, it smelled like loosened, wet earth.

Even though her ghost was outside, Sella suddenly felt like Cali might leap off the bed at any moment. Her nerves buzzing, Sella backed away, keeping her hand lit and the room filled with cozy firelight until the moment she nudged the bedroom door closed again with her foot.

She began to flee the house as if it were on fire. As an afterthought, she killed the dying embers of the stove with her magic to keep the place from burning before Cali could be properly found.

Outside, the sun was far too bright.

Sella closed the front door and slumped against the brick wall. "Well… you're definitely dead."

"I knew it!" Cali said, almost as a joke. Her expression firmed. "Was it awful?"

Sella squinted at her. No green tinge to her skin. The ghost looked perfectly alive to her, except for the faint shimmer. "No," Sella replied, her voice distant. "Not awful. Just… it is what it is."

Voices from down the street caught Sella's attention. A pair of women, each with their own baskets in tow, came strolling along the road: Ovina and her sister, Kartha, the town weavers. If they saw Sella here, the whole town would know in hours.

Sella's face went red, her heart thumping in her chest. The women were speaking loudly, but she couldn't hear them over the roaring in her ears. She could face down a body, but this had far bigger implications.

Tides high and low, Sella, do something! She thought. but her mind was blank with panic. Separated only by a couple walls, she was the only one in town who could create the poison that killed the woman inside.

It was too late. The women were upon her before her indecision resolved. With a nervous laugh, Sella stuffed her hands into her pockets as they passed. "Ovina. Kartha. Good morning."

"Mmm," Ovina said. "Morning, dear." But her glance lingered.

Could she see Cali? Did she know? The ghost was unnaturally still. The women resumed their chatter when they were far enough away. Cali shuddered, but stayed silent.

Beejee didn't. "Sella, for the love of all the ocean!" He nudged her calf with his head. "Walk to the market and say you were tying your laces or something!"

Some lookout. But his words made Sella snap out of her freeze. "Right, right!"

Sella could kick herself. She didn't usually panic like that. Everything that was happening today was off.

Sella followed the women with uneven steps. She considered explaining herself to them – *with what excuse?* – but couldn't open her mouth.

Irritation and frustration swelled in her chest. She shouldn't have come. She *knew* she shouldn't have come. "This was such a stupid idea," Sella's words were quiet and harsh... harsher than she meant them to. But she didn't pull them back. They lingered in the air between the two women like static.

"We'll have to actually buy stuff now, too," Beejee grumbled as they walked. "This ghost better reimburse us."

Cali cast a doubtful glance at her house, then heaved a sigh and trailed after them. She smiled at Beejee. "You're a cute one, you know. I'm sure Koukie is glad to have you around."

Beejee bared his teeth.

SIX

Sleep on It

LOHRNA WAS WAITING BACK at the shop. She pushed off the wooden bench by the storefront to rise when Sella walked up. "About time. I was waiting for you for ages."

Sella chuckled, shifting her bags from the market. Since she had to buy something anyway, she stocked up on tisane blends of chamomile mint, and a special jar of raw sugar crystals. Despite the thought of fresh tea, her voice was still weary. "It's been an odd morning."

Lohrna squinted at her. "You okay? You look like you've seen a ghost!"

Sella couldn't help it — she snorted, nearly dropping the jar of sugar. Beejee laughed: a sound that Sella could hear, but to Lohrna only sounded like meows and a bit of wheezing.

Lohrna's eyes shifted to the cat. "Are… both of you okay?"

Sella adjusted her hold on the linen bags of tea and the sugar jar, fumbling for the key to her shop. She nudged it open with her shoulder, cast a surreptitious glance around for Cali – who'd faded somewhere the minute they started shopping and hadn't returned – and stepped inside. "Come on. We need to talk."

"Talk, or cry?" Beejee drawled.

Sella rolled her eyes as she set her market haul on the front counter. "Close the door behind you. I'm going to make a cup of coffee."

"Um…" Lohrna followed her inside, frowning. "You're acting really weird. Are you in danger?"

"No." Sella slid the jar of sugar across the counter, then sorted the tea into the wooden cubbies behind the counter. She started the fire and poured water and grounds. This was no time for careful coffee; she needed it instantly. As she stirred, she added, "Maybe? Probably not."

Lohrna's eyebrows shot up. "Probably not? Excuse me. What do you mean?"

Sella sprinkled her 'Be Brave' mix into the pot of coffee. The pink powder disappeared into the dark liquid instantly. Sella looked at the jar for another moment, then scooped another spoonful. Today was no day for portion control. "I *did* see a ghost," she said urgently, before Lohrna could interrupt her. "This morning. I met a ghost. In my home."

Lohrna was uncharacteristically quiet as she watched Sella stir the coffee again, cover the pot, and add more fire so it boiled faster. She cleared her throat as Sella finally poured the coffee into two cups. Lohrna reached for hers, took a tentative sip. "Okay. I believe you."

The relief Sella felt was tangible. Tears sprang to her eyes, unbidden, and she swallowed past the lump in her throat. "You do?"

"I know you, Sella. You don't lie about these things."

Lohrna glanced around the shop. "So, um… is the ghost here now?"

"I'm not sure where she is. At the market, she said she was going to 'look for clues,' and then she vanished. Literally. She's…. well, she's trying to figure out who killed her."

"Maybe *she* needs a cup of this coffee," Lohrna smirked.

Sella's expression warmed. This was exactly the kind of conversation she needed. Already, with Lohrna's response and the magical coffee, she was feeling more centered.

"Can we take a seat?" Sella asked, casting a quick glance at the door. But of course, no one milling down the street dared to come inside. Today might be the *one* day Sella was grateful her business was, as Beejee often put it, a chronic failure.

She joined Lohrna on the window seat again, pressing her back to the glass so no one could see her speaking. The morning sun warmed the panes and her clothes, a pleasant comfort.

Lohrna curled against the opposite side of the thick cushion, tracing the rim of her mug with a finger. "So, wait. Seeing ghosts… is that normal for you?"

"Not like this."

Lohrna cocked her head. "How do you *usually* see ghosts?"

Sella's eyes shifted upward. She was quiet for a moment as she thought about how to address it. "They're residual hauntings. Spirits who have been around so long they can't remember their own names. Harmless, mostly." She gestured at a gold-framed needlepoint depicting a hive of bees on the wooden wall. "That was a gift from the mayor of Sarrton's wife after I banished an especially mischievous ghost from their house. And by the potions..." Sella gestured at the wall of cubbies to a small silver statue of a kelpie. "That was a gift from an entire town after I handled their poltergeist. But those ghosts were echoes. This one... definitely isn't."

Lohrna studied the gifts, taking a thoughtful sip of her coffee. "I didn't know you banished ghosts while you were gone."

A curious mix of pride and embarrassment made Sella duck her head. "I did a lot of things while I was gone." Eager to bring the conversation back to Cali – and away from herself – Sella continued: "This ghost is... almost alive. As close to it as a ghost can come, anyway. She's sentient, she's friendly, and she is wholly convinced someone killed her."

"Oh, no. You were serious about that?" Lohrna grimaced. "Where was she murdered?"

"Literally around the corner."

Lohrna blanched. "In *this* town?"

"I know."

Her friend drew a slow breath. "So, why is she looking for clues? If she's so convinced, she *must* know who did it." Hope filtered into Lohrna's voice.

Sella avoided her gaze. "No. She doesn't remember." For a moment, she thought about detailing Cali's body, confirming that she was, indeed, dead, but it felt too morbid for her bright, cozy shop. She stayed silent.

Lohrna didn't. Intrigue filled her tone and she tossed out one hand, nearly upsetting her coffee. "Then it's a real-life murder mystery!" She leaned forward so she was almost touching Sella's nose with her own. "I wonder who did it? Of course, you said we might be in danger. Oh, what if we're next?" Her black eyes grew large, but not with fear.

With anticipation.

"Why are you excited about this?" Sella nearly laughed. She clutched her mug close to her chest, almost worried her friend's enthusiasm would slip into the drink, though she knew that was impossible.

"I mean, she's already dead. It'd be sad, except she's here in the ghostly flesh, begging for your help. Oooh... do you think Benka is going to get involved? He has to, doesn't he? Wait! Who was murdered?" Sudden fear laced her tone for the first time.

Guilt flowed through Sella. She was grateful it wasn't anyone they knew well, but even thinking that belittled Cali's life. Sella's tone was hesitant. "Cali. She's a human from across the sea, according to her cat."

"Oh. Good." Lohrna paused, seemed to realize what she said, and backtracked. "I mean, *not* good. Just – well, you know."

"Yeah. I know."

Silence grew between them.

Sella glanced at the staircase. She had nearly forgotten that Koukie would be waiting for her when she went upstairs. "Look, I know it's intriguing, and Cali needs my help, but it's getting too complicated for me. Beejee and I settled here because this town is quiet–"

"And we ran out of money," Beejee cut in. He'd leapt onto the counter when they first arrived, and now he was curled on the square, felt placemat where Sella normally did transactions.

Admittedly, that placemat hadn't seen much use lately. He might as well enjoy it.

Sella ignored him. "Well, I helped this morning, but that's all. Any more, and I might accidentally incriminate myself."

Lohrna's brow furrowed. "Incriminate? What happened?"

Sella explained the events of the morning as they sipped their coffee. Words were coming easier now as courage warmed Sella's body like a small ember in a hearth.

But it also firmed her conviction. She'd helped Cali this morning. That was the best she could do. She didn't owe the woman anything else.

"But you *have* to help her!" Lohrna exclaimed as Sella finished her recount.

Sella should have known. A flash of irritation swept through her. Didn't Lohrna realize how dangerous this could get?

"I don't *have to* do anything." Sella rose from her seat. Heat bloomed in her palms, but she stifled it. "I was already seen by *several* witnesses just standing outside her door, probably looking incredibly guilty. If they report that—" Sella cut herself off, her voice firm. "I'll let Benka handle it."

"Benka? Seriously, Benka? That man spends his time investigating grandmas for their missing pearls— and feels pleased when he finds them around their necks."

Sella grimaced. "Listen, Cali seems nice. Way too nice, for someone who just got murdered. Either she's the world's most well-adjusted ghost... or she's hiding something and has an ulterior motive for seeking me out." Sella set her jaw. "She's not from here. We don't know what sort of history she fled across the sea. Her killer is probably already on a boat home." Sella pulled her arms in, the ceramic mug in her hand warmed though it was now empty. Outside, people filled the streets, and every one of them seemed to be looking directly at Sella with accusation in their eyes.

Sella looked down at her tea with suspicion. Maybe she'd accidentally soured the bravery mix — paranoia was an eerily similar recipe.

Lohrna didn't seem convinced. Her eyelids lowered. "She's probably still reeling in shock from, you know, being *murdered*. You, of all people, shouldn't judge someone's reaction to trauma. She's allowed to process it however she wants."

Sella flinched, her eyes flicking to Lohrna's empty mug. Maybe she shouldn't have doubled the bravery dose after all. Lohrna never lacked it.

"It's not my problem," Sella said, but doubt flickered in her tone.

"Sella," Lohrna replied, her voice grave. "This girl has no one. No one but you. It's not like you to ignore that."

Shame bubbled in her chest. Sella took a deep breath, eyes dropping to her boots. One foot bounced ceaselessly against the worn wooden flooring. "Lohr, I can't risk it... My shop will never recover if I'm caught up in this."

Lohrna waved a hand. "That's stupid. You're a powerful witch. Who cares what this town thinks? You might even gain public interest if you catch a killer..."

Beejee weaved his way between them, hopping onto the window seat. His tail flicked as he considered that argument. "That *could* liven things up around here," he said. "Pun intended."

Sella smiled in spite of herself, but before she could respond, the bell above the door chimed. The three of them froze, each staring at the door like the detective was here to arrest them all immediately.

"Sella, Lohrna. Am I interrupting?" Hazen asked, stepping inside. His shoulders were slumped and he looked defeated.

So, he knew. But how much?

"No," Sella said, and let her posture soften. "Hazen, it's nice to see you." She did her best to smile. "How… How did the scones turn out? "

Hazen ignored the question, and cut right to the heart of the one thing Sella didn't want to discuss. "My bookkeeper didn't report for work today. It's unlike her." When he stepped into the shop, every *thump* of his boots against the wooden floors felt like a dagger to Sella's heart. "Did you see her walk by? Young woman, reddish hair." He made a gesture indicating length and then lifted his hands to his mid-chest. "About this tall?"

Sella normally would have fumbled, but the coffee did its job. She pulled back her shoulders, appropriated a look of confusion, and replied, "I haven't seen anyone like that."

Hazen seemed to take her refusal as an indicator that she needed more details. "She comes into your shop running errands for me, so you should recognize her, at least. Goes by 'Cali'? No head horns. A human."

"I haven't seen her. I'm sorry, Hazen." Sella paused. "Is everything okay? Are you worried?"

Hazen grumbled in a way Sella could not interpret. His smile seemed forced. "A bit. But I'm sure she'll turn up. Send her to the tavern if she shows up, will you?"

"Of course," Sella lied.

Lohrna stayed silent, eyes trained on her empty mug.

Hazen nodded to them both, gave Beejee a simple pat on the head, and moved for the door. The gold bell over the door jingled as he stepped outside. With confidence, Hazen strolled right for the hotel next door, letting himself inside. Clearly, he was canvassing anywhere Cali might be.

It made Sella's heart twinge. She almost wished Cali was here right now, if only to see how some people fought for her. That someone missed her right away.

In the following silence, Lohrna pushed to her feet. Her stare was relentless. "Hazen is looking for her. *Hazen.*"

"He's her employer," Sella said, but she felt like she'd already lost this argument.

"And you're her *only friend*," Lohrna snapped. It was rare she lost her temper, but now Sella felt trapped in her disappointment. Guilt churned. Lohrna was the one person who believed in her, and now...

Well. Sella couldn't even blame her.

"I know you're scared." Lohrna's voice was quiet. "But come on, Sella. We can do better than this."

It broke Sella's last resolve – and on its heels, the coffee's courage swept in to take its place. It was like a dam broke, and cold, hard resolve solidified in every corner of Sella's mind.

"Okay." She bit the inside of her cheek. "Okay, I'll think about it. But you have to give me until tomorrow to come up with a plan of attack. I can't risk my mother's shop – not when I'm the only one in town who can make Cresablatt."

Lohrna smiled, so big it was almost wicked. She lunged forward, sweeping Sella into a hug that warmed Sella's very soul. "Oh, good! I look forward to hearing your plan in the morning!"

"Afternoon?" Sella nearly begged. After last night, she needed the morning to sleep in. She had to bake, relax, and truly clear her mind.

Lohrna didn't care about that – and considering how much energy Lohrna had on a daily basis, this wasn't surprising. "Mooooorning!" she sang, gathering her coat and bag. "In the meantime, I'll see if I can shake down any shady folks."

"Lohr!"

"I'm kidding," her best friend laughed. "Totally, totally kidding…"

With a wink, she strolled out the door.

SEVEN

A Casual Haunting

I⟨T WAS⟩ late into the evening when Sella locked up the shop and turned the sign to 'Closed.' She sent Beejee up earlier to see if Koukie was still lounging in her room, and after a suspicious pause, he reported back with an annoyed, "*Apparently* she has 'nowhere else to go.' I told her there are plenty of places, she told me to name ONE, my mind blanked on anything other than the alleyways, and now she's curled up by my fireplace."

Sella rolled her eyes.

Part of her wanted to keep the shop open later than normal so she didn't have to go upstairs and deal with the cat, the predicament she had found herself in, or the fact that maybe, just maybe, the town *was* in danger.

But the shop was a little busier than usual, which was shocking. The old weavers clearly hadn't started gossiping about Sella this morning, but she was faced with a surprising wave of guests from the hotel. On a normal day, it would be a blessing. Today, it was not.

With every person who came in, Sella had to pretend

that everything was okay, act like she wasn't worried, and explain, *again*, that no, she didn't sell nettle root tea for aches and pains. Britbark far surpassed nettles because it didn't have the chance of reactions. No, she didn't know where they could harvest nettle root themselves, and frankly, it wouldn't be a good idea.

She sighed as she ascended the stairs. The old wood creaked gently under her feet. After everything today, all she wanted to do was go to her loft, feed the cats, and pass out without having to entertain Beejee's complaints. Obviously, she wouldn't be sending Koukie into the cold. Beejee would have to accept that.

Sella waved her hand to unlock the door and light her fires before she opened it slowly, coaxing the slightly rusted brass hinges to keep them from squeaking. Through the crack in the door, she watched as her little fires overhead grew, illuminating the space in a warm, comforting glow. She rested her head against the wood door frame, only partly inside the loft, and sighed again. She felt it in her chest; she wouldn't be sleeping tonight. She needed to eat… and maybe cook her feelings out.

"Hey, Beejee." She finally opened the door fully, grimacing as the hinges squeaked at the motion.

She found her familiar mid-hiss at the orange cat. At the sound of the door, he turned to Sella. "Tell her to get away from *my* fireplace. I don't want to use claws, but I *will.*"

Sella's gaze bounced from the curled up, peacefully sleeping Koukie near the hearth to Beejee… who was all bristles and anger at the threshold. "It looks like there's room for both of you." She removed her boots and began unbuttoning her blouse. It was true: there was plenty of space to spare on the warm redbrick. "Besides, you should get some rest, if you can. I know I won't."

"Why not?" Beejee flicked his tail. "Sleep is easy. Close your eyes and do it."

Sella laughed, but the sound was pained. "Lohrna wants me to help investigate. She doesn't trust Benka to do it right." She threw her clothes aside and crossed the room to the small closet in the corner. "I told her I'd sleep on it."

Beejee huffed. "Don't bother staying awake contemplating it. Just say 'no.'"

Light rain began to tap against the window and Sella pulled a long nightdress over her head. She pinned back her unruly hair and with a warning glance to make sure Beejee wouldn't resort to violence, she cracked the window to listen to the rain. It was brisk outside, and she shivered at the temperature contrast. There was faint but lively violin music from the tavern next door. Hazen must have his doors and windows open too.

Considering today, it felt strange to think life continued on even when something so jarring had affected them.

She turned back to Beejee. "I won't get us involved. Today was bad enough as it is. The more I poke around, the worse it'll get." And yet, guilt gnawed at her stomach. She worried about the hem of her sleeping shirt. "Or, I'm just starving," she muttered to herself.

In her kitchen, an onion fell to the floor with a *thump*.

Sella frowned at it, brow furrowing. Her first inclination would be a breeze, but… well, she was far beyond "first inclinations" now. Bemusement filtered into her tone. "Hello?"

If the ghost was around, she didn't answer.

Sella side-eyed the window. Maybe the onion was just… lopsided.

Sella lit the fire beneath her oven, picked up the yellow onion, and began to peel away the flakey skin. As she chopped it, she hummed to the quiet tune of the tavern to keep the sting in her eyes at bay. The room warmed with the oven's heat. She glanced at Beejee, who was curled up by the fireplace, confirming her begrudging assumption. For a rare moment, there was peace.

Behind her, a cabinet door creaked open.

The hair on the back of her neck stood on end and a chill rushed across her arms despite the warmth of the room. She set the knife down.

"Cali?" Sella genuinely assumed the ghost had better places to be… like lurking near her body, or existing wherever ghosts did when they weren't haunting someone.

Still, only silence greeted her.

Sella closed the cabinet door. The rain was getting worse. She could barely hear the music now. Stifling the uneasy feeling in her stomach, Sella shrugged and pulled garlic from the braid that hung off one of the cabinet handles and with it, took a handful of bright green beans back to the chopped onion.

"Don't forget protein," Beejee ordered with his eyes still closed. "We need to eat too."

"You got it." She noticed his 'we,' but only smiled so as not to draw attention to his charity.

With all her ingredients in the heavy ceramic dish, she added oil and tossed them together. As she did, magic ran through her: a slight tingle at her scalp that raced down her arms and released from the tips of her fingers. Into the dish, she added her intention: *calm and easy sleep.* She placed the ceramic in the oven and flopped on the couch in front of the fire.

Moments later, a rich aroma began to fill the room and she realized how hungry she was. With a long inhale, she closed her eyes. It wouldn't be long until dinner was done: roasted and seasoned vegetables, and a side of plain red meat for the cats, all infused with magic from generations of teachings.

Outside, the rain grew louder, the music faded, replaced by the crackle of the fires drifting overhead. Her body sank deeper into the velvet couch.

BANG!

Sella leapt off her couch and onto her feet. The sound jolted everyone into sudden panic. At the hearth, Beejee was already hissing and spitting, and Koukie scurried under Sella's bed.

"What *was* that?" Beejee demanded. His tail flicked violently.

Sella squinted in every corner of her home. Nothing was out of place; the front door was still shut and locked. "I... I don't know." It was terribly quiet.

Except...

The window had been slammed closed. A chill swept up her arms, but she tried to reason it away. "There must be a storm brewing."

Yes. That was an appropriate reason. The tension drained from her limbs. It left her tired. She laughed a little, feeling silly. "The wind knocked the window shut."

Beejee's ear twitched. "I don't like it." He sniffed the air, little pink nose twitching. "Too much garlic," he changed the subject.

"No such thing," Sella countered. She adored the slightly nutty, rich flavor it offered any dish. With just a little oil, garlic, onion, and salt, any dish was transformed into something so much more. It turned a simple recipe into the feeling of coming home.

Shaking out the last of her tension, Sella stepped back into the kitchenette. She pulled dinner from the oven, immune to the high heat of the ceramic. "Okay, Beejee, Koukie, dinner's up." She removed the meat and began to dice it for them.

Koukie's orange and white face emerged from beneath the bed. She looked around cautiously, then slinked out from the shadows with grace. Tail up, she pranced into the living space with a verve Sella had not yet seen in her.

"She okay?" Sella asked Beejee.

Beejee looked at the cat, then to Sella. "She won't talk to me."

Sella bit the inside of her lip. She could only imagine what kind of stress Koukie was under being in an unfamiliar home with an unfriendly cat, her person gone, and a reluctant care-taker who neglected dinner until way too late. She set two small plates for them and gave each a small head scratch as they ate.

"I'm sorry," she whispered to Koukie.

The cat purred in response.

She smiled and rose to fix her own plate, but when she got to the counter, the plate was upside down.

Sella's smile vanished. What in all the lower levels was going on? Almost aggressively, she flipped the plate back and scooped the bright roasted vegetables with a large wooden spatula. She turned to grab utensils from a nearby drawer. The drawer, however, would not open.

She pulled again. It remained shut. Sella looked around the empty room, then huffed and pulled the handle quickly.

The drawer sprung free with ease and the motion of her heavy tug landed Sella on the floor. "Lavender be damned," she seethed, rubbing her back as she rose rather ungracefully. She pulled a fork free from the drawer and closed it with enough force that the metal within rattled loudly. She grimaced at her own overreaction.

"You're having a bit of a rough night, aren't you?" Beejee asked, licking his lips.

"I have a lot on my mind. I'm stressed." As if it weren't obvious. She took a big, undignified bite of a fork full of green beans. They crunched loudly as she chewed, impatiently waiting for the magic to take effect.

Behind her, she heard a cabinet open again. Now *this* was a classic haunting. She couldn't see Cali's ghost; she was probably too busy manipulating her environment to materialize, but Sella felt her stare. It burrowed into the corners of her mind. Another cabinet door creaked open.

"No, thank you," Sella snapped without looking back.

She heard the door shut.

She took another large bite, and with a mouthful said, "This isn't helping your case… In fact, it makes me determined *not* to get involved, if this is how you're going to be about it."

In front of her, the linen closet opened slowly. And slammed shut.

Great.

. . .

IT WAS PREDAWN, and Sella was rubbing her eyes furiously with the palms of her hands. Beejee had long since resigned himself to sleeping downstairs in the shop window. Koukie was the only one still in good spirits. She paraded across the couch with her fluffy orange tail up as if she was proud of Cali for all her hard work haunting the place.

"How am I supposed to think through what to do when you're keeping me up all night? Finding pros in the 'helping solve a murder' initiative only gets harder the less I'm able to function." Sella looked around the room. The ghost still had not made an appearance, but did spend the night opening and slamming cabinets, removing folded laundry from drawers, knocking over books, and even once pinching Sella's big toe after she threw herself on the bed with a pillow over her head.

The only answer was the sound of rain. Apparently, Cali was also trying to freeze her out. No matter how Sella tried to close the window, after around 3am, it stayed open.

Sella grumbled and poured herself another cup of black coffee. She added a dash of liquor to calm her nerves and was grateful Beejee wasn't there to shame her for drinking before sunrise. Technically, it was still night. Kind of. And special circumstances called for special reserve whiskey.

"Alright." She rested her body against the dark wood counter. "Can you at least show yourself? I feel like I'm going insane."

"That's the point," Cali's disembodied voice whispered from every corner of the room. "And the hauntings will continue until you agree, fully, to help me catch my killer."

Sella looked from corner to corner. "No more silent treatment?"

"It's very difficult to show up *and* move things." Cali's form materialized at last. She was standing by the window with her arms crossed over her chest. Her expression was fierce, eyes fixed on Sella and jaw set so hard her muscles in her cheeks twitched. "This hasn't been easy on me either. Did you know dead people also get tired? Because now *I* know."

Sella took a long drink from her mug, her eyes locked on Cali. "I know banishing spells," she said at last.

Cali's green eyes narrowed. Her small frame seemed to fill the entire window, blocking any light from the slowly rising sun behind the clouds. She squared her shoulders. "Then do it."

Sella took another sip, letting the warmth fill her throat and core. Cali was quick to call her bluff. "Lucky for you, I wouldn't do that. Banishing spells are for spirits who have no business here and need to move on. That's clearly not what's happening with you." Her fingers traced the edge of the hot ceramic as she spoke. "But considering that if I *really* wanted to, I could make you leave the world of the living... Can you please stop wrecking the place? Truce?"

Cali looked her up and down, slowly, as if assessing her intentions, her level of sincerity.

Sella held her breath.

"For now," the ghost said finally. "Truce."

Sella's body nearly crumbled as she emptied her lungs. "Thank the tides." She sighed and straightened again. "Alright, in honor of that truce... you said we were tired." Sella gestured to her bed.

Cali eyed the crumpled sheets and scattered pillows suspiciously.

"I'll sleep on the couch," Sella continued. "I usually do anyway."

"Well… That's kind of sad. Now I feel like a monster." Cali sidestepped the couch and hearth. She was making her way to the bed regardless.

A faint smile lifted the corners of Sella's lips. From delirium, gratitude at sleep being so close, or something else, she wasn't sure. "You're not a monster. You're…"

"Dead."

"I was going to say a poltergeist." Sella chuckled. She hoped to lighten the mood, but Cali's expression was impossible to read. She stifled her smile and went on with a more somber tone, "Things will be okay, Cali." She paused and felt her feet growing unsteady in her sleepiness. "The sheets are clean. Mostly. Ignore the cat hair."

"I'm used to that." Cali glanced down at the bed, then disappeared. The comforter and blankets shifted and one feather pillow dented slightly.

"Let's both try to get an hour of sleep." Sella yawned and curled up on the couch. She extinguished the fires overhead with a flick of her wrist so the loft was suddenly dark and quiet. Only the warm glow from the fireplace remained.

It was only a moment later that Sella heard Cali's small voice from her bed. "Sella?"

The witch turned over on the couch, propped her arm under her head as a pillow and waited.

"Why have you been so indecisive about helping me?"

Sella grunted a little as she adjusted her body to fit the small couch yet again. "I *want* to help. I know it's the right thing to do," she said, a little too honestly. Sleepiness made her filter thin. "But I'm afraid."

"I'm afraid, too." The ghost's voice sounded far away.

"I can't even imagine."

There was a long pause. Sella's eyes closed. Perhaps the ghost had finally fallen asleep, or gone to wherever ghosts went when they rested.

But Cali's voice spoke again, this time, a little louder. "You're the only one who can see me. I got upset when you said you told the cat-"

"Beejee."

Cali continued without a missed beat, "When you told Beejee you wouldn't get involved. If you don't help me… Well, there's no one left. I'm alone."

Sella's eyes were still shut, but her expression shifted. "I'm not going to tell you how to respond to any of this." Her voice was strained but she hoped to be supportive. "But you're not alone. Beejee and I will be here for you for as much of it as we can."

"I'm not sure you can speak for Beejee on that one." A light laugh from the bed made Sella smile.

"No, you're right." Her own small chuckle escaped her. "But *I* will be here. I'll do what I can."

"Then truce, part two. I'll do what I can, also. I'll listen to you complain about it every step of the way."

"I don't complain that much," Sella's smile grew.

"Mhm," Cali mumbled. "Sure, Sella. Goodnight."

"Goodnight, Cali." The coffee did nothing to stop sleep from claiming her as soon as the words left her mouth. All was dark and dreamless until the sound of rain faded.

EIGHT

Interview with the Witch

THE NEXT MORNING, Sella awoke to a crushing weight on her chest and the sound of a shrill voice in her ears.

Beejee was standing on her chest already mid-announcement: "-a body washed up on the beach!"

Sella rubbed her eyes and pushed him off. He landed on the ground silently, looking extremely disgruntled by her action.

Sella couldn't find the energy to care. "What?"

"The whole town is in a panic! Hazen's been asking about the dead girl, then her *body* washed up on shore. Someone must've tried to dump it."

Sella wiped away sleep from her eyes and tried to sort the series of events into some kind of linear order. "Okay…" She propped herself on her elbows and craned toward her bed. It was empty, but that didn't necessarily mean Cali wasn't there. Sella lowered her voice, "Okay, wait… Cali's body?"

"Who *else* in this tiny town?! Wake up!" Beejee hissed from the floor. He scampered away, but his voice lingered.

"Get up, open the shop. Let's not make ourselves suspect number one!"

"Right, right… right!" Sella threw herself from the couch and raided the pile of clothes on the floor, courtesy of Cali's hauntings. She pulled on a long black dress and slipped on her boots before she rushed to the door. She paused and called hastily over her shoulder: "Koukie? Koukie, come downstairs! I'll feed you there."

"As if she understands." Beejee followed Sella down the steps. He grumbled the whole way about the stupidity of the other cat, but Sella ignored him.

She flipped the sign to 'Open' and unlocked the door. With a flick, she lit the fires and started a batch of coffee. The shop filled with the warm smell of grounds and the magical ambiance of chatter, clinking cups, and faint music. It was warm despite the cold fog outside and she hoped the gentle glow that emitted from the bay window would look charming, sweet, and not at all unusual.

Behind the counter, Sella dug through her potions, looking for something she could put in the pot to make universal friends with whoever walked in. She came up empty. Making friends – either through hard work or potions – had never been her strong suit. As she hunted for an alternative, she asked quietly, "So her body washed up? That's the rumor?"

"Everyone knew she was missing, thanks to Hazen's big mouth," Beejee said, looking from the door to her and back again like he was expecting all the king's force to break through at any moment. If she didn't know any better, she'd be suspicious of the cat. He was making himself look incredibly guilty.

"Stop it with your anxiousness, Beejee. First of all, Hazen is a man of few words and you know it. Second, it's a *good* thing they found her. Now maybe she can rest."

"Excuse me?" Cali's voice rang from the corner of the shop. "I will not rest until the culprit is put to justice!"

"Oh, go to the light, would you?" Beejee murmured.

Sella startled. Thank fair tides that only she could understand him or she would be mortified.

"What?" Beejee's tone was innocent.

"Hush, you." Sella peered from behind the counter, on her toes in an unnatural posture. "Cali...?"

"Yeah?"

"Umm..." What do you say to a ghost who just found out their body was unceremoniously dumped into the sea? Sella wondered for a moment if Cali's culture required burial rites or cremation. Her heart felt heavy. With little decorum, she blurted out, "I'm sorry that, you know, they found your body washed up."

She ducked down behind the counter again and imagined herself turning into a puddle and seeping through the cracks in the old floorboards. What in all the *actual seas* had she said? Her cheeks flushed red.

"It's okay," Cali's voice called back, clearly unfazed by Sella's awkwardness. "It's not dignified, but neither is being dead, I guess. Just, you know, in general. It's just weird that someone moved my body. Were they trying to make it look like I went back home? Do they not know how tides work? Anyway, I didn't go see it."

"Too busy being a nuisance," Beejee said.

Cali went on, "Maybe someone *did* see you leave my apartment?"

Sella hit her forehead on the lower shelf. It was probably best if both of them shut up for now. She took a deep breath and began sorting through the potions.

"Hey, I just noticed the ambiance of your shop." Cali changed the subject. "It's nice. I never really listened before. It sounds… homey? Like there's people in here being cozy."

Sella continued to search, bottles clinked together loudly as she did. "Yeah, it's a unique spell…" Sella still felt disoriented from the recent news, but at least this was familiar territory. "I actually invented it."

"Really?" Cali sounded amazed. "That's creative."

"Thanks." Sella closed her eyes and grabbed a bottle at random. She opened one eye and stared at the green liquid in a clear glass bottle. The label read 'Growth.' She shrugged and added a few drops to the pot.

The bell above the door jingled.

Sella looked up, expecting Lohrna, but instead, the doorway was occupied by a lanky man in ill-fitting clothes. He looked young, but somehow still weathered. His dark hair was streaked with gray, especially near small horns that peeked out near his ears. Around his mouth, fine wrinkles formed when he offered a tight, thin-lipped smile. "Are you Sella?"

"Yes?"

"Do you have a moment?" The door shut resolutely behind him, which put her on edge. He seemed nervous, but that didn't mean anything. A lot of people were nervous their first time in her shop.

Tensing herself, Sella moved from around the counter. "How can I help you?" She kept her hand on the wood as if it could back her up.

Cali drifted towards the man from behind, assessing him with a suspicious gaze. "Who's this?"

Sella waved her hand, but beside her, Beejee stood at attention, eyeing the newcomer the same way Cali did.

"I'm Jahra. I'm Detective Benka's assistant." His strained smile never left. Sella remembered him, vaguely, but Jahra had been small when she left. She could imagine the round boy within his narrow face. Yet another face she left behind years ago, changed by time. Jahra went on, seemingly unaware of Sella's scrutiny of his changed appearance. "Benka asked if you could come meet with him. He has a few questions."

A chill swept up her spine.

"Regarding?" Both Sella and Beejee asked in unison, though his words only sounded like a meow to everyone else.

Jahra looked away and wrung his hands. "A human. She, um… washed ashore today. It looks like she didn't… Well, she didn't walk into the ocean. If you know what I mean."

"That's crass," Cali scoffed.

Sella hoped her gasp sounded real. "You mean to say, a murder?"

"I'm afraid so." Jahra took a step back toward the door. "Do you have time?"

"I'm not sure how much help I can be," Sella lied. "And I have a shop to run."

"Benka said it won't take long. He's trying to get a comprehensive idea of who this woman was. Hazen mentioned she had been in your shop before." Jahra opened the door and gestured for her to follow. There was clearly no choice. His request was simply a formality. "If you don't mind?"

"Seems like whether we mind or not, we're going." Beejee bristled. He leapt off the counter and made his way out the door.

Sella sighed. He was right. "Sure, let me lock up." She looked at Cali, trying to give her a silent warning to stay behind. But, like steam, Cali's image vanished and Sella couldn't be sure her message was received.

"After you," Jahra said.

Like he was already escorting a prisoner.

Feeling weak, Sella waved her hand to extinguish the fires inside the shop. At her feet, Beejee pushed against her leg, urging her forward. She flipped the sign to "Closed," locked the door, and reluctantly followed Jahra with her head held high.

Her feigned confidence didn't change how small she felt.

BENKA WAS A TALL, broad man. He always looked a little tired, but his eyes were sharp. They were always fixated on something — some small detail — or darting about a room of faces like he was memorizing them, scrutinizing every expression. Despite his reputation, Sella always suspected that he noticed more than he let on. Whether his unassuming posture was a ruse or not, she couldn't know, but she always did her best not to be the center of his attention.

So now, she shifted uncomfortably in her seat as his blue eyes locked onto hers like a predator cornering prey. She stayed silent. She knew enough to understand that he was making her uncomfortable on purpose.

At last, Benka leaned back in his own chair, which resulted in an almost-amusing creaking sound. He hummed, then crossed his arms over his large chest. "Sella, the witch…"

"Kitchen witch." Sella gave him a curt nod.

"Kitchen witch." Benka's voice was suddenly warm, friendly. He smiled placatingly. "What exactly is that?"

Sella's skin felt like it was bristling just beneath the surface. She maintained her friendly expression, trying not to stiffen. "I mainly do potions or magic baked into food. I work with herbs, flowers… and the bees at the edge of the forest."

"Ever go down to the beach for your supplies?" he asked casually.

She shook her head. "Not much these days. I did when I was learning from my mother. Do you remember her?"

"I do. Quite well. She was a good woman. A good witch."

A lump formed in Sella's throat. "She was."

Benka didn't dwell on her, which was perfectly fine with Sella. "You don't get to the water much anymore?"

"No." Her voice was calm and even. "I don't like the ocean."

She glanced at Beejee. He was perched on the corner of the table, staring at Benka with wide, unblinking eyes. If this were a casual conversation, she might have added that her familiar wanted to travel by sea. That he was always nagging her to leave the continent and explore the world at large.

But this was an interrogation, however Benka feigned pleasantries. The less information she gave, the better. Enough people in the town knew she and Beejee spoke to each other, but there was no reason to remind him of that now.

Benka leaned forward. "Can't say I blame you."

Sella took a deep breath through her nose and waited.

"You work in kitchens, with potions." There was a pause. Sweat trailed down Sella's neck. "Have you ever gotten into the poison business?"

Sella's scalp prickled. "Poison...? That's not 'business.' That's illegal."

"Lucrative, though."

Sella's eyes narrowed. "How do you know?"

"I've been around a long, long time." Benka leaned back in his chair again. He rested his hands on his lap. "Did you know the deceased?"

From poison to Cali. She didn't like where this was going already. "Um, no, not really," she stumbled over her words, caught off-guard. "She came into the shop once or twice, but we never talked much."

"I thought we were becoming friends... this is just hurt-ful." Cali sighed.

The ghost's disembodied voice nearly made Sella fall out of her chair. Only intense concentration kept her still – probably *too* still. For a moment, she feared Benka could hear Cali too, but apparently, the ghost couldn't appear to simply anyone.

Unfazed, Cali continued. "I think I'm charming." She folded her arms across her chest.

Sella pinched her leg to keep from snorting.

"So, you don't remember what you sold her?" Benka asked, narrowing his eyes.

She needed to focus. Sella leaned forward, trying to regain control of the conversation. "No, I'm sorry. Nothing in my shop could do damage to anyone–"

"That's not what I'm implying." Benka put his hands up in surrender. "I just want to know details about our victim."

"Favorite color: yellow," Cali whispered. "Favorite food: crackled bread."

Sella scratched her ear, trying to signal Cali to stop talking.

"She was new to town." Benka mirrored Sella's posture as he moved in closer. "Very few people knew her, so it's odd that she'd already have enemies. I'm just trying to get a better understanding."

"Maybe someone followed her from her home country? Have you checked in with Penya at the hotel?"

He leaned back in his chair again, his motions ebbing and flowing like the tides. Yet with each movement, there was a long moment of complete stillness. It was unsettling. "It's on my to-do list. Once I get a better idea of what I'm working with."

The longer this went on, the better the chance he'd connect her with a murder weapon she didn't create. "I wish I could be more helpful," Sella said. "Maybe stop by the shop for an enlightenment brew sometime."

"Perhaps I will." Benka stood and gestured for Sella to do the same.

She rose but waited. There was something more, she was certain. He wasn't going to let her leave without asking.

He did not wait long. "Actually, one more thing…" Benka held up one finger as if he had only now remembered it. "Do you know where Lohrna was two nights ago?"

Sella paused. Cali died on a full moon. Lohrna must have been where she always was those nights… a place no one in town knew, a place where no one could verify.

"Why?" Sella asked after a long pause.

"It's just..." Benka waved a hand. "A former gem seller dies by poison. Some gems go missing. You have to wonder about the one rock enthusiast in town."

All this time, she never thought Lohrna would be his suspect. Sella's pulse quickened, her blood like ice. "She was with me," Sella lied. "All night."

"Mhm..." Benka nodded, but Sella couldn't tell what that meant. "Thank you."

Sella smiled, so fake she thought her face would crack. "Thank you, Benka. I hope you catch whoever did this."

"Oh, I will."

It sounded like a threat.

NINE

Moral Ob-brew-gation

Back inside the comfort of her shop, Sella held her head in her hands. She hadn't slept, she had a new cat to feed and care for, there was a ghost haunting her, and now she needed to worry about Lohrna, too. No amount of coffee or pastries would stop the turning in her stomach or the headache forming behind her eyes.

Lohrna, however, was helping herself to her third scone, and using it as a pointer to drive home her words, oblivious of the crumbs that fell every time. She thrust the scone at Sella rhythmically as she spoke. "Benka's an *old*, out-of-his-*element, cynical* man." She bit into the pastry and took a long swig of coffee. "I'm not worried about him. I did nothing wrong."

"Of course you didn't. But why would he be asking unless he thought he knew something?" Sella peeked at Lohrna through her fingers. Her friend shrugged and another spray of crumbs settled on the wood floor.

"Ah, who knows? I'm eccentric. It bothers people."

"Being eccentric and being suspected of murder are not

the same thing! And if anyone finds out I lied, it's going to look *really* suspicious."

"No one will know. This town thinks it's so good at gossip, but no one pays attention to things outside their circle." Lohrna shrugged. "I was where I always am on full moons, and that's that." She waved her hand as if shooing away further accusations. "So, how's the ghost situation shaping up?"

Sella sighed. She wasn't going to win Lohrna's subject change. If her friend wanted to move on, they would be moving on.

"She's haunting me," Sella groaned.

"Haunting you?"

Sella looked around the shop with tired eyes. She whispered, almost a hiss as her tone dripped with frustration, "She kept me up all night. And went to the interrogation with Benka. She can't be stopped."

"My type of woman." Lohrna took another large bite. She chewed slowly this time, waiting.

"What?" Sella straightened and met her stare.

"Well, you said you'd sleep on it. So maybe you didn't sleep, but you did make a firm decision, right? You've got a unique set of skills with your magic. Plus, you're the only one who can see her. I think she's right to try getting you on her team. And, frankly, it's kind of your moral obligation."

Sella shook her head. "I don't know... We do have a sort of truce going now."

"Well, that's one step forward. Let's go look for clues!"

"That's a sprint forward," Sella complained as she sank lower.

Lohrna leaned back in her stool so far Sella was

concerned she'd fall. "How about I buy you a drink at Hazen's tonight? You can sit there silently, being a grump if you want to. I'll do all the talking, see what some of these folks know."

Sella groaned. She closed her eyes and rubbed at her temples.

"Come oooooon…" Lohrna pushed Sella's shoulder. She waited, but Sella could hear her chewing on her pastries.

Sella opened her eyes at last and glared at her friend. "*Two* drinks," she negotiated firmly, holding up her fingers to emphasize the point.

"Yes!" Lohrna rose from her seat in celebration. "Thank you! Your ghost will be so happy!"

She wanted to say that Cali was nobody's ghost, that in the short time she had spent with her, she knew Cali was her own force. But Sella was silent instead, hauling herself off her own seat.

Lohrna gave her a swift pat on the back. "I'll come back at sundown."

Sella nodded. "Yeah, looking forward to it."

"Don't tell lies, Sella." Lohrna smiled wryly. "Except when you're my alibi."

"YOU'RE CLOSING *EARLY?*" Beejee protested as Sella locked the door and turned the sign to 'Closed.' "But this tragedy is good for business. We've never seen such an influx of protective charm sales."

"That's a terrible way to look at things." But she had to admit he was right.

It wasn't just protective charms, either. People, in a steady trickle, came in to buy calming potions, sleep aids, and blends of courage. A few tried to gossip to see if she heard any additional intel, who she thought would do such a thing…

It was exhausting. Sella hoped they would never discover that she'd spoken to Benka this morning.

"I genuinely cannot stay awake any longer." Sella flicked her wrist and extinguished the little fires. "Plus, I'm getting cranky."

"Yes. I noticed."

Sella side-eyed him as she ascended the narrow staircase. "Well, we can't have a curmudgeon potion seller right after there was a murder. Once people find out she was poisoned, they'll all be looking at me with a spyglass."

Beejee followed after her with silent steps. Sella took his lack of response as a concession despite his disappointment at the missed sales.

She opened the door to their little home and flung her boots off into a corner. If Lohrna was dragging her out, she desperately needed the rest. It was the hardest day she'd had in a long time.

Sella sank into her bed and pulled the covers over her head. She let the weight of them press down on her, wrapping her limbs in a snug embrace. She turned her face to rest in her down pillow and breathed in deeply. The smell of last night's dinner still lingered in the air, mixing with the richness of rain and the bitterness of ground coffee beans. She took another long breath and waited for dreamless sleep to consume her.

Instead, she found herself stuck in a thought loop. Her

mind turned her worries over and over until they were made smooth like stones at the bottom of a riverbed. Who killed Cali? Why had Benka asked about Lohrna? To hone into Lohrna so soon, it had to be more than a few missing gems. The detective must know the method of her death, based on the bruising pattern. What if he thought Sella helped Lohrna kill her?

She lied on instinct. It was a quick reaction to protect her friend and if she had to do it over again, she would. But still, if anyone else saw Lohrna that night, if anyone could poke a hole in their alibi…

Benka knew Sella's mother, though. He didn't have a distrust of magic, did he? She couldn't tell. Sella had limited interactions with him before she left town and had hardly seen him the year since she returned.

Sella grumbled to herself and tightened her grip on the blankets. She pulled them closer, burrowing inside the heavy wool. It created a cocoon of warmth that finally relaxed her.

"This is shaping up to be an adventure no one asked for." Beejee's little paws sank into the pillow beside her. He wiggled his nose and slid under the covers to curl beside her. "Can we travel the world now?"

"Not the worst idea," she mused, eyes closed. She stroked his ears and snuggled him closer. To her surprise, he let her. Minds finally quiet, the two of them drifted off to sleep.

THEY AWOKE to the sound of Koukie meowing. It was already getting dark and the rain had begun to fall in a calming drizzle. As Beejee scolded the other cat about waking them, Sella prepared their dinner. Even as she went through the motions, though, her mind was on tonight. She hoped that it would be uneventful — that there would be nothing to see, no one to talk to, and Lohrna would give up on this quest to solve a mystery before anyone got hurt.

Well, anyone *else* got hurt.

"Aren't you worried asking questions will put Lohrna right on Benka's path?" Beejee asked through a mouthful of chicken.

Sella's eyes flicked to the familiar, but she said nothing to contradict or confirm. They both knew he was right – and it was nothing she hadn't been thinking already.

A pebble hit her window. Sella almost laughed. Lohrna hadn't summoned Sella that way since they were kids.

"Good luck," Beejee said.

"Thanks." Sella sighed. He meant it, and so did she.

"I'm coming, too!" Cali appeared in the doorway, materializing from the shadows.

Sella jumped back, clutching her heart. Fires all across the small living space burst brightly. "Tides, Cali! You can't just appear like that!"

"Sorry! Sorry!" Cali shrunk her shoulders to make herself smaller and took a step back. Despite her posture, her tone was firm, "But I *am* coming with you."

Sella tapped her chest lightly with an open palm, mimicking the beat of her racing heart. It calmed her breathing quickly. "I can't stop you, can I?" She got the feeling that even in life, Cali couldn't be stopped.

"No, I guess you literally can't." Cali's expression shifted. A bright smile widened her face.

Another pebble hit Sella's window.

"That's our call." Sella caught herself returning a smile despite her annoyance at the whole situation. She tossed a cape around her neck and pulled a hat snug on her head, covering her pointed ears carefully. It was hardly a walk at all, but she wanted to hide as much as she could. She looked to Cali. "Let's go."

TEN

A Ticket to Kill For

THE TAVERN WAS, to Sella's horror, packed with patrons. Beside her, Cali and Lohrna both looked delighted. Sella's gaze bounced between the two of them: each wore a similar smile and bright eyes that scanned the large open space, taking everything in. A part of her wondered how either of them could be in such good spirits, considering...

The three moved through the tavern slowly.

Several rustic brass chandeliers with large, dripping wax candles illuminated the large room. Round, wood pillars held up dusty rafters. Despite the neglected spaces, the stretching shadows, and rain outside, the space was warm and inviting. Crowds of different people from the town gathered at high and low tables, drinking, eating, and laughing despite the dangers of a murderer potentially on the loose. In here, it was as if all of the mystery and uncertainty was somewhere far away.

Lohrna grabbed Sella's hand in hers and gave it a squeeze. "Let's get you that drink. And keep your ears open."

"Two drinks," Sella reminded her.

Cali raised an eyebrow at Sella but remained quiet.

Lohrna guided them to a small table. Sella sat, then glanced at Cali who was waiting by the open chair. The ghost's eyebrows knitted together and her image flickered.

Sella pushed the chair out a little with her foot. Cali smiled before sitting down beside her.

Lohrna looked from the empty chair to Sella, not letting the small movement escape her notice. "Wait," she whispered, pointing to the chair. "Is that…?"

Sella nodded.

Lohrna nearly squeaked — a high-pitched excited sound escaped her and she pulled her hands close to her chest. "I'll go get drinks, and then introductions are in order!"

"Don't make it weird." Sella dropped her head into her hands.

"I won't!" Lohrna called back as she pushed her way to the bar.

The din of the crowded tavern, Sella hoped, concealed Lohrna's excitement from Cali.

"I like her." So, Cali did notice. At least she seemed to take it well. "How do you know her?"

Sella rested her chin in her hand and covered her mouth so she wouldn't look like she was blatantly talking to herself. "She's been my friend since we were kids."

Cali mimicked Sella's body language and rested her own chin in her hands. Her eyes were soft and gentle though she was clearly studying Sella's face. It felt like Benka's interrogation… and somehow entirely different.

There was something about the way Cali watched her — eyes bright, smile easy, like she was truly interested in the story. It made Sella want to go on despite her momentary discomfort. Sella mumbled through her fingers, "I was… a bit of a weird kid. People didn't like that I could use fire. She was the only other person my age who wanted me around. Even after 'The Incident—'"

"Sellaaaaa!" A voice, loud and joyous, erupted from the bar, cutting her off.

A burly man with ram horns looping around graying curls approached the table. Lohrna was hot on his heels, carrying large glasses of foaming honey liquor in each hand.

Lohrna was hissing wildly at the man the whole way, but he paid her little mind. With a big toothed smile, he pulled at the chair Cali was sitting in.

Cali yelped at the jolt, but Sella held the chair firmly with her booted foot looped around a peg. "Sorry, Cirian. This one is saved for Beejee." She gestured at a nearby table with a few empty chairs. "Join us?"

Lohrna caught up and set both drinks at the table. She looked at the empty chair, then up at Cirian with a playful glare. She patted the table. "Grab a chair! A *different* one." To Sella, Lohrna was being incredibly obvious. She had to remind herself that only she could see Cali.

"Only in this tavern is there a seat reserved for a cat." Cirian laughed, taking it in stride. It sounded good-natured, but Cali bristled at his words.

Sella tried to smooth it over. "A familiar, Cirian, is much more than a pet. He's as old as I am, after all. And you know Beejee. He'll never let anyone hear the end of it if his seat is taken."

"Take my seat for now," Lohrna cut in. "This drink looks wrong anyway." She made a spectacle of inspecting the foam, holding it to the light and squinting dramatically. "I better go ask Hazen for another pour. Go on, sit!" The bossiness in her tone reminded Sella of Aadel. Every now and then, Lohrna really looked like her mother.

Cirian laughed and sat in her empty spot. "I'll heed that order!" He took a long sip of his dark red wine, offering Sella an amused expression as he drank. "Haven't seen you in the tavern in a while!" He thumped Sella's back with a large hand, a little too hard. She coughed through the blow.

"Yeah." Sella grimaced, ignoring a now giggling Cali. "It's been a few full moons."

Cirian, the local freespirit, could always be found in one of two places: At Hazen's tavern or roaming the shops and market, buying entirely too much. No one knew where he came from, only that he blew into town one day years ago and never did seem to leave. Where he got his money was also a mystery, but it was apparent he liked to spend it.

Sella did like to create her own stories about him now and then. He had been nothing but kind to her since they met when she moved back to town. And since Hazen liked him, so did everyone in town… especially the merchants.

"What brings you in on a ghastly night like this?" Another voice chimed in. Benka. He leaned over both their shoulders.

Cirian nearly leapt out of his seat when the old man's face appeared, but Sella was still, as though she expected him all along and he was running late. She side-eyed the detective and raised an eyebrow. "Detective Benka." Her heart rate spiked, but she kept her voice level. Lohrna was nowhere to be seen. Good.

Sella took a sip of her drink as nonchalantly as she could

muster, letting the liquid run into her stomach and warm her.

Beside her, Cali shifted in her seat, looking uncomfortable.

Cirian held his hand over his heart and laughed. "Benka, Benka, Benka. You have a way of sneaking up on people!"

"Being discreet is part of the job." Benka gave Cirian's shoulder a squeeze and rose to his full height. He looked like he had just woken up. His hair was sticking up in a few places and Sella noticed sleep lingering in his eye. *So much for working hard on the case*, she thought in irritation. Benka simply enjoyed being a nuisance.

"To answer your question," Sella pivoted the conversation, "we're in need of beverages, the likes of which only Hazen can provide. It's been a grueling day, after all, what with the news of a death. And your questioning felt a little pointed, if I may say so."

"You may."

"I did."

Cirian's gray eyes darted between the two. "I feel like I'm missing something…"

"Me too," Cali whispered. "You know, it might be a good idea to try *not* to antagonize the detective."

Sella took another sip, like she was unfazed. Her hand was shaking. She desperately hoped no one could tell.

"I hope I didn't offend you today," Benka said at last. He put his hands in his pockets and shifted his feet. "It's my job to look at every angle… I'll leave you to it. Be safe out there…"

And with that, Benka disappeared into the crowd.

Cirian waited until Benka was out of sight before he chuckled drily. "What was that about?"

Sella rolled her eyes, but stopped short of sighing. She needed to play this better. Her initial lie led her into a spiral, and everything tonight placed her on the defensive. "Benka asked me about poisons today."

Cirian winced. "Did the girl die of poisoning?"

"Woman," Cali corrected him.

"I suspect so." Sella ignored Cali's amendment for now. "If Benka was asking about it."

Cirian hummed. "He should know better than to question your potions. You're certified. And way past your careless side-effect days that people can't seem to get over."

Sella smiled, this time genuinely, even if it did sting that he mentioned her tendency of past mess-ups. She briefly wondered if he had some of his own wherever he came from. Beejee would be thrilled that he referenced her certification. "I'm sure Benka only wants my help determining the cause," she said, trying to convince herself that maybe, just maybe, that might be the case. "I'm feeling a bit cautious about it all."

"Of course you are. There's a murderer on the loose!"

Sella flinched at the reminder. At that moment, it felt like everyone was watching them. The buzz of chatter of the tavern, the live music blasting from the corner, the warmth of the cup at her fingertips... all of it faded from her awareness. In the breath that followed, she looked at every table and every corner, noting eyes darting to her and then away quickly. A few patrons leaned in close to one another and whispered after they caught her eye.

Did they know she'd been questioned today?

"Sella?" a voice pulled her back. "Sella?"

Sella blinked and shook her head. The music, the voices, the feel of cold, wet air as the door opened — it all came spilling back into her awareness. "Sorry." She ignored Cali's concerned gaze, instead focusing on Cirian — the one physically present. "Sorry, I'm just tired."

Lohrna broke the tension with the scraping of her chair across the stone floor. She positioned it beside Sella and handed her another drink. "These are better." She winked at Sella, then turned to Cirian. "So, I was talking with Ovina at the bar–"

"If you go back up there, tell her she still owes me that sweater commission. I ordered it a month ago." Cirian seemed to be joking, but Ovina was known for getting behind on her orders.

"Yes, yes. I will."

"It's a gift, so tell her that I kind of need it–"

"Cirian, I got it!" Lohrna set her drink down with a thud. "Anyway, can I finish my story?"

"Right, sorry." He let out a gentle laugh.

Sella couldn't help but shake her head. She knew Lohrna wouldn't see the parallel between Cirian and herself, but it was obvious here. They acted more like siblings than friends. A small pain hit Sella's heart. She missed so much since she was gone. "So what's new with Ovina?" Sella asked, trying to get her mind back to the task at hand.

Lohrna swallowed her drink. "So, Ovina's over there saying she knew Cali."

"Yes," Cali nodded. "She's sweet. She made me a welcome basket when I first rented out the apartment."

Sella shifted in her seat. "Oh yeah?" she said to both Cali and Lohrna. She wanted to hear more about that, about Cali's first few days in Marra. But it would have to wait for another time.

Lohrna went on. "Yep! She said she was always curious about the lands across the sea. I guess she wishes she could've asked Cali more questions about it."

Sella deflated. That was not the lead she hoped for. "Well, that's too bad."

"She also said that she'd *kill* for a ticket there." Lohrna held Sella's gaze.

"Well, that certainly wasn't the best choice of words." Sella glanced across the tavern at Ovina. The old woman was laughing with her sister, clapping at what seemed to be a hilarious joke.

Cali huffed. "I'm sure it's not Ovina. People who give welcome baskets don't murder people."

Beside her, Cirian finished his drink. "Ovina uses colorful language. I just hope Benka didn't hear that. He'll draw poor conclusions." Cirian looked over his shoulder to the bar. "I hope Hazen didn't either. He's taking Cali's death especially hard."

"Aww!" Cali said. "See? *Someone's* mourning me." She stood up to look over the heads in the crowd, eyeing Hazen working hard at the bar. Her brow furrowed. "Even if he's going about it weirdly."

"Hazen's the type to strap in and work hard despite it all. Maybe even *because* of it," Sella said, mostly to Cali. "I'm sure he's hurting more than he lets on."

The night at the tavern passed slowly. Cirian and

Lohrna kept drinking long after Sella stopped. She stayed with them, speaking up when there was the rare lull in their conversation, until she finally couldn't keep her yawns hidden anymore. She left them still talking about everything and nothing.

Cali trailed her like a shadow back home.

ELEVEN

Can't Back Down Now

"I don't think your little clue hunt last night helped our cause *at all*." Beejee's eyes tracked the people outside the shop. They were all giving the front door a wide berth.

"It got Cali to stop haunting us, though." Sella stirred the coffee with a small gold spoon. She had sprinkled extra motivation into the grounds and was concentrating on infusing more energy into the dark liquid with each round her spoon made.

"I still could." Cali materialized in the bay window. "It was actually kind of fun to be a traditional ghost for a bit."

Beejee hissed at her sudden appearance. "Don't scare me like that!" He swatted at her, but his claws were still sheathed. Not that he could harm Cali anyway. Still, that was a sign he was warming up to the ghost.

"Sorry," Cali squeaked, recoiling a little at Beejee's bared teeth. "I was quiet on my feet when I was alive... I guess more so in death." Cali looked out the window. "Is it just me, or does it kind of look like people are avoiding the shop...?"

"They often are." Sella set down a small bowl of treats for the cats. Koukie and Beejee, despite himself, scampered to her. "It'll blow over. Probably."

"Hmm," Beejee protested with a full mouth.

"I have a question." Cali had already moved on. "Why did you lie about Lohrna and where she was...?"

"Lohrna had nothing to do with what happened to you," Sella replied. She took a sip of her coffee.

"I didn't say that." Cali held up her hands.

"I don't want people thinking it, though." Sella winced. "She has access to my ingredients, she loves rare gems, and you were a gem collector. Worst of all, she was alone that night. That puts her at risk."

"I died on the full moon... is she a shapeshifter?" Cali's tone was confident, as if she didn't need confirmation.

Sella's eyes rose to the ghost at her window. "That's not my information to share."

"Must be lonely for her. To keep that secret every month..." Cali went on, as if she hadn't heard Sella at all. "They're rare on this continent, aren't they?"

Beejee, still licking his lips, leapt to the counter and sat by Sella. "She's smart. Too smart."

"They're *not* rare where you're from?" Sella asked, trying to pivot the conversation away from Lornha.

"Not really," the ghost mused. She sounded wistful, almost sad. Sella leaned across the counter. "But it's open at home. They don't have to hide it. Besides, we have a lot more witches there. They advertise the suppressors they sell on subscription." She ended with a little laugh. "Got to hand it to them, they make a killing back home."

Home. The word made Sella's heart hurt for her. Her brows furrowed as she considered the word. Cali was far from home. And dead. And stuck. Yet, here Cali was, pondering how lonely Lohrna must be feeling.

Who was worse off? A shapeshifter… or a ghost?

Sella sighed and straightened. "Cali, your home sounds very freeing."

"It is, in some ways." Cali smiled gently. "Or, it was… I guess wanting to see what's out there was my downfall, huh? But Marra is lovely, too. Much that I saw in this town is so different, but it's also more… collective than I've ever known. It's sweet how everyone knows everyone. People are friendly, even though I'm a human. I wish I had been able to see more of it."

"I've traveled all over Orakan." Sella's own half smile formed. "This seaside town, though…?" She trailed off; her mind wandered to the people of the town. "I guess there's a certain magic to Marra."

"I understand."

"Ask her about the ships." Beejee pawed at Sella's dark dress.

Sella leaned down to stroke his ear. His cheek pressed into her hand and a purr escaped his throat. She gave him one final pat on the head.

He glared at her, quick as ever to change his opinion on if he wanted to be touched or not. "Beejee wonders about your journey here, if it's not too much to ask," Sella said.

He headbutted Sella in approval.

"How can you talk to him?" Cali ignored the question.

"Familiars and witches are like… How can I describe

it?" She flicked her wrist and the fires above their heads grew in brightness and warmth. Cali looked up with wide eyes as Sella continued, "We're bonded. He's been with me since I was very young. We'll be together in this lifetime and… any others."

"Will you be ghosts together?"

"Maybe. If we decide to stick around."

"I'm glad Koukie is alright," Cali said. "But it would be less lonely to have another ghost around. Someone else who can understand me." She looked back outside and squinted. "Well, Beejee, the ships are smaller than you'd expect. Lots of mice… so maybe you'd like that." She laughed, though it sounded strained. The glimmer around her shifted. "It was a very boring trip, I'm sorry to say."

Beejee grumbled something even Sella couldn't hear.

She was so busy puzzling through what he might have said that she almost missed Cali's next whisper..

"Sella? Can you tell me about Cresablatt?"

Everything in Sella tensed. She swallowed. "If you're sure you want to know." With a sigh, she crossed the shop to sit beside Cali, settling into the comfy cushions of the window seat.

Beejee jumped up to sit beside them. "Can't have you looking like you're talking to yourself now. Rumors about you losing your mind would circle faster than pixies can fly."

Koukie joined them at the window seat and purred quietly as she made herself comfortable. Sella snapped her fingers and the music grew just a little louder.

"Cresablatt is extremely difficult to produce." Sella gave each cat a quick pet behind the ear. She took a deep breath, then continued. "You need several ingredients, some from this continent and some from across the sea."

"Where I'm from?"

"Tollintal? There's specific herbs that only grow there," Sella said.

"Yes."

"Then yes… And you need to make it *exactly*. Every cut of the herbs, every crush of the flowers… It has to be made fast in the right conditions," Sella went on. "It loses its potency after a few hours."

"When you say potency…?"

"A few hours after making it, it is basically useless."

"Hmm." Cali seemed to be thinking aloud. Her voice was distant. "So, someone would need to know how to make it, make it fast, *and* use ingredients from here and across the sea?"

"Yes."

"That narrows down our pool, doesn't it? At least that should rule out Lohrna to Benka and the others?"

"In theory. It should help… but I sell a lot, if not most, of the ingredients here in the shop. I'm sure Benka is aware of that. Lohrna could've gotten them at any time, or maybe he thinks we did it together." She leaned back in her seat and felt like a sudden weight was wrapped around her shoulders. The pressure crept from the base of her neck and settled behind her eyes. "If we're not careful, this could turn out very badly for us."

"We won't let that happen." Cali's expression was light as the air that fluttered between them. "We'll find the person who did this together. You'll help me cross over and set your names back in their rightful places."

Sella's brows rose. "You think so?"

"I know so. Besides, you can't back down now. You're in this with me."

For the first time, that didn't sound so bad.

TWELVE

A Mead-iocre Plan

Lohrna glared at Sella from behind the steam of her coffee. "I feel like I should be offended that Benka thinks I'm capable of something like that." But the corners of her lips betrayed her true feelings. She was smiling despite her narrowed eyes.

Sella waited, almost amused.

Lohrna tilted her head. "But I'm also weirdly flattered he thinks I'm clever enough to make Cresablatt."

There it was. The odd beam of sunlight that Lohrna always managed to find among the clouds.

"I'm not sure that's what you should be taking away from this." Sella raised a brow.

"What I'm taking away from this conversation is that you're in! 'Practical Potions and Honey' no more! Now, we're 'Practical Potions Detective Agency!' And it's a race against time before the killer strikes again!"

"Or you're arrested for murder," Beejee grumbled.

"He likes it!" Lohrna cheered.

Sella caught her dry laugh halfway from her throat. "You could say that."

"I keep telling you to create a spell that lets everyone understand me!" Beejee stomped one front paw down on the counter. "I'm tired of my genius going to waste!"

Sella rolled her eyes. She desperately hoped he didn't see.

Lohrna gave Beejee a little pet. He bared his teeth but didn't move away. "You know, little buddy, that foot stomping gesture would have a lot more impact if you were the size of a lion. Is there a spell to make him bigger?"

That's *all* they'd need – a lion-sized Beejee. Sella rolled her eyes. "Lohrna, this is serious. Whoever did this probably wasn't from here. I don't think they'll 'strike again,' but *we* could be in big trouble."

Lohrna cocked her head and thought for a moment. She tapped her chin with a long index finger. "So this poison… it's created from things we can't find here, right? That's what makes you think it's someone from out of town?"

"That, and there's never been a murder in Marra." Sella sipped her own coffee. She closed her eyes as hints of chocolate and honey warmed her throat, flavored with bitter grounds. A little extra spice for insight hit the sides of her tongue with a punch. She swallowed. "At least, none since we've been alive," she continued.

"True; that would be weird for murders to just start happening randomly. So, it's really complicated to make and so fast it left no witnesses. Not even the cat."

Beside Beejee, Koukie was busy cleaning her long thick orange fur, unaware of the critical tone in Lohrna 's voice.

"I don't get the feeling it was random, though," Lohrna

continued. "I've been thinking about it. Yes, we get our share of travelers, and yes, if someone was from out of town, they'd be able to slip in and out mostly unassuming, but if it's someone from overseas… Why Cali? Why Cresablatt? This feels personal."

"Agreed." Cali suddenly appeared at the empty stool between them.

"Cali!" Sella clutched her chest. Her heart was pounding and her blood ran hot. So much for insight in the coffee… "You *can't* do that! You're going to make my heart stop!"

"Then we could be ghosts together." Cali's smile was wicked, but her tone was jovial.

Lohrna's eyes went wide, she followed Sella's eye line to the empty stool. "She's here? Good! She can help." She adjusted her body to face the empty space and Cali giggled at the sudden attention. "Listen, Calisyali–"

"Just Cali," Sella and Cali said in unison. They side-eyed one another, Cali with a wide grin and Sella with a frown. Sella felt like she had overstepped, despite Cali's amused reaction.

"Cali–" Lohrna did not pause at the correction. Her eyes were still locked above Cali's head, obviously thinking she was much taller than she was. "Do you have any ideas who might have done this? Any enemies?"

"No enemies." Cali raised her body a little, using the counter to lift herself so she was eye to eye with Lohrna.

It was a gesture that made Sella's heart grow warm, a sweet thing to do for a woman who couldn't see her. Cali had every reason to be angry and annoyed at little things like that, but she always took it in stride. Sella couldn't imagine anyone wanting to harm someone with a personality like Cali's.

Cali went on, "But I do know some people in town who... Well, I don't think they'd want me dead. But... they'd be worth talking to."

Sella pulled a parchment from her pocket and unfolded it across the smooth counter. She plucked a stick of lead from one of the jars on the front counter. "Names?" she asked the ghost.

"She has enemies?" Lohrna asked.

Sella held up a finger for Lohrna to wait. She wrote down two names: 'Dimas' and 'Nicte.'

Lohrna craned over Sella's shoulder. "Hang on." She was pointing to the second name. "I know Nicte. Sort of."

Sella squinted at her friend. "You know a Tollintalian?"

"I said 'sort of,'" Lohrna corrected. "He purchased a few stones from my mom's shop. Says he's a collector. He hasn't been in town long, but we've gotten to chatting a few times outside the shop. He seems nice."

"He is pretty nice." Cali agreed. "When he wants to be. When I first got here and found out he and Dimas were right behind... Well, I was a little concerned."

"Concerned?" Sella asked. "Who are they?"

"Former business associates." Cali hesitated. "I quit bookkeeping for them when I decided to come to Marra. And the next thing I knew, I got word they were on a ship heading here. Said they 'wanted my expertise' and to see what Orakan had to offer in rare gems."

"So you were in the gem business together?" Sella asked.

Lohrna looked eager to hear more. She leaned in, though she would have to wait for Sella's translation.

Cali lowered herself again, resting her head in her hand. "I was just in bookkeeping, technically. But yes. I worked for various collectors and some high-power sellers back home. Dimas was my most recent former employer. A seller. Pretty well known in Tollintal. And Nicte was basically her second in line. A son, of sorts…"

She paused, tapping her cheek with two fingers rhythmically. Sella waited, unwilling to interrupt. Despite Sella's earlier misgivings, there was something intriguing about piecing together someone's past… and enemies.

Cali sighed. "There were some things I didn't like about their business, but we parted amicably. I had always wanted to get out of Tollintal, and when I left, I thought that'd be the end of it."

Cali paused, letting Sella translate the information to Lohrna, who leaned forward, intrigue settling into her tone. "Clearly it wasn't the end of it."

Cali wrinkled her nose. "It should have been. I mean, I'm just a number enthusiast… When they got here, our reunion, I'll admit, was a little less than ideal…" Her eyes darted down to her hands and she bit her lip gently. "But, I thought we ended on good terms after that conversation. Nicte was upset… but he was always a little upset with me. We never did have the same values."

"Sound suspicious," Beejee interjected.

Sella glared at him, a true headache began to take hold behind her eyes and radiated down the side of her temples. Being the only person in the room to hear two separate beings speak was getting frustrating. "Maybe a spell to let you talk to everyone is worth looking into."

"Yes, please!" Cali exclaimed.

"I was talking to Beejee," Sella said, but instantly regretted her words. They came out harsher than she intended, and both Lohrna and Cali recoiled at her tone. "Sorry." Sella backtracked. "I'm sorry… It's a lot to be a translator for two people only I can hear." She turned to Cali. "I don't know if there's a spell for that… but I'll look for one while you're here."

Lohrna reached out and squeezed Sella's arm gently. "You don't need to apologize." Her expression turned mischievous. "Buuuuut, you do need to tell me what else Cali said."

Beejee's laugh echoed, but Sella ignored him and closed her eyes. "I need more coffee…"

Sella explained what Cali told her as the three of them sat around the counter. Beejee was sipping from a saucer of water while Lohrna sipped her coffee and hummed at each new revelation.

"So, we have some business associates in town?" she asked, looking from the empty stool to Sella. "That's promising. I can't say I could imagine Nicte murdering someone, but you never know, do you?"

"Yeah, I guess not," Sella agreed. "First things first, I think we should talk to Dimas. See what we can find out."

"They're probably staying at the hotel," Lohrna said. "We could check in with Penya."

"We can't look too suspicious, though." Sella hummed, contemplating. "Is there a way we could organically run into either of them?"

Lohrna's eyes shifted upward. "Like I said, Nicte was at our shop a few times scoping the place for rocks. But it's been a while since I've seen him there."

Cali leaned in. "Dimas is a notorious lover of mead. Honey, and all things honey-related, are rare back home. We don't have bees, so it has to be imported." She pointed to the rows of honey on the wall in one of the cubbies. "Do you sell that here, or just coffee?"

Lohrna, sensing Sella's attention elsewhere, waited before asking, "What'd she say?"

"She asked if we sell mead. I guess Dimas has a soft spot for honey liquor."

Lohrna laughed. "Of course she could sell mead! Sella's a kitchen witch. She can make anything!"

Beejee's loud meow cut through the conversation, tapping Sella with his paw as he did. "Partner with Hazen on selling your mead! We could host a Mead and Melody night. Like what your mother used to do."

"I thought you didn't want to get involved," Sella teased as she scratched his chin.

"I just want more money in the shop," Beejee purred and leaned into her scratches. "Business is looking a little rough with everyone suspecting you and the shifter are involved in a murder."

She ignored his jab, instead clenching her fist so Beejee could rub his cheek against her knuckles. "Beejee suggests a Mead and Melody night at the shop," Sella said to the other two.

A wide grin filled most of Lohrna's face. "Like your mom used to!"

"Your mom?" Cali tilted to catch Sella's eye.

Sella's mouth twitched upward. She tempered the smirk and drew her lips into a thin line. "Do you think something like that would draw Dimas in? We have to do it soon, before she and Nicte leave town."

Cali nodded. "That would do it. Dimas loves mead *and* being the center of attention. She'd come, and sing more songs than you'd ask for."

"She says it's perfect," Sella translated for Lohrna.

THIRTEEN

Lucky Brew

SELLA, though no longer literally haunted, still felt as though there was a constant presence beside her in the hours after Lohrna left. Even if she couldn't see Cali, she *felt* her presence.

It was almost comforting, especially knowing a murderer may be entering her shop soon.

Sella's steps felt lighter and her hand was quick to fly over the scrolls as she printed neatly. Occasionally, she would glance left, where she was certain Cali sat, and smiled gently. And sometimes, she would get a light tap on her shoulder in response.

"The flyers look nice," Beejee grumbled. It was a rare compliment, but then again, he *had* designed them. Sella simply printed on his behalf.

"Thanks, Beejee." She gave him a quick but gentle nudge. "How are things going with Koukie?"

Beejee's usual scoff infused into his tone. He thrust his head up, clearly scoping the shop for signs of the orange feline. Seeing it empty, he proceeded haughtily: "She's a menace."

"In what way?"

"She eats my food, sleeps in my spot by the fire, and she is utterly useless at catching mice or killing spiders. What is a regular cat good for, if not to keep pests away?" Beejee tossed his head derisively.

Sella hummed. She stopped writing and put her quill away carefully. "Beejee. Would you *like* to be able to talk to others?"

"I already do. They just never listen."

Sella laughed. "I mean, what we talked about earlier…" Her tone got more serious and she reached out to touch his front paw. "We've always just had each other. Through all our travels… for so many years, it was you and me against the world."

"And I'd like to keep it that way. In many regards. But it *is* painful to watch you translate – poorly, I might add – two entities that only you can understand. If we're going to be in this mess, I'd rather not watch you keep messing that up."

Sella snorted. Even when he was being sensitive, he was scathing. "I want you to be happy, Beejee. Would casting the spell make you happy?"

"I'm your familiar. You're my witch," he said matter of factly. "Our happiness is shared."

"Answer the question without the riddle." Sella cocked her head.

Beejee copied her posture and yawned.

Sella waited.

"Would I be able to pretend I couldn't speak? If I wanted to?"

"I think so." Sella shrugged. "You might have to practice meowing."

To her shock, Beejee seemed to consider it. He purred. "I am an excellent actor." A pause, almost vulnerable. "Do you know the spell?"

Sella scratched his head. "No, but my mother did."

"Aaaaand her scrolls are sealed in our old house, aren't they?"

"They are."

"That's… an inconvenience." Beejee huffed.

"Yeah, it is."

From across the room, Koukie meowed at the empty food bowl by the fire. Beejee hissed. Sella swallowed a laugh.

THERE WAS ONLY a day to prepare for what Sella and Beejee hoped would be a wall-to-wall packed shop. Lohrna agreed to deliver flyers for the town, gather honey from their hives for selling, and purchase small bites at the market for the event. In her place, she had sent her mother to help with decorations, which included seating and a small stage at the front of the store.

Lohrna insisted her mother didn't know she was a suspect in the murder… but Sella had her suspicions. As she watched the old woman working on clearing out little cubbies, Sella wondered if Aadel was worried that Lohrna would get too involved.

While Sella swept the shop, Aadel inspected each jar and label before putting them aside. Sella almost chuckled. She and her daughter shared that same curiosity.

Hopefully it wouldn't get Lohrna into trouble.

"Sella?" Aadel squinted at the label of a small jar she was turning over in her hand. "Could I trouble you for a cuppa? Add some of this, if you don't mind?" She handed the jar over with a warm smile.

"Of course," Sella said, and lit the fire under the kettle with her finger. She examined the jar. "Luck?"

"For both of us," the older woman murmured. "I'm glad you're opening the shop for events like your mother used to. I hope people come. We could all use a little cheer with, well... you know."

Sella nodded and opened the jar. The fresh smell of crushed grass and bitter moss filled her nose. She breathed in deeply, sensing that Aadel still had more to say.

It didn't take long. Aadel started clearing and dusting the shelves again and added, almost to herself, "We all missed you after you left, you know."

Sella's mouth twitched. She didn't know. She assumed Lohrna had, but the rest? "I think everyone was glad to have me gone after..." She trailed off as the water began to roll to a gentle boil. She wanted to say, "After her mother had showed up to the shop one day with a burn scar across her face." She wanted to say, "After Lohrna mysteriously stopped hanging around causing mischief during full moons." But that was complicated, and despite everything, it was easier to just say, "You know... The Incident."

Aadel tsked, squinting at one of the honey jars. "Oh, those spots weren't so bad. People made a hurricane out of a drizzle."

Sella waited. Some part of her, the child inside, wanted desperately to ask if Aadel trusted her. If Aadel thought she was terrible for everything that had happened. Sella wanted to fling herself into Aadel's embrace like she had when she was small, bury herself in the woman's shoulder, and let it all go.

But they'd moved past that point in their lives. Sella stuffed it down and added coffee grounds to the pot instead.

Aadel went on, unaware of Sella's near breakdown. "Who do you think could do something like this?"

"I don't know."

"You don't suspect it's someone we know, do you?"

"I don't think so." Sella watched the water carefully. Her hands warmed.

"It had to be an outsider." Aadel nodded. She seemed to be mostly agreeing with herself. "No one here could commit such an act. Especially not to a young woman like that... Do they know how she died?"

Sella's eyes flicked up, then back down quickly. "Poison, I think."

"Poison." Aadel scoffed. "That's the coward's way of killing."

Sella stirred in luck and a dash of blue calming power to both cups.

"Any killing is a coward's way," Cali muttered. Around her form in the corner of the shop, it appeared that a small wind snuck through a crack in the window. Her hair fluttered around her face, which made her look otherworldly. "We'll catch the rat who did this."

Beejee's yellow eyes fixed on the ghost. "There's the fire I expected."

Cali's wind stilled suddenly as she squinted at Beejee. "I do wish I knew what you were saying."

Beejee narrowed his eyes and slunk to the stairs.

Cali laughed. "Alright then, little guy."

"I'm hardly little. Just because I'm not a lion–" Beejee hissed as he passed Sella. He trotted up the steps, grumbling the whole way.

Sella stirred the coffee once more, then crossed the shop to hand Aadel her ceramic mug. "Benka will catch whoever did this."

"Not if we do first!" Cali added brightly.

Sella smiled, and sipped her coffee. She hoped luck would come through in more than one way.

Mead, Melodies, and Murder Suspects

THE SHOP WAS MORE crowded than Sella anticipated. She stood behind the counter with wide eyes, taking it all in. Little fires above their heads danced across the ceiling, warmly illuminating faces and casting ruby sparkles off ceramic cups. She watched Cirian chat with Hazen near the shelves; he rested a large elbow on one cubby casually. Hazen, still the taller and broader of the two, ducked a little to hear him past the din of people talking and the music projecting from the little front stage.

Benka made an appearance early on. He stayed only long enough to get a good look at everyone in attendance, then cited the rain as a motivator to get home. Sella suspected he was exhausted. Dark circles had colored his eyes and his skin looked sallow.

"I'll bet he's been up all night trying to catch whoever did this," Cali whispered to Sella after he left.

Sella's mouth had twitched, but she was quiet. She was sure he'd be back. He always seemed to find his way back.

Now, she and Cali stood side by side against the back corner of the shop, waiting for Dimas to appear.

Cali gave a description: red hair down to her elbows, very tall… very pretty. Most importantly and easiest to spot, she was human and hornless, like most of the people from across the sea. Sella's eyes scanned the room again as the crowd burst into applause. The musician at the stage took a small bow and loudly exclaimed that this next song was for the love of his life, whoever she was. The irony that she had never heard any rumor of Toppa ever so much as even having a single date made it all the more silly to the crowd. A few people chuckled.

Cali laughed as well, but Sella was busy looking at the front window. A streak of bright red caught her eye as the door swung open and a woman fitting Dimas's description walked in with a smaller man trailing close behind.

Sella tapped the counter to get Cali's attention, subtly bending her head to the door.

Cali clasped her hands over her mouth. "It worked!" she squealed through her fingers. "I knew she couldn't resist!"

Sella caught Lohrna's eyes through the crowd. Her best friend was mingling, but still on alert, so it wasn't hard to direct her attention towards the newcomers.

But Lohrna was anything but subtle. In her usual way, she stood on her tiptoes rather obviously to see over the crowd.

Sella rubbed her eyes with thumb and middle finger.

"Not exactly subtle, is she?" Cali nudged Sella's arm.

Sella froze at the cold, ghostly touch.

"Oh, sorry." Cali looked down at her own body. "I forget sometimes."

"It's okay," Sella whispered back. It wasn't the cold that caught her off guard, but the physical act of Cali's touch. She looked down at her own arm for a moment but then the newcomers caught her attention again.

Dimas parted the crowd like a shark parts fish. She was calm and confident, nearly gliding through the room as people gave her a wide berth, seemingly without intention. She smiled, wide and charismatic, when she got close to the counter.

The man scurried to stand by her side. Though his body language indicated looming anxiety, his eyes were calm and secure. He looked at Sella as though he had met her a thousand times before.

"So, this is the famous Practical Potion's Mead and Melody Night?" Dimas rested her forearms on the counter, leaning towards Sella so her voice, light and airy like wind chimes, could be heard above the music.

"I wouldn't call it famous, but as the owner, I do hope you enjoy your time tonight." Sella smiled, she hoped it didn't look as fake as she felt. "You're new in town?"

"Visiting. Tourists, if you will." Dimas stood back to her full height. "I always like to see the local entertainment when I'm out, though." She glanced about the room; she flashed a bright grin at each person who made eye contact before turning back.

Sella felt awkward, but wanted to keep the conversation going. "This should be fun for you. We've partnered with the tavern next door. Be sure to help yourself to some of Hazen's famous finger sandwiches. He's a big guy, but his little sandwiches are made with a lot of care." Sella gestured to the far corner where a table was laid out with a wide variety of tasty treats. Small signs near each listed the pricing in gold lettering. His tip jar was already overflowing, even though it was self-serve and based on the honor system.

Sella smiled gently at the little jar, but Dimas commanded her attention again. She hadn't bothered to follow Sella's hand, seemingly uninterested in any food. Her gaze was intense. "What flavors of mead do we have on the menu tonight?"

"Just mead, but it's anything but plain." Sella rolled along with Dimas' question. "The bees are local and happy. They produce excellent, high-quality honey."

"Just mead," Dimas repeated, but without any hint of malice. She sounded charmed. Sella imagined someone as well traveled as Dimas would probably see this seaside town as 'quaint' rather than 'small.' Sella wished, briefly, that she could see her home with that fresh lens. Dimas went on, "Do you make it in house?"

"Afraid we don't have the space." Sella shrugged. "Hazen makes the mead. But he uses all our ingredients."

"I'll have to trust he knows what he's doing, then," she said. "I'll take a glass of 'just mead.'" She glanced at the man beside her. "Nicte?"

"Make that two glasses, please," Nicte said to Sella.

"Nicte!" Lohrna's booming voice startled them and a few others nearby.

Sella checked Cali out of the corner of her eye. To all in the shop, Sella announced loudly, "Sorry about that…"

Lohrna nearly bounded through the crowd to the counter, glass raised high above the heads of those around her. "Nicte! I'm glad you could make it!" She gave him a quick pat on his shoulder, and he took it in stride.

"We wouldn't miss an opportunity to see local entertainment," he echoed Dimas's words. "Or try some honey wine…"

Sella slid two glasses across the counter.

A small flame floated between them for a moment, shining light on the thick, golden liquor. It sparkled brightly in the light, and the flame moved on.

"What lovely magic." Dimas's eyes watched the little fire float away. She took her first sip. "And lovely flavor. Happy bees do make happy honey, I suppose."

"I'd like to think so," Sella said. "It seems you already know my dear friend, Lohrna." She held out her hand. "I'm Sella. Certified Kitchen Witch."

"These flames must come in handy in the kitchen," Dimas said. She looked down at Sella's hand for a beat before she stretched out her own. "I'm called Dimas. This is Nicte, as I'm sure you heard."

"It's not our custom to shake hands in Tollintal," Cali explained Dimas' hesitance.

Sella withdrew her hand as soon as Dimas let go. She felt color rise to her cheeks at the lack of knowledge with customs from across the sea. For all her travels, she still had much to learn. Though, she wished Dimas were more well-read on customs in Orakan and avoided this whole awkwardness. "It's nice to meet you." She tried to recover. "How long are you in town?"

"We'll be leaving soon. I hear there is a mine in the valley up north," Dimas said. "Besides, we… have worn out our stay."

Behind them, the stage was quiet while the next musician set up her instruments.

Lohrna leaned in as the music began again, a folksy melody that filled the space with gentle strums. "What makes you say that?" she asked, her voice uncharacteristically quiet.

Nicte and Dimas exchanged a wordless look. Dimas sighed, her shoulders sunk in… but to Sella, it looked like a practiced pose. Everything about Dimas was intentional, calculated. A way to get people to like her, to empathize with her, to be swept away in her charm.

It was unsettling.

Dimas continued, "We came to this side of the world to procure products for our business." She glanced at Lohrna, then added for Sella's benefit, "We're gem sellers. It's a bustling trade back home." She waved her hand casually as though it was any other boring job — not terribly important or lucrative – though her well-crafted, clean attire and jewelry-studded frame implied otherwise.

"That sounds interesting," Sella inserted, prompting her along.

Dimas took another large sip, smacking her lips. "It's something. We came to Marra first, considering a former associate of ours had recently moved here. I was hoping to get some insight from her about where we should visit – which mines were most successful."

Sella caught Cali raising an eyebrow. It took all her concentration to avoid glancing Cali's way.

"Speaking of," Lohrna cut in, directing her gaze at Nicte, "did you ever go down to the shoreline? There's lovely seaglass there. It's not rare here, but considering you're from a desert, I'll bet it could fetch a good price simply for the novelty–"

The sound of large, booted steps announced Hazen's appearance, stopping Lohrna before she could go on. He seemed unfazed by his own interruption. "Great night, Sella. I'm impressed we were able to pull this off on such short notice."

"What can I say? You and I are brilliant, Hazen." Sella refilled his cup "I'm glad you get a night off."

He took a swig of mead and wiped his mouth with the back of his hand gruffly. The way his attention descended on Dimas clearly stated it wasn't a social call. "You're Cali's former boss, then?" Hazen held out the same hand to shake.

This time, she did not wait before taking his hand firmly. "I am."

"She was a good kid. A good kid."

"She was a good woman," Nicte corrected.

"Ah, everyone's a kid to Hazen," Lohrna said lightheartedly. She squeezed Hazen's forearm, a silent signal. "Cali worked for Hazen… before… you know…"

A silence descended upon them. Cali rolled her eyes and crossed her arms. "Way to bring the mood down."

"Shocking that this could happen in a place like this." Nicte shook his head. "It doesn't seem like a dangerous place."

"It's not." Hazen's eyes narrowed and the air grew thick.

"More mead?" Sella asked brightly. She filled all their cups.

Beside her, Cali smiled. She leaned in close to Sella, arms still crossed. "You're a pro."

"If you're insinuating anything, we've already discussed the situation with your detective." Nicte met Hazen's glare with a scowl of his own, his gentle facade temporarily broken.

"And I advised you to not leave town yet," Benka said, appearing as quickly and quietly as an apparition.

Lohrna jumped. "I thought you went home!" she squeaked.

Benka looked better than he had only a bit ago. The bags under his eyes were gone. Sella wondered briefly what kind of charm or potion it was… Nothing she made here. "I did. But it occurred to me that I left without paying my respects." He looked at Sella, then to the group. "This is quite the gathering we have here."

The music lulled and everyone but Dimas shifted uncomfortably in the brief silence.

Benka focused on Sella. "I am glad you're hosting this, and I look forward to many more to come. It is a beautiful way to honor those who came before us." He pushed gray hair over his thick horns and stayed very still until Sella sighed just to break the silence.

"Thank you, Benka. Consider your respects paid." Sella gripped the counter with one hand. Her hidden fingers searched the shelf.

Cali leaned down to inspect Sella's wandering hand. She pushed a thin vial into Sella's outstretched fingers. Sella knew this one by touch. It was labeled 'Trust the Process.' She poured a few drops into the jug of mead hidden below, but kept her eyes fixed on Benka.

"Mead?" She lifted the trust-spiked pitcher from behind the counter.

He shook his head and stuffed his hands into the pockets of his large coat, still speckled with rain from outside.

"Don't leave town," he said again to Dimas and Nicte, a solemn warning.

"We couldn't even if we wanted to." Dimas tossed a lock of hair over her shoulder. "You beached all the boats."

"Inclement weather," Benka responded without pause. "The sea is too rough."

"They're docked on your orders, are they not?" Dimas said before taking another quick sip. She met his eyes with a calm but firm expression. "The hotel is crowded and the people are becoming restless. The ships' captains should be the ones to make the decision if their boat is sturdy enough to travel."

For a moment, Sella regretted giving Dimas any liquid courage.

But Benka merely shrugged. "The ships are unfit to navigate this weather. " And with that, he wandered his way back through the crowd and out the door.

"He certainly has a way about him," Dimas said diplomatically. She turned to Nicte. "I guess we're in town a little longer. The captains don't seem interested in breaking his orders."

"He has no authority over us. We aren't Marran citizens," Nicte said coolly.

"Stars," Cali hissed.

It echoed in Sella's ears as Dimas said the same thing. "We'll cooperate however we can." Dimas narrowed her eyes clearly telling him to sound more helpful. She wasn't quite as subtle as she thought she was. "Though we do have scheduled appointments coming up…" She looked around the shop again and sighed dramatically, her shoulders rising and falling in a huff, making a show of her sacrifice.

Sella ignored her comment. "More?" She held up her ceramic jug filled with magic and mead.

"Always." Dimas smiled, her posture shifted once again to that of grace. She held out her cup eagerly.

"Told you," Cali whispered.

"Gnarly business, all of this," Dimas said as she sipped her refill. Her long lashes slowly blinked over the rim of the cup. "I do hope, for all your sakes, they find whoever did this. Poor Calisyali…"

"To Calisyali," Nicte raised his cup.

Hazen's stiff demeanor softened, enough for Sella to notice. He rubbed one eye and held his cup out with the other. "To Cali," his voice boomed as the five clinked cups and music blared in the background.

"Aw, this is sweet." Cali leaned over the counter. "But we have work to do. Ask them some questions… Oh! Ask them who they think did it."

Sella side-eyed Cali, playing it off like she was assessing the party, and then waited for them to all take a drink. "Do you have any theories on who could have done this?"

Hazen took a deep breath, his barrel chest expanding and then collapsing as though his core had given out. "I don't have any theories… I don't have any thoughts but grief over this senselessness."

Lohrna held his arm again. "You're a good man, Hazen…. Hey, I think Cirian is looking a little lonely anyway." She gestured to the man across the way who was looking at them with curious eyes, clearly trying and failing to eavesdrop.

Hazen grumbled, but squeezed Lohrna's hand and

nodded to them before he made his way back through the crowd.

Lohrna clinked her class against Dimas'. "Sorry about him. He feels more than you'd expect."

Dimas waved her hand. "It's fine," she said in a way that made Sella think it was anything but.

"You knew Cali, though. Before she was here," Lohrna said as the crowd applauded the second musician. "You must have some insight."

"Not really." Dimas shrugged. "Cali kept to herself… She wasn't in the habit of sharing much."

Sella's brows furrowed. That didn't sound quite right.

Dimas went on, "There is a former partner I was never enthusiastic about. They say it's always a lover."

Cali puffed. "How banal."

"What was his name again?" Dimas asked Nicte casually. She took another drink.

"Rorin," Nicte said. "And it wouldn't surprise me. Somewhat of a temper on that one. Jealous."

"Hmm…" Dimas' eyes glanced off to the ceiling, following another little flame as it passed by. "He did have some… let's call them 'issues'… if I recall. But he wasn't exactly the sharpest thorn on the cactus."

"You know, I thought I saw Rorin the other day," Nicte said, as if he had suddenly remembered it.

"You saw *Rorin?* Here?" Dimas's composure broke for the briefest moment. Considering how bad their acting had been until this point, this revelation felt off-script.

"What?" Cal's voice was so loud, Sella was certain everyone had heard. "Rorin is here?"

Sella frowned. "Is that bad?"

"It's just odd." Dimas looked to the far end of the shop. Her tall spine almost seemed to expand to see over the heads and stage to the large window. It was a futile effort; she'd never glimpse him in the dark through the rain, especially with the reflections of warm fires inside. "That is odd…" she whispered.

"He *was* far away. Like Dimas said, it was so 'odd' and out of place. I just assumed it was a trick of the light. But now that I think about it, it really might have been him."

Lohrna's eyes were wide. She scanned the faces of everyone in the group, but stayed unusually quiet.

"Where would we be able to find him?" Sella asked, feeling bold. The trust and truth in the mead began to finally work on her. "Where did you think you saw him?"

Nicte paused, scratching his ear thoughtfully. It was round at the tip – a bit odd to see, and only reminded Sella more that she was meddling with affairs she probably shouldn't be.

It was far too late now.

"I saw him at the hotel, if it was even him. But he looked like he was in a hurry and left. The place was booked, anyway. I figured it was simply someone who looked like him being turned away. He didn't have any of Rorin's usual… let's say, arrogance, about being told 'no.' But he was muttering about staying in that house by the shore since it looked empty. The woman said it was a witch's house."

"Your mom's?" Lohrna mouthed, not too subtly.

Sella's head tilted, enough to acknowledge it.

Nicte and Dimas were too busy sipping their drinks to

notice. Dimas held her cup out when she finished. "Another glass and I just may go on stage and sing."

"She will, too," Nicte said seriously as Sella refilled both their cups. "Be careful with this one."

"Oh, hush." Dimas' eyes narrowed playfully. "You know you love me."

"That's true," Nicte conceded.

"I knew it!" Cali pointed dramatically between them. "I *so* called it!"

Sella nearly burst out laughing, a small chuckle escaped despite her best efforts. She gestured to the small stage, trying to recover. "Feel free. That's what the stage is for."

Raising their glasses, Dimas and Nicte made their way back through the crowd.

Sella released a sigh when they left, scanning the other guests. Some side-eyed her, clearly trying to overhear her conversation with the two humans. When she met their gaze, they looked away.

On the counter, Beejee pushed at her arm with his head. Apparently, he'd decided to rejoin the party. "There's a group toward the back," he said softly. "They've been looking at our ingredients for far too long."

"Maybe they want to purchase something?" Sella shrugged, though she knew it was unlikely.

Beejee narrowed his eyes.

"Alright. I'll go check." She moved around the counter as the music began to fade. Applause broke out and Sella drew closer to the two women gathered by one of her shelves. She recognized them immediately, Ovina and Kartha. The two sisters came in on occasion, usually begrudgingly, for help with their arthritis – one of the many reasons Ovina was usually late with her knitting commissions.

"Can I help you find something?" Sella asked.

They both bristled at the question; she clearly caught them off-guard. She did her best to smile politely. They were also the ones who saw her outside Cali's house. She hoped they didn't remember.

"We have a remedy for almost anything, if you're looking for something new?"

Ovina, the eldest, held her shawl around her shoulders closely. She squared to face Sella. She was several heads shorter than the witch, but deep wrinkles formed between her brows. "We are not in the market for remedies."

"Rude," Cali muttered at Sella's side. She moved closer to Ovina, looking her up and down. "How could someone who gives welcome baskets and makes sweaters be so uncouth?"

Sella blinked, her own courage fading fast. This was the most hostile Sella had ever seen the older woman. Ovina was usually so kind and, if anything, aloof most of the time. "Is–is something wrong?" she stuttered, her words drowning in the sea of music.

"We couldn't help but notice you have a variety of *foreign* ingredients here. Things we haven't seen before," Kartha said. Her tone was accusatory as her eyes moved to Lohrna across the room. "You should be more careful keeping these things out like this. You never know who might be stealing from you, right under your nose."

"Beejee keeps a keen eye on customers," Sella spoke carefully. Her entire body felt hot under the old women's scowls. "And it's true that I sell remedies from other lands."

She followed Kartha's gaze. Lohrna was locked in what looked like a deep conversation with Nicte. Sella's heart was pounding. She went on, almost forcefully, "My recipes are different from my mother's, but more effective because of the variety of ingredients, I can assure you."

Kartha scoffed but said nothing else. She waved her hand for her sister to follow her back into the center of the crowd as Dimas took the stage.

"What in all the stars was that about?" Cali glared at the women's backs. "Are they implying that you've sold poison due to carelessness? Or that someone's been stealing from you? Beejee would *never* allow it." She nearly laughed, a little exhale. "This is ridiculous. I can't believe they spoke to you like that. And to think! The gift basket was so lovely…"

"I don't know what to think right now." Sella pinched the bridge of her nose. She closed her eyes and let Dimas' voice, beautiful, but louder than anyone else who came before her, overtake the pulsing in her ears.

She glanced at the ingredients that the women were eyeing. At least three of them were components of Cresablatt. Sella swore under her breath and grabbed at the powdered nightroot, stuffing it into her pocket before she could think.

"They're ignorant," a little voice said above Dimas' booming voice.

Sella turned to see Isra leaning against the bookshelf with one small elbow. Her sleeve was covered in dust from the shelf, one Aadel clearly missed in her cleaning spree, but either Isra didn't notice or she didn't mind. "Isn't nightroot used for treating joint pain?"

"You know your stuff. And… thanks." Sella felt her anxiety begin to fade.

"Well, your mom was nice enough to teach me a thing or two to help my grandma before she passed and everyone else moved away." Isra shrugged. She pushed herself off the bookshelf, a gesture so nonchalant and confident, she seemed taller. "I wouldn't worry about these people; they're small-minded. Lohrna couldn't hurt any living thing. And besides, you're a kitchen witch. It's not like you're *actually* an elemental witch. That would be a problem… but you're certified."

Sella's face paled, and she released a heavy breath. The news that people were really talking about Lohrna this way, dropped so casually, cut deep into her stomach. She tried to hold herself tall. "Thanks, Isra."

Isra placed a hand on Sella's forearm, a warm gesture. "Don't let these guys get to you. If anyone should be suspicious of anyone, it's us of *them*." Her eyes drifted to the stage as Dimas shoved another singer off. "Oh my…" She laughed. "It looks like the human is having some troubles."

With a wave, she strolled back into the party, leaving Sella to her thoughts.

THE PARTY ENDED LATER than Sella wanted. But after escorting Dimas away, the crowd trickled out little by little with each passing song, until at last Sella made Cirian and Hazen walk the stragglers home. No one would try anything with a group, especially not with the large pair in tow.

Just a precaution.

With the downstairs tidied and the door finally shut and

locked, Lohrna broke. "Tides high and low, Sella! I couldn't say a word with whatever you added to the mead! I had to put my tongue in a vault!"

A half smile crossed Sella's face. "In mead, there is truth."

"And in your truth potion, a little more."

"Just a suggestion, really." Sella shrugged.

Lohrna sighed. Her shoulders deflated, but she looked proud. "You're better than I would've thought, I have to admit."

"This was all your idea," Sella said. "I just… added in some detail work." She pushed her hair back over her ears.

"Okay, okay." Lohrna yawned. "Listen, I don't want to sound like a little coward or anything, but it's late and–"

"The bed's already made," Sella interrupted gently. "Come on up."

FIFTEEN

Sounds Spooky

LOHRNA WAS SNORING in Sella's bed, loudly. But the witch and ghost were still wide awake.

"Even if he *is* in town, I don't think it was Rorin." Cali's usual smile adorned her face in a way that rarely seemed to reach her eyes. Sella wasn't sure how real her smile was. It felt genuine now, but…

Sella's brows furrowed as she scanned the ghost's face for any sign of distress. No one, not even Cali, could be this casual about the possibility of a former lover killing them. When Cali showed no signs of cracking, Sella simply asked, "What makes you think that? Dimas and Nicte didn't exactly paint him like a great guy."

"He wasn't." Cali glanced out the window. A small laugh escaped her lips as she held her head in one hand, elbow resting on the high back of the velvet couch. "That's why he's not in my life… or… death… anymore. He has some deeply held prejudices. But when I say he wouldn't hurt me, it's not a compliment. He's just too selfish for that. He wouldn't risk his own skin for anything."

"Sounds like a winner," Sella muttered.

The ghost's image shimmered. Cali looked away. "That's why I was so surprised that Nicte allegedly saw him here. Even *if* word of my death were to travel that fast, Rorin would never come to pay his respects. The trip would be an inconvenience."

"So, he really wouldn't care?" Sella pushed, just a little.

Cali shrugged, voice distant. "You know the type, I'm sure."

Sella didn't know the type at all. Her previous relationships, though brief, were loving and supportive. They usually ended because Sella moved to a new town, or they felt like her attention was elsewhere – on spells, potions, knowledge – not love.

She glanced at a large pink crystal on her desk. Her latest ex gifted it before she came home. Sella told herself for nearly a year that she would give it to Lohrna, but she never did. She liked the way it caught the light, the way it reminded her that someone out there cared once, even if the spark of affection had grown cold. Her smile grew genuine, reaching her eyes.

Cali followed Sella's eyes to the crystal. She pushed herself from the couch and approached the desk with silent steps. "This is beautiful. I take it you've had better luck than me. Is he still in your life?"

"She," Sella corrected. "And no. It's probably time to part with that one."

Cali's expression was wistful. She ran two fingers across the desk as she walked by the crystal. "Maybe it's nice to remember." She stopped in front of the pink gem, leaning down to study the details.

"Maybe. Sometimes," Sella said. Sometimes, it was simply painful. She changed the subject back to Cali. "So, this Rorin... Any ideas about why he might be here?"

"I wish I had someone to give me something like this," it was a whisper so small Sella almost didn't hear it. Cali turned to Sella, clearing her throat as if she hadn't realized she'd spoken. "Ah, I don't know what would bring him here, but it has to be something big."

Sella wondered what could be bigger than Cali's death, but she said nothing.

"We'll figure it out!" Cali's melancholy was gone, replaced with another easy, fake smile. "Did Lohrna imply that he might be near your mom's house?"

A dry laugh escaped Sella's throat. She rose from the couch and crossed into the kitchen, lighting a small fire under a metal teapot. "You caught that?"

Cali crossed her arms, waiting.

"Yes, the place he described sounds like my mom's old house. She's been gone a long time. But the house itself is shut down. Guarded by a powerful magic… I honestly don't know if I can even break that spell, so I doubt he's hiding out there." Sella leaned over the counter and rested her chin in her hand. "Is he a skilled camper?"

"He'd like to think he's skilled at everything." Cali waved her hand as she spoke, as though mentioning him was bringing flies into her space. "I wouldn't put it past him to rough it in the woods if the hotel really is booked."

"That's actually fairly dangerous." Sella moved in closer. "Especially if he doesn't know the area."

Cali shrugged it off, but copied Sella and leaned her body across the counter as well. The corners of her eyes crinkled in a mischievous expression. "So, tell me about your mom's abandoned house guarded by magic. It sounds spooky."

Sella was startled into a laugh. "It's actually pretty homey… or, it was, once. I haven't been since I got back into town. Beejee and I do need to go anyway… break the seal and gather a few things. I can see if Rorin is lingering in the woods while we're there?"

"What do you need in the house?"

"My mom's scrolls. Spells and recipes. Hopefully, something to help us out… and let Beejee talk to you."

Cali squeaked, startling the cat. "I'd love that!"

Beejee leaped onto the counter beside Sella. He butted his head against her chin. "No one can truly be this happy about everything," he drawled.

"Well," Sella said to Cali as she scratched the familiar's ear. "You may end up regretting that enthusiasm. He's a sassy thing."

"That's why I like cats." Cali looked at Koukie, perpetually resting near the hearth. "Some call it sass, but I like that they're honest."

SIXTEEN

One Small Setback

SELLA AWOKE EARLY but decided against making any pastries for the shop. Nearly no one ever bought one, and she didn't want to risk waking Lohrna, who was still snoring gently in her bed, one arm flung over her face. By her side, Koukie was curled up in a tight orange ball, sleeping peacefully.

Sella slipped on her clothes and waved Beejee and Cali to join her as she quietly left the loft.

"Hazen's here early?" Cali noticed as they descended the stairs to the shop level. Through the windows, Sella caught his large frame, backlit by the early morning fog. A light wind blew his curls around his face and he frowned, crossing his arms across his broad chest as if to keep the wind at bay.

Hazen was through the door as soon as Sella unlocked the store. She hadn't yet polished off the shelves, many of which still held crumbs from the night before, and though it was mostly tidy, she felt a wave of embarrassment flush across her face. She'd never so much as heard of Hazen's tavern ever being anything less than pristine. From one proprietor to another, this felt like being a bad host.

"Good morning," she said, trying to draw his attention away from the minor messes. She moved out of his way so he could fully enter the shop. A crunch under her boot told her that she did not sweep well enough the night before and she cringed. "The usual?"

Hazen sauntered to the counter. He yawned as he passed her, too tired, thankfully, to notice the crumbs. "Make it a double. I'm delivering to Cirian this morning, too."

Sella's steps quickened to reach the counter before he sat. She slid a mug across the way to him and set out a taller ceramic mug with a lid beside it. "Anything extra added?" She eyed him carefully as she began to heat the pot of water. Something was off. Something new.

Hazen sighed, shoulders heaving as he released a heavy breath. "Anything for poise?"

Sella's brows lifted. "Poise?" She bent below the counter. "Let me see what I've got."

Under the counter, Cali bent down to join her. "He seems like he's worried about something." Cali whispered, though Sella knew she could scream and only she and Beejee would hear.

Sella glanced at her for a moment, impressed that she was able to gather so much from so little. She grabbed a jar of honey labeled 'Timelessness' and shrugged, rising from her squat quickly. She poured a little of the honey into each mug and waited for Hazen to continue. When she was met with only silence, Beejee nudged her calf behind the counter. "Long night?" Sella finally asked.

Hazen rubbed his eyes with his thumb and index finger. His head bobbed. "You could say that. We made a fair amount of money though. That's the good news."

Behind the counter, Beejee purred triumphantly. Sella flashed her familiar a quick smile, then focused on pouring the dark coffee grounds into the pot. "I sense there's bad news coming." She stirred the grounds, releasing a burst of nutty aroma through the air.

"There is," he said, matter of factly. "I'll just come out and say it. People had a great time last night, but as we walked them home, I couldn't help but notice a few consistent rumors. I thought you should know."

Beejee leaped onto the counter at her side. His green eyes narrowed.

Sella focused on stirring the coffee into each mug carefully, mixing the thick honey throughout the dark roast. Steam rose from the mugs and swirled through the air like ribbons. "What kind of rumors?"

"People are suspicious about Lohrna spending a lot of time with the foreigners," he said as Sella pushed his mug closer to him. "Did you hear that some of Cali's jewels were stolen when she died?"

Cali scoffed. "They were hardly valuable. Any gem collector, even Lohrna, would know their true value. Hardly worth the risk of murder."

Sella cast a quick glance at Cali. If anything, that implicated Lohrna more than Nicte or Dimas. Lohrna was only a casual collector. She probably had no idea what was genuinely valuable. Sella drew her attention back to Hazen. "I heard that rumor, yes."

Hazen took a sip of coffee. He hummed as soon as he

swallowed. "Well," he went on, "Lohrna and her rock hobby, you with your potions... It doesn't bode well for her that she was so friendly with Cali's former associates."

Beejee looked up at Sella. "So, how much money are we talking about here? It better make last night worth it with all this."

Sella ignored him. "But that doesn't make any sense," she poured herself her own cup of coffee now, silver rose in front of her face as she held it to her chin. She took a deep breath in to monitor her own composure, to be sure her words held a gentle tone. "Lohrna was nice to them because Lohrna *is* nice. Everyone knows that."

"I just thought you ought to know." Hazen took another sip. "It'll probably amount to nothing, like all rumors around here."

Cali huffed. "I'm glad we know. But this is stupid. How could anyone suspect Lohrna of hurting anyone?"

"Well, then." Hazen rose from his stool, placing a few coins on the counter. Sella didn't have the heart today to argue his overpayment. Her eyes were fixated on them like they were poison. These coins were probably from the night before and all they brought were more destructive rumors and a lead she wasn't sure she could trust. Hazen grabbed the other coffee. "I better get this to Cirian." He tipped his head to her. "Come by the tavern soon, it'll be good for people to see your face out and about."

Sella nodded back but did not meet his gaze. "I will."

After the bell above the door silenced, and Hazen's figure cleared their view, Sella deflated onto the counter. "This is a mess!" she groaned.

"Should we wake Lohrna?" Cali suggested.

Sella turned her face to look up at Cali, her body still melded to the wood counter. "No…" She sighed. "I don't think knowing this will help her."

"If anything," Beejee said as he nudged Sella up with his nose, "it'll just make her more reckless."

Sella peeled herself from the hardwood. Her body still felt weak, her mind numb. "You're right." She turned to Cali again. "He thinks it'll make her do something more drastic to solve this. No, we'll leave her out of this for now."

"That doesn't feel right." Cali crossed her arms. "But if you say so. You know her best."

AN HOUR LATER, no one else had entered the shop or even bothered to walk by. Beejee's tail twitched, but he was silent. Cali busied herself with inspecting all the little details within the shelf cubbies, occasionally asking for the story behind a trinket or potion when she found one that particularly caught her attention. Sella, meanwhile, was on her hands and knees, inspecting the floor for any debris left behind from her latest burst of sweeping.

Lohrna's footsteps overhead alerted them to her arrival long before she descended the stairs. Sella pushed herself up from the ground and dusted off her dress before she snapped her fingers. The flames above them grew a little brighter.

"Coffee?" she asked as Lohrna reached the last step.

"Please!" Lohrna greeted them with a bright smile. A mess of curly hair framed her face, her eyes shining bright.

Sella couldn't imagine anyone thinking that this face could be capable of anything nefarious, let alone murder.

Her insides twisted as Hazen's words echoed in her mind. She tried to reciprocate her friend's easy nature despite the feeling gnawing at her. "How about a dose of self-love?"

"Sounds great!" Lohrna looked around the shop with squinted eyes. "Is Cali here?"

Sella pointed to the counter where Cali now sat. "Second stool."

Cali waved and tapped the space next to her.

"She's inviting you to sit," Sella said as she scoured the shelf for her special blend.

"Don't mind if I do." Lohrna moved around the counter to sit beside the ghost. "So," she went on as Sella began to brew her second pot of coffee for the day. "Mead and Melody! What did we learn? What did we gather?"

"We made money, but not enough to escape this town. Oh, and everyone thinks you might be a murderer because you like rocks, so there's that," Beejee said.

Sella's ear twitched, but she ignored him. She closed her eyes and her hands wrapped around the large pot. She infused courage, hope, and love into the water – a little extra to keep them going. When she opened her eyes, she did her best to look happy, pushing Hazen's warning from her mind for now. "Well, Nicte thinks he saw Cali's ex at the hotel. That seems like a massive red flag. But, then again, we know he got into a quarrel with Cali before she died, so we should probably take what he says with that in mind."

Cali shrugged.

Beside her, Lohrna leaned her elbows on the counter. "True. The whole thing seems awfully convenient, doesn't it? I mean, Cali's former business partners show up. She ends up… you know. And next thing you know, these same people are saying they saw her jealous and temperamental ex here?" She paused, eyeing the coffee patiently. "Maybe he really is here... because they lured him to frame him!"

Beejee looked back from the seat in the bay window. "She has a point."

Sella poured two hot cups of coffee and slid one to Lohrna. "You're right. And Cali's pretty convinced it couldn't have been Rorin. Framing him would make some sense. You learn anything else from talking to them during the night?"

Lohrna laughed. "Just that Dimas likes to drink and Nicte's a bit of a coward when it comes to his boss. Once Nicte got more truth blend in him, he definitely had less than flattering things to say about Cali." She turned to the empty seat beside her. "Sorry. Nothing too serious. I guess he thinks you're a bit on the principled side." She changed the subject. "They're upset about being stuck here."

"Who isn't?" Beejee yawned.

"This whole thing feels like it was a waste." Sella sighed. She thought for a moment, taking a long drink. The corners of her mouth twitched, betraying the start of a smile form- ing. Even though it felt like several steps back, she couldn't help but think they had to be right around the corner of something big. It made her heart flutter, if only for the briefest moment. "At least when I go to my mom's, I'll check for signs of Rorin. You never know, right?" She leaned her body to look out the shop windows and into the barren street. "I'll probably close up early and do that soon. It's not like anyone else is coming in today. Or even out and about."

Lohrna sipped her coffee slowly. She turned to the stool

beside her again. "She sounds excited, doesn't she?" she asked the ghost.

Cali laughed. "You do sound kind of excited."

"I'm not *excited*…" Sella half lied. "I just want to get to the bottom of this. Because Nicte is looking pretty guilty to me if we don't see anything out there."

"Don't forget the framing theory." Lohrna gestured with her mug to Sella. She mumbled something else under her breath and took another big gulp as she looked to Cali's space with a wide-eyed 'told you so' expression.

"I'm not excited!" Sella's voice nearly squeaked.

"One small setback and she's back in the game," Lohrna said to Cali, ignoring Sella's protest. "That's how she's always been. You can't keep this one down. She likes the challenge."

"I'm right here!" Sella threw her arms up.

"Don't worry, Cali, we can keep talking like *she's* the ghost." Lohrna laughed.

"Okay, that's my cue." Sella grinned back despite herself. "I'm out of here. Lock the door on your way out if you leave. Come on, Beejee."

SEVENTEEN

Spells and Seaglass

THE HOUSE WAS NESTLED JUST below a small, moss-covered hill. It looked humble, surrounded by large, lush trees to its right and stacks of faded white box beehives scattered in front. To its left, a short drop led directly to the ocean. Waves crashed onto the pebbled shore like a heartbeat in Sella's ears.

It was an unassuming cottage: quaint and cozy. The hum of bees, and the breeze through tree branches from the ocean created a sort of song. The rhythmic ocean waves, however, calling gray clouds closer, felt to Sella like a warning.

Beejee stood at her side but offered little comfort. He was quiet in contemplation.

"This feels weird," Sella said, lifting herself to her toes so she could scope out the small house. It looked like any other in town: with a gray and brown stone exterior, thatched roof, and stained glass windows facing out like large colorful eyes. Through the buzz and waves and wind, however, Sella could hear faint chimes. The sound of the cloud of magic surrounded the house. It was impenetrable – the door would only open for Sella. And only under certain conditions.

"What enchantment did she place on this?" Beejee asked.

"The door will only open for us…" Then, the sound of chimes grew until Beejee's ear flicked. "Only after I quiet the music."

Sella spent years learning how to be still, how to quiet the anxiety of others through food and drink, but no matter how she tried, her own inner thoughts raced — she leaped from one city to another, one recipe to the next… Calming herself, let alone calming magic, had never come easy.

"You have to be calm of mind," Beejee said, rather unhelpfully.

Sella side-eyed him. "This may be a lost cause…"

"I'm not going home until we try." Beejee stomped as Sella threw him a sly half-smile. "I want to be able to talk to the ghost girl."

"And Lohrna?"

Beejee's gray fur bristled but he still sat down on the mossy earth. His ear twitched. "You and I both know your mother was worried about you when we left. She didn't want you to have her wand, not then, but that doesn't mean forever." He was so quiet she was not sure it was him at all at first. "When your mind races, you get anxious."

"I know." Sella thrust a hand out for him to quiet but he went on anyway.

"And when you get anxious, you get dangerous," Beejee repeated words to her that she had told herself a thousand times.

She didn't need to be reminded. She thought of it all the time, especially on full moons. Even now, decades later, in the stillness and peace around them, Sella could hear her mother screaming at her. She could feel the anger, hear the fear in her mother's voice. How could she be so stupid to let Lohrna go with her into the woods at night?

Sella's hands warmed now as they had then. But then, she let it grow. Tears like a tidal wave burst from Sella's eyes. Fire erupted from her fingertips.

Her mother's face never fully healed. But her mother never told anyone in town what had really happened. It was left to rumor and speculation. Sella, the little witch who messed everything up.

Sella flexed her fingers, releasing the heat as she did. She took in a breath so deep it hurt and sat beside her familiar with a heavy exhale. She filled her lungs with the fresh air and she tried to ground herself to the earth, to the sensations around her. The smell of the salt misting from the sea, the lavender flowers in a forever bloom, the soft musk of damp dirt beneath them. She closed her eyes and exhaled slowly, emptying her lungs completely. She paused and counted to four before she breathed in again.

She listened, trying to filter out any sound but the bright sound of magic in the air. It sparkled in her mind's eye like a fog of glitter. It surrounded them, the house, the bees…filled her chest, rushed through her veins as though carried with oxygen. Sella's fingers curled into gentle fists.

"You're *still* not quiet of mind," Beejee hissed.

"I know that!" Sella snapped, eyes still closed.

"Do you think I could go in?"

The voice startled both of them, but Sella remained seated while Beejee scurried behind her.

Sella exhaled before looking up at Cali's figure, silhouetted by the light gray clouds above, hair moving in the gentle breeze by the sea and of her own creation. "Hi, Cali." Sella tucked her hair behind her ears and straightened her pointed hat. "Can we try to not sneak up on us?"

"Sorry." Cali knelt beside Sella. She looked at the house and rubbed her nose with the back of her hand. "I'll keep working on that."

Beejee uncurled himself from Sella's legs and sat between the two of them. He glared at Cali but said nothing.

"Cute house," Cali mused, ignoring Beejee's intense stare.

Sella pulled her legs up to her chest and wrapped her arms around them. She rested her chin on her knees like she used to when she was little. She felt small beside the ghost. Small in front of her old home. Small and weak and foolish again.

"Is this where you grew up?" Cali didn't notice Sella's racing thoughts, or at least, she gracefully pretended not to. She made a show of looking around, glancing over the beehives and into the tree line. "It's pretty."

"Yeah, it is pretty, I suppose." Sella buried her chin deeper into the folds of her arms. "And yes, this is where we grew up, Beejee and I."

"Sorry— I feel like I seem a bit distracted. My home is a desert," Cali said. "It's nice to be by the sea, all the rain, the green…" She chuckled to herself, a light sound like the chimes of magic around them. "You know, it hurt my eyes to see so much green when I first docked here. I thought I'd never get used to it. But even though it hurt, I still loved every second of it."

Sella glanced at her from the corners of her eyes, but it was clear that Cali's gaze was fixed on the scene around her, so Sella looked ahead to the small house once again. "Funny…" Sella smiled, lifting her head at last. "I've always wanted to see a desert. All the plants growing low to the sandy ground… seeing the sun all the time… Sounds beautiful to me, even if the sun would hurt *my* eyes."

Cali laughed. "Yeah, but those plants sting you if you get close and the sun is hot. Like, really, really hot. Plus, all the buildings are made of clay and stone, none of these beautiful wood exteriors, and whimsical thatched roofs."

"Here, the rain makes you tired and we miss the blue of the sky most of the time." Sella chuckled. "And don't get me started on these roofs during windstorms. I wouldn't describe winter here as whimsical."

"Fair enough." Cali's good mood continued, the happiness clear in her voice. "You never know what you have when you're in it, I guess. Sounds like we should have done a swap."

"Yeah, I guess so…"

Between them, Sella noticed that Beejee's tail stopped flicking. She unfolded her arms and scratched behind his ear. He purred. A thousand questions raced through Sella's mind. Why did Cali finally decide to come here? What was her favorite part of the trip? Did she like the food here? She heard from hotel guests that it was so bland by comparison… But all her questions seemed so trivial. And she didn't want to pick at Cali's old life. Not when it was something she could not return to.

So they simply sat in semi-content stillness. Silence filled with the sounds around them and Sella tried to find the right words for 'I'm glad you got to see the water and trees before you died,' but anything she came up with sounded horrible. She toed at the thick grass beneath her booted foot until there was a small circle indent in the damp earth.

Cali broke the quiet. "So, you think I could go in? Find what you're looking for? It sounded like you were having trouble…"

Sella considered it, she tilted her head to one side, then the other, trying to get some different perspective on the magic surrounding the house. "I don't think I'd want to risk it. Only I can open the door. Ghosts aren't common, especially human ghosts… but I wouldn't put it past my mother to think of keeping them out, too."

"What would happen if I tried?"

Sella's mouth twitched. Nearly anything could happen. Her mother's magic was deep and potent.

"She can't die twice," Beejee said.

"I don't want to risk it," Sella reiterated. She stretched her legs out in front of her.

"If she really would ward it against you, anyone, even ghosts… There's something in there your mother didn't want you to have… not until you're ready, isn't there?" Cali tilted her head to catch Sella's gaze.

Sella met her eyes. "Yes. Her wand."

"Don't most witches need one to practice?" Cali asked. "Where's yours?"

Pride, warm and uplifting, rose in Sella's chest as shame

took root in her gut, twisting in her stomach like an illness. She decided to be honest, to try to release the conflicting emotions brewing within her. "I don't have one." A confident tilt in her lips lifted her tone. "I have never needed a wand. I'd just be more powerful with one."

"Impressive!" Cali smiled. It was warm and kind. Wrinkles formed at the edges of Cali's green eyes and Sella noticed how bright they looked, framed by her auburn hair, like part of the scenery around them. Cali held her gaze, her calm, happy expression fueling the fire in Sella's chest until the shame began to dissipate.

Beejee moved closer to Sella, breaking her concentration. "She sure knows a lot about witches. Suspicious."

"They're more common in Tollintal," Sella said aloud. She laughed, turning to Cali. "Sorry, Beejee is concerned about your knowledge of witches. Orakan people don't do a lot of dealings with witches unless they have to. No one but Lohnra has ever questioned my ability to use magic without a wand."

Cali looked at Beejee, gentleness still radiating from her bright eyes. "You're observant. I knew a few witches back home. I don't know a lot about them, but I know the basics. You've got yourself one powerful witch here if you've both been flying solo this whole time."

"I know it!" Beejee thrust his head away from her.

"Well," Cali said, changing the subject, "we can just sit here until we come up with a plan. I've got nothing else to do. I don't mind."

Sella looked at Cali for a moment, studying her expression. "Thanks. I think I'd like that." She turned back to the house and took a few deep breaths until, at last, she felt her breath grow deeper on its own. Her jaw relaxed, the space between her brows unwrinkled slightly.

Time seemed to move differently as she relaxed, but whether it was going faster or slower, Sella couldn't tell. The three of them sat, listening and waiting, as though there was nowhere else in the whole world to be.

Beejee rose to his feet, extended his neck to sniff at the air. "Do you hear that?" he asked.

Sella's eyes scanned the house. The magic was calm – no chime in the air, no sparkle about the doors or windows remained. "I hear everything… except the magic."

"Exactly." Beejee looked up at her.

"Does that mean we're in?" Cali stood and turned to reach for Sella's hand.

Sella smiled, but looked at her hand, then back to Cali's hopeful face.

"Oh, right… I still can't come in." Cali's hand withdrew. She turned to the house with a light twirl of her dress. "Well, go on then!"

Sella pushed herself up and gave Cali and Beejee one final warm look before she moved forward, past the bees and lavender, along the cobblestone path.

Sella's hand tentatively reached for the door handle. She paused when her skin made contact with the cold metal knob. She waited. She wasn't sure what she was expecting, but the utter ordinariness of it made her stop. How many times she had touched this door and come inside after a long day, how she rushed in looking for comfort on hard days, or sauntered in with Lohrna quick on her heels ready for dinner time… Now, she knew the home would be empty, void of the warmth and love that had been there once before. Now, her mother was gone. No one to tell her how to proceed, how to be. Now, it had been years since she stepped inside and she didn't know what to expect.

Sella turned back to Beejee and Cali. Cali winked and waved her forward. Beejee stayed still as stone. At last, he blinked, slowly, and Sella stepped inside.

The door behind her shut, but she was greeted by brightly burning flames in the fireplace, candles lit on tables and shelves, and sunlight streaming through the stained glass windows that cast a rainbow glow across the worn wood floors. Sella tilted her head to see outside; it was still overcast… The magic around the house must have made the inside look like a comfortable summer day. She moved within the house, surprised to find that none of the surfaces were dusty or blanketed with spiderwebs like she had imagined after so long unattended. She leaned close to a candle at the table and studied the flame. It looked real enough… she reached out a finger to the flickering light. How did this magic work?

From the kitchen, she heard a small clatter of ceramic, then a gruff cough. Sella stopped still as fear overtook her. She waited like a statue, though her heartbeat began to pound in her ears.

"Don't be afraid," a voice called from the kitchen. It was not her mother's voice. "If you don't calm down quickly, the magic will expel you from the property."

Sella forced herself to take a step. Then another. She moved soundlessly toward the kitchen's entrance. She positioned her hands to be ready to ignite fire if necessary.

"And definitely don't start fires!" The voice added

urgently. From around the corner, footsteps, light, and quick, approached.

"Who's there?" Sella's voice was firm, her fingers twitched.

"Calm mind, my dear, calm mind…" A small figure, about half of Sella's size, and limbs so thin they looked like threads of glass, appeared in the threshold. What exactly it was, Sella could not discern.

It appeared genderless, androgynous in all of their features, with glassy skin, fine wrinkles at the forehead, and smile lines revealing what looked like several rows of sharp teeth when it grinned at her. Silver, pupilless eyes squinted into the grin and the creature raised a small hand to show no malintent. In the other hand, it held a steaming mug of what appeared to be a dark green herbal tea. The smell of stone in rain filled the space between them as white steam rose from the surface. It was familiar to Sella in a way she could almost access in her memories. So close, and yet, intangible as the steam itself.

Her heartbeat was still racing; the cold in her stomach and heat in her hands battled for her attention. "Who are you?" Sella asked, voice vibrating with fear though she tried her best to sound brave. She drew in a shaking breath, inhaling more steam. The silver steam seemed to be gravitating toward her like a spell. "What are you doing in my mother's house?"

"Who I am is a difficult question to answer, isn't it? Who are you, for instance, when you are with strangers? Who are you alone? With Lohrna? Who *are* you truly?" the creature asked. It waddled toward her and held the mug out. "Tea?"

"No, thank you," Sella said cautiously. She was surprised

at her own politeness, given the situation, but the creature seemed to have a quick way of disarming her that confounded her. Her eyes flicked to the steam in the mug. It was so familiar… A calming spell, perhaps? One her mother used to make her? She took a step back and relaxed her hands to her side. As she felt its effects kicking in, her heartbeat slowed and her breathing returned to normal. The ice in her core began to melt. "I'm confused… I'll ask again: Who *are* you? What are you doing here?"

"My name is too difficult for most to say," the creature said kindly. "Your mother called me 'Seaglass.' A nickname. How she gave it to me is a story for another day." Seaglass began their waddle again toward the table and hoisted themselves onto a chair with the steaming mug held precariously in their hand. They tapped the table, indicating for Sella to sit.

Sella followed to the table, but stayed standing, watching Seaglass's face for any change in expression or shift that could cue her into the creature's inner thoughts or intent. But they conveyed nothing except what seemed to be genuine contentment. Seaglass patted the table again and gestured to the open seat across the table. "This only works if you stay relaxed. I tried brewing your mother's specialty blend. But I'm afraid I'm not as skilled as she was. The proportions are off… Sitting will help."

Sella's lips pulled into a hard line. She sat, unblinking at the small creature in front of her. Patches of colorful light from the windows illuminated the back of Seaglass's head with an otherworldly glow.

Seaglass blinked and lifted the tea into a 'cheers' motion before they took another long sip.

Sella waited, but her frustration was growing, clawing at her chest and fingers. She bit her bottom lip. Under the table, her hands balled into fists. "Can you tell me why you're in my mother's house?" she said as calmly as she could muster.

Seaglass swallowed loudly. "Certainly."

Sella waited. And waited. Her impatience grew. Anxiety tingled at the edges of her scalp. "Will you please tell me?"

"Yes." Seaglass sipped at their tea.

Sella began to wonder if this was an exercise in futility. Or perhaps a final test her mother set. How would she handle a fright, then confusion, then utter frustration? One final test to see if she could push Sella into dangerous action.

But Seaglass nodded as if empathizing with her. They began to speak again, "I thought it would take you longer to open the door. My apologies if you perceived my absence when you came in as deceitful. I've been here since your Tria went away."

Sella cocked her head. 'Went away' sounded much more peaceful than 'dying early.' She waited for Seaglass to continue.

"She asked me to keep charge of the house, continue its protective magic in her place... and I have. There's a lot of knowledge in here that she didn't want falling into the wrong hands."

"Including mine," Sella whispered.

"Yes, of course. But, you're not the only witch in this town." Seaglass waved their hand and took another drink.

"What?" Sella leaned closer. "There's another witch here? Since when?"

"Oh, yes, another witch. But they're not fully in control of their gifts like you. She wields your mother's wand–"

A flare of heat flashed through Sella's cheeks. Her nails pinched into her palms. "She has *my* mother's wand?" Her words dripped from her lips like poison.

"But that shouldn't upset you; it's not really why you're here. And you don't need it." Seaglass swirled the tea in their cup carefully. "Your mother always knew you'd find your way back here, Sella. I would meditate on the reason Tria gave her wand away to a lesser witch rather than her own daughter."

Sella didn't need to think on it. She blurted out, "Because I'm dangerous." Tears needled the edges of her eyes. She blinked them away. Her mother, her own mother, gave her wand away to another witch. Who it was hardly mattered. Her mother thought she was too dangerous with it. She had to be right. Too dangerous. Too in tune with fire. Too careless.

Seaglass shook their head, as though reading her mind. "It's not for me to say. The little witch needed guidance, that's all I know for now."

Sella had to stop herself from biting her tongue too hard. Already, blooms of cuts began to form within her mouth as her teeth found cheek. Even in death, her mother found a way to tear her down.

She took a deep breath to calm herself and push away the thoughts weaving deeply through her mind. Could she even trust anything Seaglass had to say? A witch here was nearly impossible… She tried to cut it, and the news of the wand's whereabouts, from her mind for now. "How long did you know my mother?"

Seaglass smiled a grin full of shark teeth. "Oh, I've known Tria for a very long time. Since she was a child."

"She never mentioned you." Sella's back straightened as she did her best to lean away from the steam that followed her.

"No." The creature shook their head. "I can't imagine she would have. It's considered a dangerous thing to know a Niminé. But I promise, it's not all you have heard."

"A Niminé?" Her eyes scanned the creature now more closely. She bit the inside of her cheek again and winced. The taste of iron filled her mouth but the wound healed nearly instantly.

She felt so foolish. She should have noticed it before. She had only ever read about Niminé; her mother never spoke of them. But she knew them. How could she sit across from one and not see it?

They were a close relative of sirens, as far as anyone who got close enough to study them could tell. A deadly ocean dweller, responsible for unnatural sea storms, shipwrecks in sight of shorelines, and the eerie teal glow that surrounded some small islands and trapped those who landed in their sands. They were thought to be immortal, and known to use witch's magic… Apparently, they could also come ashore.

"Some stories are true, some are not." Seaglass seemed to be uncannily following Sella's thoughts. "But yes, we can come to land. I promised your mother I would tend to the home when she left. I have grown quite fond of it here. It's been so long, the sea feels like a memory."

"You can stay," Sella said cautiously. Suddenly, any position of power she felt she had fled her limbs, dispersed through the air like smoke. She was strong, even without a wand. But she was no match for a Niminé. "I have my own place," she continued as though that justified it.

"The flat above the storefront… Indeed." The creature nodded slowly. "There may come a time when you use that as storage for your other needs, as your mother did. Should you need a place to stay, this door will always be open to you as long as you can open it. I want you to know this. However, I do not want anyone else knowing I am here." Seaglass smiled and finished the tea in a few long gulps. A bony finger pointed to a large wooden chest on the far wall by the fire. "The scrolls you seek are within. There is no magic needed; it will open for you."

Sella followed their finger to the chest. She let out a heavy breath, and with it, let go of all the tension trapped in her body. Her back relaxed into the seat just as she pushed herself up. She stretched her toes in her boot and rolled her neck. "This other witch, who are they?" Sella reached her full height at last. The calming spell took hold but her skin still felt electric with restlessness.

"Have they not relieved themselves to you since your return?"

Sella shook her head. "No…"

"Perhaps the witch worries." Seaglass cocked their head. "You are very strong, my dear. It must be harrowing to know they have the wand your mother meant to give to you once. Now, to the chest, child. I'm going to make myself another cup of tea."

Sella's fingers curled. She wasn't done with this conversation, but it seemed Seaglass was. "Thank you," was all she could manage to say.

"Of course. It's good to finally meet you, or at least, this you that I see now, Sella. I hope you come visit again. Bring your familiar when he can speak. I am sure he is full of words."

Sella tried to smile but only the corners of her lips cooperated. The confusion still lingered in her mind. She wanted to get the scrolls and race away from the house like it was filling with water. She tipped her head to the Niminé graciously and opened the chest. It was stuffed with papers: some folded, some rolled, all worn and delicate-looking.

"You want the one with the teal wax seal," Seaglass said. "And maybe the one folded into a rose. Just in case."

Sella glanced back at Seaglass but they were already sauntering off into the kitchen with the empty mug clutched in two small hands.

She felt the crease between her brows begin to fade when she heard the sound of a kettle being placed on the stove. She turned back to the chest and found the two spells. They were small enough to place into her pockets, and she did so before shutting the chest and swiftly walking to the door. With her hand on the knob, she turned to the kitchen and called, "Seaglass, thank you."

Of course, my dear witch, a voice in her head whispered.

Sella took a deep breath and crossed the threshold back out into the lavender garden. The door closed behind her and she heard the faint sound of crackling behind her. The surge of magic made the hair on her arms stand up and she knew the house was once again enchanted to only open for her.

"How'd it go?" Cali asked once Sella had crossed the path back to her and Beejee.

Sella looked back at the house. She sucked in air and

scratched her ear. "Very oddly, in a way I can't really explain right now…" She pulled the two spells from her pocket and examined them. The first was a simple rolled parchment, sealed with a teal green wax at the crease. The second, an intricately folded parchment that resembled a rose. She turned it over in her hand, looking at it curiously.

"What's that one?" Beejee asked, sticking his nose in the air to get a better look.

"I'm not sure. A Niminé in there told me to grab it."

"A Niminé?" Beejee and Cali both asked. Beejee's tone was grave; Cali's curious.

Sella ignored them for now. She put both scrolls back into her pocket. "Let's see if we can find any signs of Rorin." She looked out into the treeline. "I'll explain everything when we're with Lohrna… For now, I need to let my legs do some work."

Beejee grumbled at her response but trotted off ahead toward the forest.

"I guess it's time to move." Cali shrugged and followed him away from the house.

Sella looked back at the house once again. It was strange to think that all this time, there was someone in there, tending to its upkeep and taking care of it. She couldn't help but smile a little.

"YOU DIDN'T FIND anything in the woods *at all?*" Lohrna asked. She deflated in the doorway and Sella had to hold her by her arm to lead her inside the upstairs room above the shop.

It was a weird detail to focus on, Sella thought. Lohrna

hadn't mentioned Seaglass, the witch, or even the impressive feat of Sella calming the magic.

Sella locked the door to the loft behind them and ushered her friend to the couch. She lit the fireplace with a swish of her hand and ignited little fires overhead. The room grew warm and inviting as rain began to patter on the large circle window.

"We found some footprints!" Cali said, though Lohrna could not hear.

Sella repeated her words, went to the kitchen and began preparing tea. The clinking of ceramic cups filled the space. "But that was basically all." Sella spooned a little honey into each mug. "It's not nothing, but it's inconclusive."

"You didn't follow the tracks all the way to the end?" Lohrna flopped dramatically on the couch. "Why?"

"It was getting dark." Sella looked up from her work with gravity in her eyes. She wanted to finish with, *You remember what happened when we were kids?* But instead she held Lohrna's gaze. "I didn't want to run into a bear, or a group of pixies. You know how they get after dark."

Lohrna draped herself over the back of the couch and sighed. "But a few tracks sounds like it could be a promising lead."

"Or a hiker." Sella shrugged.

"Maybe Nicte's not clever enough to think of framing Rorin? Or has no reason to... Do you think Nicte's eyes were playing tricks on him?" Lohrna looked hopeful.

"Can we focus on the real issue? When are you making my potion?" Beejee yowled from the edge of Sella's bed.

Sella removed the two scrolls from her pocket and placed them on the slab of wood in her kitchen. "It's hard to know for sure," she said to Lohrna, ignoring Beejee for now. "There wasn't really anything to go off of." The tea was finished and she set the mugs on the table, but Lohrna didn't move.

"We'll have to start asking around… We can go to Hazen's tomorrow morning. He's doing breakfast," Lohrna said. Her round eyes drifted around the room. "Is Cali here?"

Sella pointed to the corner of the kitchen where Cali stood. Cali winked and hoisted herself onto the counter. She let her legs swing under her like she was enjoying a carefree spring day.

Sella smiled back and got to work on unrolling the sealed scroll.

"Wait– We can worry about Rorin later. Did you say that there's a *Niminé* living in your old house?" Lohrna gasped. "A real, live Niminé?"

"The weirdest part is that they said they knew my mother from childhood," Sella explained to the group as she read the spell to herself. She busied herself with gathering the ingredients scattered in cupboards, drawers, and even small wooden boxes on the counter. Beejee joined her on the counter, inspecting each item as she placed them in a row.

"So wait, I thought they were just a legend?" Lohrna continued as Sella moved about. "And your mom *knew* one? Personally? That's… wild."

"I'm still trying to sort through that too." Sella laid out all the ingredients and then leaned in closer to the parchment and squinted at it. "I'm not sure I got the code perfectly," she said to Beejee quietly. "She was always writing these spells all secretive…"

He looked at her, then back to the scroll. "I think it's worth a try."

"Do you need help?" Lohrna asked from the couch.

Sella glared at her over the parchment.

"Right, right…" Lohrna looked in Cali's direction but not quite in the right spot. "The last time I 'helped' with a recipe, it… let's say it backfired."

"Horribly. And Beejee will never forgive you," Sella added.

Cali laughed, covering her mouth with her hand. "What happened?"

"We were trying to make a stinky bomb," Lohrna said, almost proudly. "We wanted to clear out the hotel, see what guests were there… and have a good laugh."

"I'll never forget *or* forgive," Beejee said.

Sella stood straighter, hands resting on the counter as if to contain herself. It was mostly a show to up the theatrics of the story. She looked at Cali with a pained expression. "It was an experiment, and it failed terribly. The bomb went off in our faces and we smelled like rotten eggs for weeks."

"Weeks!" Lohrna loudly repeated.

"Oh no, I'm sorry for laughing," Cali spoke through her fingers, laughter concealing most of her words.

Lohrna joined in with laughter she couldn't hear. "Yeah, so I was basically banned from the kitchen ever since."

Beejee bared his teeth. "She shouldn't be here at all. She could contaminate it. What if you all start speaking cat?"

Sella glanced at him and started adding ingredients to a mortar. "I don't think we will all start speaking cat," she said, loud enough for Lohrna and Cali to hear.

"Ooh!" Lohrna pointed to the familiar. "*That* would be neat! Then we could speak to you in a code, Beejee!"

Beejee hissed, but under his breath, he added, "That actually would be useful."

Sella closed her eyes and focused on infusing magic into the mixture. She whispered the incantation written on the scroll quietly while she imagined fire, red sparks, coming from her fingers to heat the herbs and spices. No fire was released. Just heat, as the spell indicated. She opened her eyes and gave it three quick stirs. She closed her eyes again and focused on the intention of sharing, communication, and thought morphing into words. She gave it another three stirs and waited until she felt the stone warm under the pads of her fingers.

The room was quiet, but if Lohrna or Cali were talking still, she could not tell. She was hyper-focused on the task at hand, infusing her intention with the recipe. When the heat became unbearable, she removed her fingers and opened her eyes. Her fingertips were red and burned, but the mixture smelled of hope and strength.

She looked at Beejee and asked, "Are you sure you want to try?"

Beejee trotted across the counter to the bowl in response.

"You have to eat it while it's hot," she reminded him.

Beejee snorted, but plunged his face into the bowl before he could consider anything else.

Lohrna and Sella held their breath as they watched the familiar devour the meal. On the opposite counter, Cali had pulled her legs to her chest and held them close with her arms. She peeked out from behind her knees to watch.

When he was finished, Beejee rose and licked his lips.

"Well, how do you feel?" Sella asked, stroking his ear gently as she spoke.

Beejee looked around at each of them. "That mixture was disgusting… Can everyone hear me?"

To Sella, he sounded the same. She turned to Lohrna. Her friend's mouth hung open, her eyes wide.

"Beejee!" she said brightly. "You have the most beautiful voice!"

"Oh good… it worked," Beejee said, coming to the edge of the counter. "Now then, there are some grievances I've been meaning to unpack with you for *years!*"

"Hey now," Sella cut in, crossing around the counter to stand between them. "Beejee, you can talk to people! That's not going to be how we celebrate!"

Beejee battered the counter with each word, his little paw, however, made almost no sound, especially over his yowling voice. "I! Have! *Grievances*!"

Lohrna laughed and sprung up from the couch. "I'm sure you do, old friend! And I can't wait to hear about them!"

"Another time." Sella stretched. "I'm exhausted…"

"Magic can take it out of her," Lohrna explained to the area near where Cali sat. She still didn't quite have her location down.

Cali nodded. She unfolded her legs and leaned forward on the counter. "Sorry…" She looked at Sella with concern in her eyes but stayed still. "Do you need anything?"

Sella shook her head and then looked at her bed. "I'm passing out," she said. "You guys can stay up as late as you want."

From under the covers, Sella listened to the sweet sounds

of Beejee talking to Lohrna and Cali, translating for the ghost and even Koukie. Sella worried, briefly, that the tea on the table would grow cold. But everyone seemed more interested in talking than drinking anyway.

Despite everything that happened that day, it didn't take her long to drift off to sleep with a smile on her lips.

EIGHTEEN

Boo-sy Breakfast

THE MORNING CAME TOO QUICKLY. Lohrna hurried them out the door, certain that if they got to Hazen's any later, all the good food would be gone.

Beejee elected to stay at home and keep watch over the shop. The new ability to speak to anyone he wished was something he realized could get him into trouble. He was used to speaking his mind whenever he wanted to without, or at least with very little, consequence. Learning to keep his thoughts to himself would require practice.

After he snapped at Lohrna for putting his food bowl down in the wrong location, Sella agreed that this was for the best.

Their walk to Hazen's tavern was short but crowded. It was a day most people took off, save Hazen and a few other shops who hoped to capitalize on everyone's free time. It was an ideal morning to spend having a snack and drinks and seeing if they could learn anything new after the woods proved to be mostly a dead end.

Lohrna, Sella, and Cali meandered their way into the

tavern and out of the morning mist to an almost full room. Tables were filled with patrons enjoying Hazen's weekly breakfast spread of meat, cheese, and fruits, and many seemed already rosy-cheeked from their morning beverages.

They were running late, as Lohrna had feared, but found seats at the bar top. Sella scooted her stool close to Lohrna's to make room for Cali. The ghost sat atop the bar, her legs dangled over the side as they flagged Hazen down for two breakfast plates.

Hazen put their plates down in exchange for their silver coins and gestured to the buffet at the side of the great hall, but said nothing. He turned to help the next person at the other end of the bar who raised their glass for a refill.

"I'll get us breakfast." Sella picked up the plates. Her eyes grew wide when she caught Lohrna's faraway stare. She tried to lead her friend's gaze to the people at the bar and back to indicate for her to mingle, but Lohrna simply smiled flatly in return.

Sella sighed but felt a small grin cross her face gently. Lohrna was in one of her moods. Maybe that was for the best. Sella wasn't sure what would be more suspicious – Lohrna at the bar looking forlorn, or Lohrna asking pointed questions about the murder. She decided to let it be. There was no win except to show their faces and keep Lohrna acting as natural as possible.

She moved through the crowd to the long table with food spread on slabs of wood. Sella picked at the contents, filling her plate with fruits and cheese, and Lohrna's with mostly meat. She glanced about the room as she did, but tried to not focus too much on any one particular group to avoid looking like she was actively eavesdropping. She overheard bits of conversations and her ears twitched, trying to focus on what caught her attention.

"--From out of town–"

"Well, I heard that–"

"--Recovery after the melody night–"

"Did you hear Tiritan sing?"

"I had no idea!"

"--Just like old times—"

"But we have to keep a watchful eye!"

"--Killer's still out there–"

"Nasty business, isn't it?" the voice was so close that Sella startled and clutched the plates closer so as not to drop them. She turned to the small figure beside her with eyes wide. "Sorry to scare you again," Isra said with a kind voice. "My mom used to say I should wear a bell." She laughed, her expression easy.

Sella felt her shoulders loosen. "Maybe, maybe. You're quiet like a cat, that's for sure." She continued filling the plates, watching Isra from the corner of her eyes. "Nasty business, meaning the murder?"

"What else?" Isra reloaded her plate with bread and butter. "Scary to think someone could still be out there, hurting people. At least you have a way to protect yourself."

Sella eyed Isra cautiously, unsure of where the conversation was going. "Did you know Cali?" She was trying to pry for information in a way that hopefully sounded natural.

She looked away as Isra continued, "Not well, but we chatted most mornings. She seemed sweet. A little scatterbrained for being a numbers person." Sella thought that sadness crossed Isra's face despite her easy smile. She went on, "Did you know her? I recommended your shop to her. She said she'd try it."

"She came in a few times… I never got to know her well."

"I would've thought she'd be more memorable than just that. Maybe make more of an impression on you." Isra sounded like she was scolding her. It put Sella on the defensive. "She was always very talkative with me. And she… let's just say she stood out in more than one way."

Sella felt a twist of pain in her chest. She hated that she always acted cold toward Cali when she was alive. In fairness, most of her income came from hotel guests and out-of-towners. She wasn't in the habit of inviting small talk with them or particularly noticing anyone new. "I must be horribly uninterested in others," she said, mostly to herself. But as she spoke, she tried listening again to the conversations around them. She heard nothing in particular, only empty chatter.

"Maybe so." Isra's tone was soft. She spoke quietly, only loud enough to be heard over the noise. "Are you scared at all? Being a witch… does that make it easier? Or is it harder, with some of the prejudice in Orakan?"

Sella paused. She turned to Isra and watched her closely. Though her horns curved up from her forehead into long spirals, she still was so small compared to Sella. It must feel like a dangerous world to someone like her, Sella thought.

Isra's expression grew worried the longer Sella was silent. Sella wanted to reassure her, and a feeling of protectiveness came over her. "Witches are considered a little suspicious everywhere, I think. Except Tollintal. I've heard it's better there. But I've traveled to many big cities where this kind of crime is more common. I can tell you, being a witch doesn't make it easier." She set down one plate and reached a hand to Isra's shoulder. She gave it a small squeeze. "We'll be okay. Just be careful, always. Here or anywhere."

"If nowhere's safe… and even you're careful with your magic fire," Isra whispered. "Then maybe I may as well travel?"

Sella sighed. "Maybe. It's a big world. There's a lot to see."

"Thanks… Maybe I'll try Tollintal someday."

"SELLLLAAAHHH," Lohrna's voice called. "I'm STARVING!"

Sella laughed, grabbing both plates. "Chin up. And lock your doors."

"How generic." Isra's voice was lost as she continued to pile cheese from her family's farm onto her plate.

Sella side-eyed her but she didn't linger on Isra's words. She had other things to worry about.

"Thank goodness," Lohrna said when Sella set her plate down. She began shoveling food into her cheeks. "How's Isra?"

Sella glanced back at the small girl. "Scared. I think most people are."

"Fair," Lohrna said. "Must be hard for her in that big empty house in the woods, especially. Did you know that after her grandma passed, her whole family basically left town?"

Sella hummed. She looked around the tavern for Cali and caught her leaning in close to one particular table of women. She found Sella's eyes and smiled brightly, giving her an excited wave and gesturing dramatically to her ear.

Sella nearly laughed at her enthusiasm. It was infectious, despite everything. She looked at Lohrna before she let her giggle slip.

Her friend's expression betrayed a hint of disappointment, but she changed the subject quickly. "Well, Cirian isn't scared!" Lohrna gestured with a thumb three seats down at Cirian who was laughing loudly and toasting a friend in the seat beside him.

"Cirian," Sella nibbled the corner of her cheese slice, "is always jovial."

"Also," Lohrna said after a large swallow, "my fellows over here are also pretty nonchalant about it all."

A patron on the seat beside Sella leaned forward on the bar counter to make eye contact with Sella. "It's no worries over here. The girl was new to town, and she's got human 'friends' staying in the hotel. It had to be personal, someone not from here." He was a large man, with wind and sun-cracked skin. A fisherman, most likely, but Sella didn't recognize him. Perhaps he moved here after she left.

She raised her brows. He had a point, but his confidence was off-putting. There was something about his demeanor that made her skin crawl.

The other man next to him, clearly another seafaring man based on his clothes and one cracked horn, nodded in agreement. He was seemingly unaware of the brewing tension and barreled ahead, "Benka'll catch 'em if he can get enough evidence. Or they'll move on soon enough and the gossip'll quiet down, finally. I'm sick of everyone throwin' out the idea that it's one of our own just 'cause the foreigners have a so-called 'alibi.'"

Behind the bar, Hazen stopped pouring a drink. He narrowed his eyes at the pair of men. "Arda and Yorro. I'm ashamed that you would speak like this in my tavern – like she's not worthy of getting justice. She wasn't just some out-of-towner," he said coldly. "And if you think you're safe just because of that, or because she was a small girl, then you could end up dead wrong. We have no idea what the motives were."

Beside Sella, Lohrna stilled midchew, hand still raised to her mouth with a mini sandwich she crafted. She looked between the pair of men and Hazen with wide eyes, waiting in silence for the pressure to collapse on itself.

Sella, too, was quiet. She watched the scene, scanning each of their faces for any twitch, any change in expression that could give away their next move. She felt like she was watching feral alley cabbits face off over scraps. Each side was slightly puffed at the chest, but no one wanted to make the first move. They were busy cautiously sizing the other up. When the tension grew too great, Sella heard Lohrna swallow and then cough. An obviously fake means of breaking the silence.

Hazen spoke first. He continued to pour the drink, but he kept his eyes on the sailors. "Cali was one of us," he said firmly. "And whoever did this *will* be brought to justice."

"Yeah, okay, Hazen," one of the men said. Arda, by the way Hazen had spoken to them. Sella could hear no sarcasm or unkindness in his voice.

"Sorry… you're right," Yorro added.

Arda and Yorro got up and added a few extra coins to

the counter as if they were paying for the inconvenience they caused. They bent their heads to Sella and Lohrna respectfully and then made their way to the door.

Lohrna side-eyed Sella. "Phew!" she exhaled. "That was… a lot. To be honest, if I were a man, I'd probably feel similarly. They're used to being in a small town where no one troubles them…"

Or suspects them of murder, Sella thought with bitterness rising in her gut.

Lohrna didn't notice Sella putting her food down or the sour expression that crossed her face. She lowered her voice and leaned in close, "Did you hear anything of value while you were out?"

Sella shook her head. "Not really. The town is split, it sounds like. Some are frightened, some only seem to like that something has happened here at all and are happy to gossip." She turned back to the table of food. It was growing bare. Her eyes found Cali again. "But Cali's on the case," she said, nearly inaudible.

Lohrna held her plate up. "Seconds and more eaves-dropping?"

"Let's go."

They both rose and walked, slowly, to the food table.

"Hazen's lost his mind…" someone said quietly.

"--Fair, though, he worked with the girl--"

"Seems suspicious--"

"--Just smell your food before you eat it--"

"--She's too trusting, and you can't forget The Incident--"

Sella felt her scalp begin to prickle. She slowed to hear

more, but Lohrna was already ahead, moving through the tables with ease, her plate raised high above her head.

"--No alibi. And I heard she was down at the beach that night--"

"--That's where they found the body--"

"--Lock down the hotel--"

Sella heard enough. She shut herself out of all the chatter until they were back at their seats with plates refilled.

"Can you believe these people?" Hazen said when they were nearly finished with their meals. He rested his forearms on the counter, his posture defeated. "Some of 'em are acting like wild trolls since this whole situation."

"It's nature," Lohrna said, sympathetically. "People are nervous. They get weird when they're nervous and don't know what's happening."

Sella's expression softened at her friend. This town didn't deserve Lohrna. She was too kind. Too understanding for them. They had shown her no such warmth since rumors of her involvement began.

"Someone here knows something." Hazen broke Sella's thoughts. He was scanning the tavern with narrowed eyes. "Someone saw something, even if they don't know what they saw. Someone here is hiding their knowledge of poisons… I know people are looking at you two." His voice lowered, "But I also know you aren't capable of something like this. Your mothers raised you right, girls."

Sella felt the muscles in her face untangle, but she couldn't shake what she overheard. That she was too trusting. The focus wasn't on her. It was on Lohrna. And she couldn't stand it. Her jaw tightened. "Thank you, Hazen."

She poked at her plate, avoiding looking at either of them. "Really, that means a lot."

"It's just the truth." Hazen leaned even closer. "But I keep looking around at everyone. It's exhausting thinking it could be any of us. People we know well, or *think* we know well. I keep wondering what will happen next."

"You don't think it's over, then?" Lohrna asked. "You think people will keep getting hurt?"

"I don't think anyone capable of doing something like this will stop. Do you?" Hazen shrugged. "I wish Benka'd hurry up and get to narrowing things down."

Lohrna agreed, but Sella shifted in her seat. Benka getting closer to his truth probably meant a nightmare for her friend. If he caught her in the lie about where she was that night, it could be a quick undertow sweeping her away. A stab of pain shot through Sella's veins, electrifying her whole body.

"I don't think Benka's on the right current," Sella felt herself saying, as if possessed. It was true, of course, but she didn't want to announce that she and Lohrna were, as far as she could tell, suspect number one and an accessory.

Hazen paused. He leaned closer. "No?"

"No," Sella said. She was already in it; she figured she'd better see it through to the end. "I don't think any of us are."

"Intuition?" He tilted his head, curls falling around his horns as he did.

"I guess you can call it that." Sella looked around the room briefly. Part of her wished she would find Beejee in the crowd. She felt like she might need more backup than

Lohrna could provide. "I just think this whole thing is deeper than it appears."

"Still ponds?" Hazen asked.

Sella agreed, "Still ponds."

"Rough seas, loose boards." Lohrna continued the well-worn metaphors of their seaside village. "Water gets into ships slowly."

Hazen let out a small huff. He looked at Cirian down the counter. Sella watched him, following his eyes to Cirian's empty plate. "Excuse me." He tapped the counter with his knuckle and looked each of them in the eyes like he wanted to say something else, but couldn't. He left them alone and without closure.

Unfazed, Lohrna took a bite of her food and talked from the side of her mouth. "You know, Sella, I think you're right. This whole thing seems much more mysterious than it appears. Let's hope it gets easier to untangle all these ropes."

"Let's hope." Sella looked to Cali.

"I'll fill you in later!" Cali called loudly over the din of the crowd, a voice like a little wind chime in a storm that only she could hear.

NINETEEN

Dead End

THAT EVENING, the four gathered in Sella's upstairs and sat around the table, lit by glowing fires that surrounded them from all angles so that no dark shadows lingered despite the complete darkness of the night outside.

Sella served them a soothing herbal nighttime tea that smelled of sweet lemon and cut grass. She set a tray of golden, flaky biscuits at the table. Gentle steam still rose from their middle when Lohrna ripped one in half.

Cali eyed them enviously, but Lohrna bit straight into hers and made an inconsiderate amount of joyful sounds as she chewed. Beejee licked butter off his, and beside him, Koukie was busy snacking on the cut chicken liver that Sella had placed there for them.

Cali leaned forward and smelled the tea that Sella set in front of her, mostly for her to experience being part of the group, but also for her to try to get some of the calming remedy through the steam. She seemed to be feeling more at ease as she inhaled deeply. Sella noticed her shoulders loosen and her jaw unclench. At last, Cali's posture lifted her whole body as she took another long, deep breath. She looked around the table and waited for Sella to sit before she broke the silence, finally. "So, I didn't really learn anything all that interesting. Except, apparently, there's some sort of incident with you? It seems like we're still at a dead end, huh?"

Sella grimaced at the mention of The Incident but ignored that part of Cali's observations. "Unfortunately, we didn't learn much today, except that the whole town is processing things a little differently… and Hazen's pretty heated about it."

"You didn't laugh," Cali grumbled. She sunk into her chair.

Sella's brows furrowed. "Laugh?"

"Laugh at what?" Lohrna asked, scooting her chair in closer to look around the table.

"'Dead end?' I'm dead? Come on." Cali leaned across the table with open arms. "Get it?"

Sella's laugh was harsh, a forced sound. She held her forehead with both palms pressing into her eyes. "Cali made a 'dead' pun," she explained at last.

"Ah," Lohrna chuckled lightly. "Good thing you still have your sense of humor, Cal."

"It's Cal now?" Sella asked.

"What? I think we're good enough buddies that I can nickname her nickname…" Lohrna shrugged. "Right?" She looked at the empty space where Cali sat.

Cali laughed. "I like it. It's stronger sounding than 'Cali', but not as strong as 'Calisyali.' Maybe that should be my new name in death? New life, new name?"

"Up to you," Sella said to the ghost. To Lohrna, she added, "She likes it."

"Knew she would," Lohrna said, but her tone was a smug victory that revealed to Sella that she had been more nervous about it than she let on.

Beejee nudged his plate across the table, creating a clanking, scraping sound that silenced the group. When he looked up at them, he said, "Back to the business of the murdering murderer with murder on their mind still quite possibly running amok about to murder in our village."

Lohrna's brows rose. She slid his biscuit closer to him as if more butter would solve his bad mood.

"Right." Cali nodded. She took another deep breath, exhaling loudly before continuing. "I was thinking, we should go back to the forest tomorrow. We have an idea that someone's been there; it may be Rorin. I think we can find out more as to why he's here. Even if I think he didn't do it."

Lohrna rested her chin in one hand. She gave Koukie a quick scratch behind her ear. "I feel like we are in a forest, wandering about without ever looking back. We have no answers and all the trees look the same." She lifted herself higher and sipped her tea carefully. She looked up at the ceiling, and Sella followed her gaze, cringing at the small spiderweb she spotted among one of the low rafters. Lohrna went on, but her eyes were fixed on the web. "So we have Nicte and Dimas out and about… but even though we don't exactly buy the amicable ending, it seems unlikely they did it, according to Cal. *But*, they're each other's alibi… and they seemed pretty keen on leaving town soon. Then there's this Rorin business. Why is he here?"

"It is usually someone close to the victim that does the killing," Sella agreed.

"Hey now! 'Victim' seems harsh," Cali cut in.

"Sorry." Sella pushed the tea closer to Cali so she could sink back into the steam. "You're right. But, to be frank, it usually is the partner or ex-partner. Especially if they're in town when it's not expected. You have to admit, it doesn't look good."

"I just don't think he's clever enough to make Cresablatt, let alone have the follow-through to see it done, then sneak off." Cali shrugged.

Lohrna raised a brow. Her eyes shifted from Sella to the empty seat. "What's she saying?"

"She doesn't think he's got it in him. Not smart enough," Sella summarized.

Lohrna laughed. "Yeah, we should focus our search on women. They're the real brains of the operations!"

Sella rolled her eyes, but felt herself smile nonetheless. "I feel like it has to be an out-of-towner," she agreed, in part. "Let's hope Benka's feeling similarly. I don't *love* the idea of this all being left up to us."

"I kind of love it." Lohrna bit into another biscuit. She spoke from the corner of her mouth. "Plus, I think you're shaping up to be quite the detective!"

But she didn't feel like she'd accomplished anything at all so far. If anything, it felt as though she made matters worse with every decision.

Lohrna went on, "It makes sense for it to be someone we don't know. No offense, Cali...."

In her seat, Cali leaned in, waiting for the rest.

"We just haven't had something like this happen... like

ever. And then all of the sudden, three people from your past are here? Seems like more than a coincidence."

"We'll check for signs of Rorin tomorrow," Cali agreed. "I don't know. I don't see it. Maybe Nicte. He and I always squabbled about stupid things. And he's clever. Really clever. But Rorin?" She sighed again. "I'll keep an open mind."

Sella looked back at the little silver web. "Let's hope we have a little more time to keep working on this…"

But it felt like cold saltwater was rising around her. She kept kicking, trying to stay afloat, but her legs were getting tired.

TWENTY

Scones by the Creek

IN THE PALE MORNING LIGHT, Sella watched as Cali carefully stepped over ferns and branches on their way through the mossy woods. She wasn't sure if Cali was simply used to stepping around and over things, or if she was physical enough for it to matter. Either way, watching her be careful to not disturb the foliage around her, and to be cautious in her movements, made Sella feel a warmth within her. It was endearing that a habit carried on from her life was one of being considerate of plants, even when she didn't need to be.

Sella shook her head. She also had to remember that this was the same ghost that bullied and haunted her into helping her. Still, she smiled when Cali looked up at her after skipping over a small ring of mushrooms.

"What do you think will happen after we catch who did this?" Cali asked.

Sella paused midstep. She felt her jaw twitch at the sudden question. She was unsure of how to answer. "What do you mean?" she asked.

Cali looked deep into the thick branches. Her voice was nearly a whisper. "What do you think will happen to me? When I find peace or whatever. When I move on…? What's next?"

Sella shrugged but tried to keep her expression warm. She leaned closer. "Sorry, but… that I don't know. Witches don't have special knowledge of the afterlife, unfortunately. I know tradition says we are reborn with our familiars in each lifetime. But… since my mother's death, I haven't seen any sign of that being true…" She paused, realizing as she spoke that the pain of her mother's death was still a thorn in her heart. There was no time for that. She buried it again. "I wish I could be more helpful."

Cali let out a bigger huff this time. "When you banish ghosts, you don't know where they go?"

"The afterlife, I assume." Sella continued her journey. She was a few paces ahead of Cali now, and though she heard no movement behind her, she felt her presence coming closer. "Are you nervous about it? The afterlife?"

Behind her, Cali scoffed.

"It's alright to be scared." Sella didn't turn to face her. Cali was finally being vulnerable, at least partially. She couldn't look her in the eyes while she did. It would be too hard. For her, for Cali. For them both.

"I'm not scared," Cali asserted, but her voice cracked. "Just curious."

Sella kept walking. "I understand." Though she knew she couldn't possibly understand, and hopefully wouldn't, for a very long time. "Sorry, Cali. I wish I had more answers for you," she added, hopeful it would help Cali to simply know she tried, cared, *wanted* to understand.

At last, Sella looked back. Cali's usual cheerful demeanor was gone. The ghost was fixated on the circle of mushrooms with a furrowed brow. She kicked at one gently. It did not move. Her face scrunched.

"You sure you're okay?" Sella asked, knowing she would probably lie in her answer.

Cali was already smiling. "Of course! Let's keep going. I think I hear water…. Rorin would probably be holed up around there."

Sella watched her carefully. A lie and a quick diversion. That seemed to be Cali's way of coping with things. Deflect until she couldn't anymore. Sella kept her eyes on Cali, watching her smile stay fixed to her cheeks but the corners of her eyes were like stone. "Cali…?" She reached a hand out, but Cali withdrew, her fake smile still etched on her face.

"Yes?"

Sella's hand fell to her side. She sighed.

Neither of them moved or spoke for a long moment. They held each other's gaze, one with a smile, the other a frown. This was going nowhere. Sella knew she wouldn't win against Cali's stubbornness.

"There is a creek up ahead," Sella broke their standoff. She squinted through the trees but could see no sign of anything moving. She changed the subject, hoping if she lightened the mood again, Cali would keep opening up slowly. "We used to play at the creek all the time when Lohrna and I were kids."

"I wish I had a creek to play in as a kid. Tell me some stories?"

"One time, Lohrna thought she was going to drown.

She jumped in with pockets full of rocks and sank to the bottom…" Sella laughed. "She was thrashing and splashing about wildly. But then she stood and it was only shoulder deep."

"That sounds like her. She's funny like that."

"She doesn't always think ahead," Sella agreed. "But she's got a good heart. I wish she could be her true self to people here, though. I think that's why she puts on such a silly facade…"

"It's not fair that no one here knows she's a shifter, what she's going through… Why hasn't she taken a suppressant? You can make them, can't you?" Cali asked. There was no unkindness in her voice, only concern.

Sella kept walking. She turned over her shoulder. "Yes. She hasn't ever taken me up on it, though. I don't know why…" She trailed off, then changed the topic again before Cali could say anything. She didn't want to talk about Lohrna's condition. Or how it was her fault she got that way. As they neared the creek, Sella said, "My mother and I used to come here to get fresh water for our recipes."

"Was she a kitchen witch too?" Cali rolled with the quick change. Sella was grateful it worked.

"She was much more eclectic. She practiced a lot of different forms. That's a lot more rare, at least here. But she called herself a kitchen witch." Sella paused for a moment. She had never said any of that aloud before. It felt odd. Almost criminal. She moved on before she could feel guilty. "I heard there's a lot of different types of witches across the sea?"

Cali nodded and Sella turned back to watch her steps.

Sella continued, "I think humans tend to be more accepting of witches. Here in Marra, folks want us to stick to baked goods and ancient potion recipes."

"We definitely have a lot more open witches of all varieties in Tollintal," Cali said. "But don't worry, I won't tell anyone your mom was an eclectic witch."

Sella raised a brow at her and they both laughed.

The sound of slow-running water grew louder, and through the gap in the trees, the creek came into view. It was peaceful but wide. The clear water sparkled as it glided, unhurried, over smooth, colorful rocks. Mossy boulders, tall as Sella, dotted both sides of the shore, decorated with little white flowers that reached toward the rays of sunlight as the thick clouds passed over. In the distance, a bird called in a singsong tune.

Sella held out her arms like the creek was her masterpiece. "What do you think?"

Cali stood beside her with her eyes wide, mouth open. "Wow… This is beautiful."

"If Rorin is hiding out here, he's probably close to the water." Sella's eyes scanned the shoreline.

"Eh," Cali shrugged. "Can we just sit and take in the moment for a bit? This is beautiful and like nothing I've seen before… I don't really want to think about death and murder or a dumb ex right now."

Sella looked at her for a long moment, but Cali's eyes were closed, her face lifted to the sky. As clouds drifted across the sun, her face muted, then lit up again. "Sure," Sella said at last. "For a bit."

The two sat on a boulder at the edge of the water,

watching the water glisten by. Sella felt unease settle into her muscles. She wanted to keep moving, to find what they came for, and hopefully get some answers.

But Cali looked so content to simply be by the water's edge. Her eyes drifted lazily from one point to another, taking it all in. She looked down at the water, then to the trees and the flowers growing slowly between them.

As Sella watched her, the tension in her legs and shoulders started to fade. She took a deep breath and slowed her mind. The theories swirling within her mind could wait. Rorin could wait. Her mind was quiet and she found herself missing Beejee. He didn't want to have to trudge through the woods again, Sella understood, but it was rare they were apart. She felt a small pitch of loss in her heart and her mind wandered to Lohrna. She couldn't lose them… They needed to find something of value today. Anxiety spiked in her body again. Her fingers twitched.

The sun began to shine again and a school of small golden fish darted by. Cali watched them with a fascinated expression. The wind rustled the leaves above their heads. Cali looked to the sky and said, "It sounds like breathing."

Sella smiled, looking up too. "Yeah, it does…"

They fell into a comfortable silence, listening to the world around them breathe.

IT WAS midafternoon when Sella finally broke their quiet. She reached into her pocket to pull out a small scone. "Do you mind if I eat?" she asked.

"Of course not." Cali looked at the scone with wide

eyes. "It looks good, though. Can I be super weird for a moment?"

Sella shrugged. "Go for it."

"Can I smell it?"

Sella's laugh caught her off guard. She held the scone out to Cali for her to sniff as though she were a lost cat she was trying to tame. Cali took a big sniff. "Lovely."

"Cinnamon and cranberry." Sella held it up to the light for her to inspect the little flakes of burgundy and sprinkles of dark cinnamon throughout.

"I think I'll miss eating most. Do you think ghosts can eat once they cross over?"

Sella took a small bite. She chewed carefully before answering. Cali didn't seem like she was rushed and Sella wanted to be thoughtful about her answer. "I don't know much about the afterlife, or even ghosts for that matter. Maybe it's because you're human? Maybe it's the way you died? But the only ghosts I've ever dealt with were much different…" Sella paused and looked at Cali with a gentle smile. "I don't know if ghosts can eat when they go, but I know all the ghosts I banished must be happier there than here. The ones who get stuck… they seem to become less and less themselves over time. They're not happy in the end."

Cali's smile faded. Her lips drew into a thin line and a crease formed between her brows. She looked at the clouds. "Maybe next time, lie to me," she said quietly. "Just tell me 'yes.'"

Sella followed her eyes to the sky. "Can I start over?"

"Yes."

Sella let out a small chuckle, though her body felt like anything but happy. "You know what, Cali? I heard they have the best buffets on the other side. All you can eat, but you never get too full. You get to eat scones and drink tea every single day. And wine and chocolate flows from gold fountains at night."

Cali laughed, a genuine sound. She pushed Sella's arm with solid fingers. "That's better!"

THE CLOUDS DARKENED as they moved on and made their way along the water's edge, looking for any sign of disturbances. Sella was glad to have a happier Cali again. But their previous conversation didn't sit right with her. She kept glancing back at the ghost as though she was about to fade away.

Cali caught her stare and raised a brow.

"Let me know if you see anything." Sella covered for her awkward watchfulness.

"You got it," Cali called from a boulder ahead. She was standing on top, looking below with squinted eyes.

They kept moving, Cali leaped easily from boulder to boulder, keeping her vantage point high. "Hey, Sella! Look at this!" She was pointing to the tree line. "Is it dangerous?"

Sella stood on her tiptoes to see. In the woods, a dark shadow moved through the trees. It stopped and turned to them. Dark fur covered its huge body. It stood on all fours with thick, curved legs. It seemed to look at them knowingly, briefly, before it turned forward and kept walking through the trees.

Sella moved to Cali on the boulder. "It's not dangerous

right now. As long as you don't sneak up on them, they're quite peaceful and reclusive."

"Oh, that's good." Cali watched the creature continue its journey until it was out of sight. "Not that I would need to worry so much about it."

"And I have my fire," Sella said, her voice calm as she felt. "I'm usually safe."

"As long as no one sneaks up on you," Cali teased.

"Bears and witches have that in common." Sella nudged her shoulder with her own and found it as solid as before.

"HEY!!" A man's voice called from the treeline.

Sella nearly slipped on the moss as she turned swiftly to face the direction of the voice. Her fists were clenched, heart racing.

"Hey!" It sounded again. "Watch out! Watch out for the bear!"

Sella's brow furrowed. She stood a little straighter, her fingers relaxed. "Yeah, I saw it," she called, just as a man emerged from the treeline. Another thick cloud covered the sun, and without the harsh shadows, she could see him more clearly.

He was tall. A mess of curly black and gold hair fell into his eyes and over his ears, but she could see was hornless; human. He smiled at her. "Good thing." He continued to approach them, half watching his footing on the mossy rocks, half keeping his eyes on Sella. "I almost spooked the creature a moment ago."

"That's Rorin!" Cali hissed, inching closer to Sella as if to hide herself. "What is he doing here? I was sure this errand was–"

Rorin unknowingly cut her off. "What're you doing out

here?" His voice was concerned. He stepped closer. "Are you lost?"

Sella hated to admit, he was handsome in the way that she figured probably made people feel at ease around him. He seemed so nonchalant about their encounter. She wondered for a moment if he had ever met a stranger who didn't immediately enjoy his company. She, or anyone finding him in the woods, should be questioning why *he* was out here. Not the other way around.

"I'm not lost." Sella reflexively squared herself to him, shielding the ghost behind her. She wasn't going to let herself be fooled by charm. There was something about his expression that dripped with disingenuousness to her.

"Ah, okay, my apologies for the assumption," he said, his voice no longer a shout now that he was closer. He did not seem to notice her change in body language and he kept approaching her with easy movements.

"Are *you* lost?" Sella asked. "I see you're not from around here."

Rorin let out a deep laugh. He tousled his hair and the corners of his eyes wrinkled. "Yeah, no horns… pretty clear giveaway, huh? I guess us humans from across the sea can't blend in in Orakan."

"He seems awfully jovial, given the circumstances," Cali whispered. "Ask him why he's here."

"I can't just ask that," Sella whispered back, but immediately regretted it.

Rorin looked at her quizzically and she realized that to him, she looked like she was scolding herself.

She changed the subject. "Where are you from?"

"Tollintal. Across the sea. It's a short trip... Have you been?"

"What are you doing out in the woods?"

"They call me Rorin... You are?" he asked as if he thought her questions were rude without an introduction.

"Sella." She lifted her arms like it was obvious. She was already exasperated by his antics.

"Nice to meet you, Sella." He finally stopped advancing, but he was already closer than Sella wanted. "Yeah, I'm not from here, that's evident," Rorin let out another strained laugh. "But why I came here is... Well, it's a long story." He shifted his feet as though uncomfortable on the uneven pebbled shore. "It sure is beautiful here, though. I wish my stay could be longer—"

Sella didn't wait for him to continue. "You may need to, the boats are all docked for now."

"So I heard." Rorin smiled. He scratched the back of his neck.

Sella wanted to cut to the heart of it, to smack the smile from his face with a quick swipe. She cast a glance at Cali. The ghost was transfixed on Rorin. With a huff, Sella decided to wait and see what he had to say. She tilted her head and crossed her arms, waiting impatiently.

"I, uh, got a letter," Rorin said carefully. He reached for the pocket in his coat but then paused. "An old friend of mine wrote to me and said she needed to see me... regarding a few personal matters. But when I got here, she... well, she..."

"Was already dead."

Rorin's expression turned pained and his shoulders

slumped. "News must travel quickly in a small town like this." He looked away. "I still can't believe it's real. I never thought anything like this would happen to me." He was looking at his feet in a way that made Sella think he was trying to look sympathetic. It turned her stomach.

Sella rolled her eyes. She was glad he was looking adrift pensively and didn't catch her disgust. He really was making someone else's death about himself.

Unaware of his company's repulsion, he continued, looking at the folded letter in his hand. "Did you know Calisyali?"

Sella glanced to her side. Cali nodded fervently, so Sella lied, "Yes, she was my friend."

"Then maybe you'll understand…. I thought about destroying this. Burning it… or something, once I heard the news…" Again, he paused dramatically.

Sella crossed her arms, her patience was running thinner by the moment. "So why didn't you?"

"It paints me in a bad light, but it might be helpful, if someone trusted I was telling the truth." His face shifted. Sella thought it looked like desperation. "I swear, I didn't hurt Cali. I'm not dangerous," he added, somewhat urgently.

"I never wrote him a letter," Cali whispered, inching closer to Sella. She peered over her shoulder to get a better look at Rorin. "We have nothing to discuss," she added. "I would've been happy to never see him again, honestly—"

Rorin went on with a dry, hollow chuckle, "This all sounds crazy, and you have no reason to trust me, I get it. I'll leave you alone and figure it out myself. Just, be careful of the bear." He looked into the woods.

"They're more afraid of you than you are of them," Sella called as he turned to walk away. She glanced back at Cali, who urged her on silently. Sella jumped from the boulder and landed in the shallow shoreline with a splash. "Hey, Rorin! Stop!"

He turned back to her, eyes wide and hopeful. Sella could see now what Cali meant. He seemed harmless enough. Maybe a little simple, a little selfish. Too selfish, it seems, to risk it all on revenge or a bruised ego.

"Look, Cali was my friend. If you have something that can help me bring whoever did this to justice? I need it. I can't promise that nothing bad will happen, but you should come with me." She moved closer to him. "This letter might help clarify a few things for us. Our town is really frightened right now."

"But I didn't write a letter!" Cali hissed.

"I know," Sella grumbled under her breath.

"I could just give it to you." Rorin unfolded the paper slowly. He read it over himself and then folded it back up. He reached his arm out with the paper extended.

Sella recoiled at the notion. "I don't think that's a good idea."

"Listen, I don't want to make this more complicated than it needs to be. I was planning on leaving as soon as the boats were free to go. I am trying to do the right thing here and get this letter into someone's hands. Someone who can help. Can you help, or not?"

Sella stood still with narrowed eyes. "You're not exactly a brave heart, are you?" But the words tasted disingenuous in her mouth. She wasn't sure she was brave either, but his level of hesitancy seemed ridiculous, given the circumstances.

Rorin squinted at her, his full lips hardened.

There it is, Sella thought with a half smirk. The temper everyone who knew him spoke about. The arrogance.

"Do you talk to everyone like this?" Rorin's tone was indignant.

Sella scoffed and drew her arms tighter. "Is he always like this?" she asked, unabashedly, to the ghost beside her.

"I told you we broke up for good reasons."

Once again, Rorin was left to puzzle out if Sella had lost her mind or not. He looked entirely unsure.

"Alright," Sella said, louder. "I need you to come with me and explain your side of things. I can't exactly show up to our resident detective and say I found some man wandering the woods and he gave me a letter, alright?"

"That's what you'll have to do."

"You think you can just get on the next ship out of here? They'll lock it *all* down before you can purchase a ticket, and judging by the way you snuck up on me and the bear, I honestly doubt you can make it long out here… They'll find you." Sella took a step forward, trying a different approach. Her voice was calm, and kind, "Rorin, if you want to go home and put this all behind you, you really should come with me back to town."

"Sella," he said with enough force in his voice that she stopped in her tracks. "I really don't think that's a good idea."

"Use your fire," Cali urged her. She took a step from behind Sella's shoulders to get a better look at Rorin.

But Sella simply shook her head. She couldn't. Not

here, not on him. Sure, he seemed like a big, selfish jerk, but fire was too uncontrollable once it left her fingers. Especially if she got angry. She squeezed her hands tight and bit her lip hard before she finally gave in. "Fine." She threw her hands in the air. "Give me the letter, you coward. But you better hope you're more adept at hiding than you are with manners because it won't take them long to find you." She advanced on him, hand outstretched.

Rorin set the folded paper in her hand. He smiled, trying to be as charming as he had before. "You'll give me a head start?" He sounded like he was trying to flirt.

Sella nearly gagged but decided to leave him with at least one bit of advice: "Good luck out here, Rorin. Watch out for bears... and pixies. They're small, but they're spiteful."

"YOU'RE sure he didn't do it? He seems like suspect number one to me. I don't like him or trust him one bit," Sella said as the two of them walked back through the woods. Rorin had held firm in staying behind, but he did hand over the letter, which they read as they walked.

"Yeah, he's too dumb to have thought this out, plus, this letter? I didn't write it. Whoever did is clearly trying to frame him. He's even dumb enough to fall for something so obvious. This isn't my voice at all." She pointed aggressively to the words on the paper and read aloud. "'-Desperately need to see you; I am concerned for the safety of my family?'" She looked at Sella. "I am never *desperate* for anything, and quite frankly, my family couldn't care less if I was alive or dead. Why would I be concerned for their safety? It's like he hardly knew me."

Sella's eyes glanced at Cali by her side. Her head was lowered again, reading the letter in Sella's hand. It was impossible to guess her emotions. Sella kept walking, but her eyes were fixed on Cali. "Are you going to pass over that…? Your family?"

Cali waved her hand and furrowed her brow at Sella. "They practically disowned me a long time ago. I'm fine about it."

Sella waited and Cali only met her gaze with silence. "What happened?" she asked at last.

The corners of Cali's lips turned up, trying to hide another expression, one Sella couldn't place. "I'm the youngest of seven," she explained. "Everyone in my family, and I mean *everyone*, is a Wyvernrider. No one could get over that I didn't want a military life." She shrugged. "Honor and glory and Wyverns are overrated anyway."

Sella let out an audible exhale. She could understand, at least in part, disappointing family in wanting more, or less, than what they wanted.

"What?" Cali folded her arms across her chest. The hint of a smile faded and she looked squarely at Sella with a fire in her eyes. "You're going to tell me I should be lucky to know wyverns too? That it's a shame I liked numbers and rocks and quiet more than prestige and fame?"

Sella let her hands fall, though she wished she could reach out to calm the growing insecurity rising in Cali. Sella knew Cali was repeating words spoken to her over and over again. By her family, by friends, by Rorin… It was an echo of things everyone told her, and it still stung her in death.

Sella sighed. "I think it's fine to want whatever you want. If that's sorting through numbers by candlelight…? I mean, that's not for me, but that's because I hate math, not because I don't understand the desire for a peaceful life." Tension in her face eased as Cali's arms withdrew from around her body.

"Well… thank you. Math isn't boring, by the way, it's a puzzle." She paused, only for a moment, before she continued, louder. "Anyway, my family is all power and might, which is why Rorin is *so stupid* to fall for this." She kept walking, and Sella met her pace, examining the letter once more.

Cali stood on her tiptoes for a better look at the paper. She read aloud as though just a moment ago they hadn't been on the verge of something deep and real. Sella's cheeks flushed with embarrassment. Had she said the wrong thing?

Thankfully, Cali didn't seem to notice. She read, "'I'm afraid they're after me. You have to come to Marra on the fastest ship.' First of all, who is 'they?' And second, it goes on to say I am with his child? Pulling out *all* the stops! Whoever sent this really wanted him to come here, probably to take the blame. And quite frankly, I don't think they were terribly smart about it."

Sella felt her color return to normal slowly. "Nicte and Dimas are looking really suspicious right about now. They knew who you dated, and knew his reputation for having a less-than-ideal personality."

Cali nodded, but she seemed disheartened by the comment. Her head was low, and her pace slowed a little. "I didn't think they'd have it in them to hurt me. Even if we didn't always see eye to eye."

"The world's a messed up place. I can't imagine a family

not wanting you around no matter the reason… I'm sorry. It has to be hurtful."

"It's not your fault."

"I'm sorry *for* you?" Sella suggested.

Cali stared at her with narrowed eyes. "That's worse."

Sella scratched her pointed ear. "Yeah, I guess it is… For what it's worth, I'm glad I met you… I wish it was under different circumstances."

"Even though I haunted you into helping me?" Cali asked.

"I do wish you were slightly more reasonable about the whole thing from the start, that's true."

"I was murdered." Cali's tone was warm, almost light-hearted. "I think I can get away with a minor haunting."

"No, you're right. As usual." Sella watched Cali from the corner of her eye and before she could think about it, she reached a hand to her shoulder. Her fingers hit faint resistance, then passed through the ghost like cold smoke. "I'm sorry!" Sella pulled her hand into her chest and clutched it as if afraid it would venture out again without her permission.

"That's okay. You were trying to comfort me. You're always doing that for everyone. You're always trying to take care of everyone. I've noticed." She looked down at her shoulder and Sella thought she caught Cali's green eyes turning watery, but Cali looked the other way before Sella could tell if they were truly tears or not. "What're we going to do about Dimas and Nicte?" Cali asked, still looking deep into the forest.

Sella held her own hand as the two walked together. Her mind drifted to what Cali said about her family, about Rorin not really knowing her. Her heart was heavy. "I'm not sure. For now, let's focus on getting out of these woods without running into any bears or potential murderers."

"And then have a cup of tea?" Cali asked.

"For you to smell?" Sella raised a brow, trying to keep things light.

Cali smiled, her eyes were clear. "It's not nothing."

TWENTY-ONE

The Witch's Mark

"Dear Rorin," Sella read the letter aloud to Lohrna and a visibly cringing Cali. "This letter is urgent. And private. I'm afraid they're after me. You have to come to Marra on the fastest ship. I desperately need to see you. I am concerned for the safety of my family and I'm afraid they will come find them after they're done with me. They travel fast. I did not want to tell you this before I left, and I am sorry to have kept it a secret, but I am with child. Yours. I know you never wanted kids, and I promised myself that I would bring this secret to my grave, but now I need to see you. WE will need to see you. You have to keep us safe." She paused, looking up from the letter. "It goes on for a while; some of it is pretty damning. Good motivation for murder."

Cali's eyes narrowed.

"I mean 'good' like 'traditionally,'" she corrected herself. "It does come off as a setup to get him to take the heat on this. But Benka isn't going to believe that we just don't *think* he did it."

Lohrna rubbed her temple with two fingers. She looked

over the letter herself and asked, "Okay but who is all this 'they' talk?"

Sella shrugged, she looked at Cali. Her eyes darted off when Sella made contact. That was unusual. "Cali?" Sella prompted.

Cali huffed. She crossed her arms. "Listen," she said, her voice a little strained. "I didn't want to mention this. I feel it's hurtful."

"Hurtful or not," Sella said, "we actually need to know some context here."

Cali paused. Lohrna's eyes bounced from the letter to Sella, to the empty space where Cali stood. Finally, Cali spoke, "Rorin had a run-in with some witches back home. He was a bigot and an idiot, and frankly, he got off easy."

"But...?" Sella prompted.

Cali's arms uncrossed. She moved about the room, pacing, her image flickered for a moment. "But Rorin wouldn't let it go. He kept antagonizing them. Over a stupid gem sale. Kept writing about it in the papers, talking to people in the street about it. He was trying to delegitimize their operation. But there's strong witch support back home. The whole thing ended up biting him swiftly – a real 'snake in the tall grass' situation."

Sella had never heard that expression, but she under- stood the meaning vividly. He struck her as the kind to trudge forward, not looking where he was going, unaware of venom hiding in small things.

Cali continued, "He never saw it coming, and I, unfortu- nately, got caught up in the social explosion."

"The 'they' are witches?" Sella asked.

Lohrna's eyes widened. She set the letter down. "That could be dangerous."

Cali looked away, red flared across her cheeks. "They put a witch's mark on me. It wasn't fair, or, in my opinion, justified. I was only dating the man. I hadn't harmed them in any way. But none of them would scrub it off."

"I didn't see any mark on you," Sella's brows furrowed. She tried to remember her face any time that Cali had come into the shop. But the details were fuzzy. She would have noticed a witch's mark immediately. It would have been obvious. She turned to Lohrna and filled her in on Cali's story.

"A witch's mark? Really?" Lohrna gasped. "I didn't know they *actually* did that."

Cali started to pace. She spoke with her hands as pressured speech poured from her. "I was eventually able to purchase a spell to cover it. Temporarily. I only wore it when I came into your shop… I didn't want you to think I was ignorant. Or hateful. I'm not, I promise."

"I don't think you're any of those things," Sella said. She was honest. It didn't seem like Cali possessed a hateful bone in her undead body. But it was true that if Cali had come into the shop with the mark, she never would have given her a chance.

"So this mark, it's one only witches can see?" Lohrna asked. "I've read about them before, but… Sella, have you ever met a witch who's used that spell?"

Sella shook her head. "No, never."

"Kitchen witches wouldn't even know how to cast it," Beejee added, leaping to the table.

"So," Lohrna went on, facing in Cali's direction. "They scarred your face… like *permanently* over this scuffle?"

Cali looked away. Shimmering tears seemed to form in the corners of her eyes.

"That would get you in a lot of trouble," Beejee said. "I know *I* wouldn't let you in the shop if I saw it, no matter how much we needed the money."

"Beejee!" Sella scolded him but Cali simply agreed sadly.

"I know… I understand. It makes me a target wherever I go. I knew I'd run out of the counterspell eventually. I had planned to talk to you about making me more… once you got to know me."

Sella felt her stomach turn with regret. Frustration at her own self-centeredness spread from her core to the tips of her limbs. If she had only been able to step out of her own head more. If only she hadn't been so busy feeling sorry for herself, she might have been able to help make Cali feel like she wasn't alone before she died. "I'm sorry I didn't get to know you then," she said at last. "And I'm sorry some witches can be so spiteful."

"Just like everyone else," Lohrna interjected defensively, coming to Sella's aid against her own words. "Witches are no more or less anything than anyone else. They can simply do more about their grievances."

Sella shrugged. "You're right. But it's still not fair to mark Cali by association."

"I agree," Cali spoke with her hands, gesturing wildly as her voice grew agitated. "I swear, I wouldn't have dated Rorin if I knew the extent of his temper. I wish they had listened to me!"

"Do you think a witch would have followed you here?" Sella asked, redirecting Cali's frustration as best she could.

Cali paused. Her eyes scanned the room as if looking for the answer written on the walls. "I doubt it. The mark seemed mostly like a way to inconvenience me. To ostracize me from their shops and places they frequent. I didn't think they'd really hurt me... Though I guess that theory is as good as any at this point."

Lohrna tapped the table. Beneath, her leg was bouncing quickly. "Cali." Lohrna's tone was suddenly urgent, "You said this letter isn't in 'your voice' and that there are details that don't line up. Any way we can corroborate that? Some detail that we can find so we can disprove that you wrote this?"

Cali looked over the letter again, her face scrunched a little as she leaned in closely. "This is hard... The details are wrong, but with no one here who knew me well enough, it's impossible to disprove." She bit her lip, eyes shifting again from top to bottom of the paper.

"She's looking," Sella told Lohrna. She noticed that her friend's mug was empty and she went to the kitchen to light a little fire under the kettle.

"OH, Zelti's grace!" Cali cried out, she was frantically pointing to the top of the letter. "It's dated! The letter is dated!"

Sella poured the steaming water into a pot of fresh herbs and tea leaves. "Yes. But I already noticed that. The timing is accurate if you were wanting to set Rorin up to take the fall."

"No, it's not that." Cali looked up with a bright smile. "I write my sevens with a dash—" She pointed to the letter again. "This is *not* my handwriting! And the numbers don't lie!"

Sella crossed the space between them, hot teapot still in hand. She looked at the letter, and sure enough, the seven was indeed without a dash.

Lohrna reached for the pot but Sella pulled the kettle away. "It'll burn you," she scolded. She poured the tea into Lohrna's mug. "She says the numbers aren't the way she writes them," she explained. "That could prove she didn't write it."

Lohrna looked into her mug, her reflection bouncing off the dark, steaming liquid. "That's great news! That could totally work!" She blew on her tea carefully. "So, where do we get a writing sample for evidence?"

"Hazen." Cali's voice triumphed. "Any of his paperwork that I did, all of it, will show my numbers written differently."

"We need to talk to Hazen," Sella and Cali said.

TWENTY-TWO

Free Samples

Hazen had not been in for his usual early morning coffee and chat since the day Cali died. Other than his brief stop-in after the Mead and Melody night, which proved to be more of a drop-in visit to warn her of cruel rumors, he kept his distance. Under normal circumstances, she would be bringing it to him as a gesture of goodwill and sympathy, but she was so busy and tired she completely forgot any rules of engagement in a polite society. Now, as she watched him from the window turn to enter her shop, she felt the sting of her own inconsideration. She wondered if she could tell him what she had been up to when all this was solved. He'd understand then.

The bell above the door chimed, and Hazen came in with a tilted head to fit. He eyed the shop thoroughly, as though it was his first time in.

Sella waved him in, Beejee even attempted a very human-sounding 'meow'.

"'Mornin'." Hazen approached the counter.

"Good morning, Hazen. The usual?" Sella asked. Her fingers in her pocket gently ran across the folded letter.

Hazen nodded. "And a scone, if you have them."

"Blueberry or apple and cinnamon?" Luckily, she had spent the night baking. She was certain she'd have come with some delicious offering if she was going to ask for his help. She figured baked goods might soften the blow of having to dig through paperwork and talk about the loss of his employee.

"Let's say one of each," Hazen said. "I'll bring one to Cirian."

Sella started his coffee order and glanced at the stairs behind her. "While this is steeping, I'll grab those scones. And no charge today. I actually have a favor to ask instead."

Hazen grumbled, though not unkindly, as Sella made her way up the stairs and into her loft.

On the large wood island, her scones waited on a massive ceramic plate. She pulled them off the counter but stopped before she turned to leave. Beside where the scones had laid, she saw three small purple flowers. Ones she had not picked.

She looked around the room, but it was quiet, seemingly empty.

"Not all hauntings need to be annoyances," Cali's voice said quietly. "I thought they added a little charm."

Sella smiled at the flowers. Her body eased and yet she felt electric all at once. "They are charming." She wanted to add, 'like you,' but instead, she simply said, "Thank you, Cali. This place could use some sprucing up."

"I noticed. It was no small feat gathering them and

bringing them all the way here. Next time, we'll have to go to the market and I'll have you purchase us some." Cali said with a light laugh. "Bring them downstairs if you want, I can't make it that far."

"Will you stay up here for a bit?" Sella asked. She lifted the tray of scones carefully.

"I think for now," the ghost said.

Sella's chest expanded, and a warmth flooded her core. "They're lovely; I think they should stay here so you can see them." But an overwhelming part of her wanted to keep these little flowers in her safe space, away from talk of murder, handwriting, and deep, terrible unfairness. At least, for now. "Thank you," she said again, hoisting the scones over her shoulder with delicate balance. "I hope you get to rest." And, with that, she descended the stairs again.

Sella's smile was still lingering on her face when she set the tray on the counter. Hazen cocked his head but said nothing as she poured the coffee in his usual yellow mug.

Hazen took a sip and let his head fall back. "Ah… This is much needed…"

Sella's expression shifted quickly to a frown. "I'm sorry." She looked away, shame creeping in on her moment of happiness. "I could've been more supportive after every-thing that happened. I should've brought you coffee at the tavern."

Hazen waved his hand as if shooing away her words. "What's this favor you have to ask?"

The bell above the shop chimed again, catching them all off guard. Three people walked in, looking lost.

"I'll wait," Hazen said, gesturing to the new customers.

"Thanks," Sella whispered. She moved around the counter with Beejee hot on her heels. "Good morning, how may I help you today?" She greeted them warmly, thankful she already lit the fires and started the ambient music long before they officially opened.

The first, a tall woman, withdrew her hood. Speckles of rain dripped from her coat and Beejee grumbled.

The woman didn't seem to notice him at all. "I'm in need of a sea sickness remedy, I'm afraid."

The others beside her – probably her nearly grown children, Sella gathered, by their similar appearance – lingered along the cubbies on the wall. They were pointing at some of her trinkets and speaking in hushed tones.

"Of course." Sella waved her way between the two. She pulled a blue powder from the shelf. It was labeled 'Beejee's Blend.' "Are you traveling soon?"

"We may," the woman said. "I have family in the east islands. With all this business going around, my husband thinks it's time for us to take a little vacation. He's in a bit of a hurry about it."

So that's why she didn't recognize them. They must have moved here from the islands after she left. Beejee kept a watchful eye on them.

Sella moved through the shop and ducked low behind the counter. She called, "How many people? How many days?"

"Two," the woman called back. "Two people, one day. But one day of the feeling is enough, let me tell you."

Sella packaged the powder in two separate parchment bags. She sealed them with wax she warmed with her fingers. As she worked, she considered their situation. It seemed innocent enough, but were they fleeing under a guise?

"Oh." Sella heard Hazen's voice as she waited for the wax to dry. "You're seasick, Hatha? A fisherman's wife?"

Hatha laughed. "Arda never lets me forget it. Me and our boy can't stomach the sea. We'll have to make do with Arda's little boat. It's a short trip but all the commercial boats are docked. You know how those smaller boats get knocked about in the waves."

Sella looked up from behind the counter. The woman looked pale just mentioning it. Sella withdrew again to finish writing instructions on the packaging.

"Well," Hazen said, "this kitchen witch is the real thing."

Under the counter, Sella felt a rush of pride. But her alarm bells were also ringing in her mind. She didn't like the idea of a man fleeing with his family on short notice. Especially since Benka had given orders for all boats to stay in the ports.

"I've heard…" Hatha's voice was cautious. "The certification certainly doesn't hurt."

Beside her, Beejee grinned to the point of near cackling. He shared none of her concern and simply headbutted Sella triumphantly.

Hatha continued, "Especially not after—"

Oh, tides high and low. They really never would let it go, Sella thought. She prayed her next words weren't what she predicted.

"--The Incident."

Sella wanted to scream.

"Ancient history," Hazen said, lightheartedly.

Sella popped back up. "Two of the Beejee Blend." She set the pouches on the counter. "Take them in any liquid, preferably not liquor, just before you set off."

The woman turned one of the packets over in her hand. She studied the seal and glanced back at her children who were showing each other jars of honey. "We may be a minute… These kids…"

Sella made her best customer service face. "Have a scone while you wait to decide on honey. We have lots of good options here. Happy bees make happy honey."

The woman eyed the scones, but Hazen gestured to them warmly and she took one before finding her way back to the other two. They spoke low enough that Sella could not hear.

The door chimed, and Isra, an empty wire basket in her hand, walked in with much more confidence than the others before her. She smiled when she saw Sella.

"Finished with deliveries?" Sella asked.

Isra nodded, and set the wire basket on the counter beside Hazen. "Good morning," she said to both of them.

"Scone?" Sella offered.

Isra glanced at them, then at the woman who was in the process of taking a big bite of her scone at the other end of the shop. "Not today. I'm just getting a few herbs, if you don't mind. The old mare is lethargic again."

"Of course." Sella gestured to the cubbies. "You know what you need."

Isra joined the others at the wall of wood squares. Sella noticed her point to the lavender honey that the oldest child was holding. She said something to them with a brightness in her tone.

Hazen finished his coffee with one last sip. He rose, and prompted quietly, "The favor?"

"Yes," Sella whispered back. She pulled the letter from her pocket. "This is going to be a lot to explain, and I need you to trust me on some of the weirdness of it."

Hazen raised an eyebrow, but let her continue.

Sella recounted her trip to the woods, running into Rorin, and receiving the letter. She left out Cali's ghost, the wild speculations, and especially Lohrna's involvement. "But I have reason to believe he's not the one responsible. I think it's a setup," she concluded.

"More of that intuition?" Hazen raised a brow.

Sella nodded, but did not elaborate.

The door chimed again and Aadel, along with another older woman, entered. "Oh, it's good to see business booming!" Aadel said loudly.

"*Now* we're busy," Beejee grumbled, low enough that Sella hoped only she could hear.

Sella shrugged at him. Two sea sickness packets and a bundle of herbs were enough to pay for a breakfast at Hazen's. She'd take it.

Sella waved Aadel and the other woman in with a gentle smile despite her feelings of inadequacy sneaking up.

"Told you she's reputable," Aadel whispered, rather less than subtly, to her friend.

To the other woman's credit, she smiled back at Sella and looked at the little fires above with delight in her eyes. She turned back to Sella but did not speak.

"She's looking for something to calm the nerves," Aadel said, holding her friend by her forearm. "I've told her that she needs to come in, but again, the nerves."

Sella reached out to the woman's arm. She gave it a light squeeze. "No need to be nervous. Almost no one knows what they're looking at here during the first few visits." She gestured to the lower shelves. "Anti-anxiety blends are at the bottom. I have the flavor profile of the teas on the label. You'll let me know if you need more help? And help yourself to a scone while you look, if you'd like."

Aadel patted her friend's arm. "I can take it from here, Sella." She guided her friend to the crowded cubbies, stopping by the woman with the jar of honey. "Oh, that's the good stuff," she said loudly, with all of her daughter's enthusiasm.

Sella made her way back to the counter at last. Hazen was starting to look impatient. His leg bounced on the rung of the stool and he already pushed away his empty mug.

"Right." Sella opened the letter to show him. "Do you think you could gather some of Cali's handwriting samples? I don't exactly want to bring this to Benka without proof that my… intuition… is right."

"That's a fair thing to worry about," Hazen said quietly. "Benka's not exactly subtle about who he's starting to openly suspect. I wouldn't want him thinking you're also an accomplice." His eye contact was intense, and Sella knew exactly what he meant. Lohrna was in high water. And it was catching up to Sella fast. He grumbled at last, rubbing his beard gruffly. "I'll gather as many writing samples as I can. Give me a few to find it all. Cali was in the process of organizing before…" His voice trailed off. "Let's just say I haven't touched the paperwork since."

"Thank you, Hazen." Sella held his hand briefly. "And

take as many scones as you want. I promise, no spots this time."

The rest of the day was quiet. Outside, the rain began to fall harder. It would be rough seas. Sella hoped that Arda and his family wouldn't be going out in a storm like this.

TWENTY-THREE

Fish in a Pond

"WAKE UP!" Beejee yowled the next morning.

"It's too early," Sella groaned and pulled a down pillow over her head.

"Wake up!" Beejee nudged his nose under the pillow. "Hazen is out in the streets. He's lost his mind."

Sella threw the pillow aside, she blinked into the bright of the early morning. "Hazen what?"

Beejee ran to the window and pawed at the glass. "Sella, he's out there ranting to everyone that we're not safe until the killer is found," Beejee turned back to her again. "He's calling for an official King's task force. He's losing it!"

Sella scrambled to her feet, she went to the window and opened it to hear Hazen from the ground below shout, "And *another* thing! Cali was stuck here. Like a little fish in a pond waiting for the net! She should've been out to sea!" His words were slurred, his body motions too fluid and unstable.

"He's drunk," Sella whispered, but anxiety in her chest betrayed her. She knew Beejee could feel it too.

"Hazen doesn't get drunk." Beejee looked up at her. "He hardly drinks."

The witch pulled her hair behind her ears and then turned to the wardrobe in the corner. She pulled out a green dress and threw it on before pulling on boots and her hat. "Come with me, Beejee. We better get to him before this gets out of hand." She secured her hat low to cover her brow.

Cali appeared by the window, looking down. "Poor Hazen," she said wistfully. "I never would have thought he'd miss me like this. He doesn't need to. I'm okay."

Sella looked at her and her heart sank at the sadness in her voice. It was a break in her usual cheerful tone, another small fissure in her mask. "Why don't you come with us?"

"What are you going to do?" Cali asked.

"Nothing scary. A calming drink." Sella grabbed a small jar from her shelf and stuffed it into her pocket. "We can't have him riling everyone up. Or worse, have Benka catch him before we do."

"Is there an ordinance against public drunkenness?" Cali asked as she followed Sella and Beejee down the stairs with silent footsteps.

"A steep one." Sella glanced back. "Since last time… someone was out of control like this. It wasn't good."

Cali hummed as if about to ask a question. But as they went out into the street together, Hazen turned to them at the sound of the shop door opening.

"Oh, good!" Genuine relief filled his voice. He held a large pitcher with one hand and pointed at her with the other. "The witch is here to save the day! With magic!"

Sella hurried to his side. She looked at him for a

moment, at his unsteady feet, and then she rushed in to hold his large body upright as he began to lean too far. She heaved his body, but he was huge and heavy. Unstable on his feet, he sauntered with one arm draped over her shoulder. It felt like a log trying to crush her. Her body shook, from exertion, from fear, as more of the town's eyes fell on them. She felt like prey. Everything in her body told her to freeze.

But she needed to keep moving. She needed to get him back in the tavern, and soon. "Hazen," she whispered as people passed them with wide eyes, predators on the prowl. "What has gotten into you?" Her legs spread, and she finally stabilized him, but her hands still quivered beneath him.

"We're all just fish in a pond!" His words were slurred. He clutched the ceramic jug closer to his chest, his free hand went to his side. "Fish. Belong. In. An. Ocean."

"Okay…" Sella let go of his arm around her shoulders. He was too heavy, and becoming too chaotic to hold. She hurried to his other side and held his free arm tightly with both of her shaking hands. "Fish in a pond, an ocean, right… Let's chat more about this inside. Is the tavern open?"

"Open? We're *always* open! No rest for old Hazen. No rest for Cali. She was a good one!"

"Aww," Cali said, suddenly appearing by Sella's side.

Sella's lips drew into a thin line. She sucked her teeth as she strained to pull Hazen along. "Come on, then," she grunted. "Let's chat about fish and death in the tavern. Quickly now!" She positioned her body so she could leverage herself into steadiness.

Below, Beejee moved between his feet to keep each of his legs always a little lifted and easier for Sella to guide.

They moved in an awkward dance through the street as townsfolk and hotel guests stopped and pointed, some whispered to each other. In agreement with his utterances or in horror, Sella wasn't sure. It didn't matter right now. She had to make it to the tavern doors, to get safe.

They approached and she heaved herself into Hazen to keep him standing as she felt him slouch. "The door!" Sella cried out as she pushed and shoved Hazen back upright.

From the side of the street, Lohrna darted out. "I got you, Sella!" She moved in front of them quickly to push the double doors. They opened with a groan and Sella, Lohrna, and Hazen all fell forward to get him into the safety of the tavern.

Hazen landed on the stone floor with a loud thud. He was asleep before Sella could even fish the calming spell from her pocket.

"Close the doors!" Beejee called as he and Cali entered the empty tavern behind the others.

Sella hurried to the doors and began to pull them shut as Benka's pale face appeared down the street. She glared at him between the fast-closing gap and then the heavy doors slammed, blocking out the street, the sun, and the spectators. Sella sighed and straightened her back against the closed doors. She looked down at the sleeping man. "What in all the lower levels was that, Hazen?"

His snores were the only response.

Beside him, the ceramic pitcher was still intact, turned on its side and leaking a clear liquid.

Lohrna squatted beside him and poked at his arm with one finger. "My mom told me what was happening and I had to come help. I haven't seen Hazen like this since..."

She paused and turned to Sella. "Hey, this is pretty uncharacteristic. I'm worried about him. Should we go get Cirian?"

Sella sighed and finally pushed herself off the doors when she realized she sunk into the thick wood doors. "Maybe. It will take forever to pull him to the back with just the two of us."

Between them, Beejee trotted forward. He sniffed at Hazen's boot, then up along his body with a pink, twitching nose. "Sella," he called, "Come here. He smells… enchanted."

Lohrna's eyes followed the length of his body and then to the pitcher. She picked it up and studied its contents with one eye closed. She sniffed, stuffing most of her face into the opening. "Beejee, come put your nose to good use over here."

For a moment, Sella felt the static in her body dissipate. It was good to see the two of them working together, talking. But then the reason for their teamwork crushed down on her and her brows furrowed, muscles tightening again. She shook out her limbs, trying to regain control of her nerves.

Beejee went to Lohrna's side and sniffed at the jug before recoiling quickly with a hiss. "Garawock."

"Garawock?" Sella stepped toward them, but Lohrna already had her nose back in the jug. "Lohrna! Get your face out of there!"

"I *knew* it smelled off." Lohrna took another deep inhale before she finally heeded Sella's warning and held the ceramic at arm's length.

"Lohrna, what were you thinking? You know that stuff

knocks you out cold!" Sella snatched the jug from Lohrna's grasp and eyed it suspiciously with a single brow raised.

"Knocks you out after it makes you go stupid and out of control," Beejee added. "Not that *you* need help with either."

Lohrna, still positioned on the floor, side-eyed the familiar. "You know we can understand you now," she grumbled.

Beejee stopped in his tracks. He turned to Lohrna slowly. Sella thought she sensed an apology coming as he sighed. He'd always been able to freely speak his mind, or been able to make jokes at everyone's expense with little consequence. Sella knew this would take getting used to. But instead of an apology, he turned back and trotted to the door. "I hear a crowd outside."

Cali gave a friendly wave and then disappeared. Her unbodied voice echoed, "I'll go check it out."

Sella set the ceramic jug on a nearby table and studied Hazen's sleeping form closely. He was breathing steadily, that was a good sign. It felt like her ribs were finally able to unwrap around her lungs and heart. "How did Garawock get into Hazen's drink?" she wondered aloud.

Lohrna stood and dusted her knees off. "Weird, right? First Cali's death from Cresablatt, and now this?" She shook her head. "Think this might be the other witch's doing?"

"Yeah, maybe, " Sella said. The other witch *would* probably know how to make this potion. She tucked her chin to her chest and curled her arms around herself. Still, she felt exposed. "But why kill Cali? Why poison Hazen?"

Lohrna huffed, hoisting herself onto the tabletop. Her back slouched and she curled her legs up onto the table. "I guess we have multiple questions on our hands now." She stared at Hazen with a worried expression. "First, are they even connected?"

"Stay here." Sella's voice was exasperated. "I'll go back to the shop. I have what we need so he won't be hurting too much when he wakes up. Nothing can stop what's done, but he'll at least feel better than he would without it." Sella didn't wait for Lohrna to acknowledge her. She slipped outside before her friend had time to ask another question for her to worry about.

She closed the door behind her with a loud thud, but the town's gossip was already louder. Voices rang in her ears like loud bells. She searched the crowd that began to gather on the side of the street. Some were pointing, others hurrying away small children, clutching their skirts as they ushered them along.

Sella glared at the crowd. She noticed no one was trying to come into the tavern. No one was moving to help. Were they afraid of Hazen's behavior, or of her? She didn't have much time to wonder. She caught Cali's eyes through the crowd and motioned her head for her to follow back to the shop.

They entered Practical Potions and Honey. Sella locked the door behind her with a finger snap.

"Is Hazen alright?" Cali asked.

"He will be." Sella was already working behind the counter. She added a dash of yellow powder to a stone bowl, a splash of dark liquid, and a sprinkle of dried herbs. "The poison isn't deadly, but he'll be in a lot of pain in the morning if he doesn't get this soon." Sella closed her eyes and stirred the mixture together with a gray pestle. She imparted healing, sleep, and strength through her hands as she worked to mix it together. She breathed in deeply. A rich earthy smell filled the shop. It was done.

"Glad you can help," Cali said once Sella's eyes opened. "Hazen doesn't deserve any of this." She glanced out through the windows of the shop. "Wow, people are really starting to gather out there..."

"Hazen had his share of public embarrassments," Sella blurted before she could stop. She halted. Of course she managed to blurt that out. Not wanting to betray any of his trust any more than she already had, she bit her lower lip. That was all in the past. He had come a long way since he was a young man. She packaged the small dose into a little glass jar. "Anyway, this town just loves its gossip. There's not much else to worry about." She looked past Cali as more people appeared in the street. "Just... stay close to me."

"I don't think I'm in danger, what with..." She gestured at her body broadly.

Sella's eyes flicked to her. She knew annoyance was plastered across her expression. She couldn't hide it. She was in no mood for jokes and already felt silly for her protectiveness over the ghost at all.

"Of course." This time, Cali's tone was serious.

"Alright, come with me."

They hurried out of the shop and through the crowd of people who couldn't be bothered to mind their own business. She almost gave them a snide remark, but instead, she bit her lip and marched through them, back to the tavern's doors, with squared shoulders.

Behind her, she caught moments in conversation louder than others.

"Of course it's her," a man whispered.

"Always is. So careless with her recipes," said another.

"We've had peace for ten years, now this?"

Sella let herself in and gave them all one more quick scowl before she shut and locked the door behind her. "I got it." She held the little vial aloft. "How's he doing?"

"Still passed out cold." Beejee guided her back to Hazen's sleeping form on the floor.

Sella passed the potion to Lohrna, still crouched beside him. "Here, if you can, try getting at least some of this in his mouth."

Lohrna nodded and positioned Hazen's large head in her lap, rather ungracefully.

A hard knock on the doors startled them. Beejee scurried closer to the door and held a gray ear to the wood. "Benka!" Beejee hissed.

The Letter

The knock sounded again, this time louder, more insistent.

"Benka!" Sella whispered. She backed away from the door slowly, as if a monster was on the other side.

"You have the letter," Lohrna said. "We can explain—"

Sella let out a guttural bark. She side-eyed Lohrna with a scowl.

"What?" Lohrna moved closer to the door. "He's reasonable, right?"

"Lohrna!" Sella hissed.

"Authorities!" the voice behind the door boomed through the wood. "Open up!"

Lohrna reached for the door but Sella smacked her hand away.

"This is private property." Sella hissed. "He doesn't belong here."

"Maybe he can help with Hazen? Does he need medical attention?" Cali asked, crouching down beside the large sleeping man.

Sella looked at Hazen, then back to the door. "There's no cure. Really he just needs to sleep it off. He's a big guy. Whoever did this only wants to stir the pot."

Lohrna and Cali both looked at her with skeptical expressions but said nothing in return. Sella turned to the door and bit the inside of her cheek worriedly. To open the door or not? It felt like there was no win. She was backed into a corner.

"Sella, *Kitchen* Witch!" Benka stressed the word 'kitchen' as if he implied it was a lie. As if she was more dangerous than she led on. She felt her fists clench and heat rise in her fingertips. "Open. This. Door." Another long series of bangs reverberated through the tavern.

"Sella?" Lohrna grabbed her arm and tugged at it. She looked at Beejee, then to the door.

Sella unclenched her fists and gave Lohrna's hand a small squeeze. "Okay." She sighed. "But don't say anything."

Lohrna nodded.

Cali rose and shifted herself away behind a table, as if Benka would be able to spot her when he came through. Her brows knit together and a small wind began to blow about her hair. A sure tell that her anxiety was spiking.

"I don't know about this," Beejee hissed as Sella strode to the door, more confidently than she felt. The letter in her pocket felt suddenly like lead. Like it was pulling her down into dark depths.

Still, she opened the door a crack, catching a burst of sunlight and Benka's stern face in view. "This is private property," Sella said, hiding most of herself behind the door. "You're not invited."

"I don't need an invitation. I am not a vampire. I am the law." Benka tilted his head so he was closer to Sella's eyeline. His eyes were gentle, but his expression firm, with his lips drawn into a tight line and deep wrinkles forming on his forehead.

"Are you ordering me to open this door?" Sella asked.

"I am," Benka replied with a lazy, almost sad nod.

Sella bit the inside of her cheek again but slowly opened the door just wide enough for his thin frame to fit through. She glared at the onlookers and as soon as he was through, she swung the door shut with a loud thud.

Benka strode into the tavern with deliberate steps. He looked from Beejee, to Lohrna, to Sella. "Always you three, isn't it?" He moved around Hazen and casually placed his hands in his pockets.

Lohrna shrugged but kept her mouth sealed.

Beejee jumped onto a table to get a better look at the detective. Sella noticed he was also positioned between Benka and Cali, puffed up at the shoulders to make himself look bigger. Thankfully, he also remained silent. The turbulence around Cali began to still as Beejee remained between them.

"Hazen falling into bad habits again?" Benka asked. He was squatting down now to assess the man's face.

"Garawock, actually." Sella pointed to the jug on the floor. "It works quickly and makes you act out of control, even with a limited dose."

"I'm aware of how Garawock works." Benka picked up the jug and took a deep inhale. His expression was impossible to read, but he set it down with a definitive movement that Sella hoped meant he was satisfied. Hands back in their pockets, he stood and looked at each of them slowly. "A lot of poisonings happening all of a sudden." As if they didn't know.

Lohrna's gaze caught Sella's. She swallowed hard and let out a long breath through her lips. Her eyes flicked to Sella's pocket.

Benka's followed. He looked up at Sella and waited.

Sella blinked. She considered her options, and none looked good. She could ignore it entirely, but then again, Benka was already implying, more than he ever had before, that they were on his shortlist of suspects. She could hand it over and pretend that Cali had written it in the hope that he would hunt for Rorin and buy them some time. But she couldn't imagine explaining that to Cali either. She was convinced he was innocent, and she didn't want to let her down, or let her actual murderer get away with it.

Or she could tell the truth and hope for the best, as wild as it all sounded.

She felt like she was at a crossroads and every direction led to danger. It was only a matter of what type of danger she thought she could get out of. Before she could paralyze herself further, Sella let out a heavy exhale and fished the note from her pocket.

She opened it and gave it a quick once over. "Benka, you're going to have to listen to me about the contents of this letter," she said as she folded it back up.

Benka nodded. "I'm listening."

Sella and Lohrna exchanged glances and then, Sella explained. How they got the note, though she omitted the ghost and substituted her witch's intuition. She told him how she had shown it to Hazen first, since he knew Cali best, that Hazen had said he would get handwriting samples, and he had comparisons for him to view. She handed the letter over and waited for him to finish reading it.

"I was going to give it to you," Sella explained when Benka finished reading. "I just didn't want the town going after Rorin if Cali didn't write the letter. I didn't want anyone falsely accused."

This time, it was Benka who sighed. "It doesn't matter if she wrote it or not. Rorin, an ex-partner, still showed up here. More than likely, he confronted her about the letter. It sounds like enough motive is contained here, no matter how factual the information." He paused, and toed Hazen's boot with his own as if that small movement would wake him. "And it is awfully convenient for you that Hazen can compare the handwriting, yet, here he lies, asleep, the place clearly in disarray, and with recent memory loss." He looked at Sella's wide eyes and nodded. "Yes, I am aware of the other side effect of Garawock." He folded the letter and placed it in his own pocket.

Sella straightened her posture, trying to meet Benka's imposing stature. "Well, we can look at his paperwork. Calli was his bookkeeper. I'm sure we could compare writing samples right now."

"You know that is outside the limits of my ability. We will have to wait for him to wake up and provide permission before we can rummage through his finances," Benka said. He took a step closer to her, and his tone grew darker. "Sella, I've been lenient with you because of the immense respect I had for your mother, but this is pushing my amiability."

Sella's stomach dropped. She took a step back. It felt suddenly like the walls were caving in on her, that her only way out was through him. And he did not look like he was going to retreat. A spark lit at her fingertip.

"Rorin didn't kill Cali," Lohrna cut in. "You have to trust us on this. Look into Dimas–"

"I am aware of the other Tollintalians." Benka quieted her with his hand raised. "Their alibi is firm. Unlike yours."

"Mine?" Lohrna bristled, her posture shifted as though she was about to run. She looked at Sella with desperation in her eyes.

"Yours." Benka looked from her to Sella. "And yours."

"Show some respect!" Beejee's voice roared from his tabletop, so loud that Lohrna flinched. He was on all fours, fur bristled, and teeth bared. "You are speaking to a witch!"

"*Kitchen* witch." Benka corrected with a raised finger. He clicked his tongue on the roof of his mouth and tilted his head to the familiar. "I always thought you could talk."

"It's actually new," Beejee spat.

Benka hummed dismissively. He crossed the floor between Sella and Lohrna. "We'll send out a search party for Rorin. And you'd better hope we catch him."

TWENTY-FIVE

Practice Makes Perfect

AFTER CIRIAN'S help getting Hazen into bed and cleaning the tavern, it was already dark. Lohrna and Sella found themselves in the only place that seemed to feel safe: the little loft above the potions shop. The air in the loft was warm, the smell of cinnamon and honey drifted from the oven, and outside, through the crack in the round window, soft rain pattered. Everything seemed at peace here.

"Sella?" Cali asked from her seat at the table. "Can you drape that sheet over me? I'm tired of Lohrna looking through me. And also bring the glasses so we can see eye-to-eye," she added with a laugh.

Sella hesitated over her work in the kitchen. "Are you sure you have the energy to keep it on?"

Cali smiled and nodded.

Sella looked from her to Lohrna, then cleaned her hands on her apron. "Lohrna, Cali has requested something a little… Well, just go with it." Crossing around the butcher block island to her cabinet in the corner, she shook out a well-worn sheet and fetched a pair of thick-rimmed glasses from a drawer in her desk.

She glanced outside, but it was dark, and only her indistinct expression reflected back at her. She briefly wondered if the town below was asleep, If the hotel guests who were trapped here until the boats could leave were going stir-crazy in their rooms with the tavern closed. She shook her head and went to the table.

"This might take a second to get used to, but..." She fluttered the sheet over Cali's head and it retained the shape of her figure. A distinct head and shoulders appeared beneath the fabric.

"Ooh!" Lohrna let out an excited yelp as she watched Sella attempt to place the glasses over the sheet. "This is brilliant! Why don't we do this all the time?"

Sella glanced back at her, still working on adjusting the glasses securely. "It's difficult to maintain a more physical form. This is kind of like a haunting situation," she explained.

Lohrna shrugged. "I'm sure it'll get easier with practice."

Sella paused, hands still around Cali's head beneath the sheet. She wished she could see her expression, read her eyes at that moment. *With practice,* Lohrna's words repeated in her mind. Would there *be* practice? Surely, Cali would move on to the next stage once they caught her killer. Right?

She moved her hands away and inspected her work. The glasses were a little crooked, and she let out a small laugh at the ridiculousness of it all. "This'll have to do."

"I like it!" Lohrna grinned brightly. "It's a good idea!

Now I can see you, Cal. Kind of. Eventually, we'll have Sella dig through old spells and find a way for us to talk, too."

"I can't wait," Cali said, though Sella was not quite sure with what tone. With her expression hidden beneath the sheet, it was nearly impossible to tell her true feelings.

Sella moved back to the kitchen and busied herself with making a large pot of tea. She gathered dried lavender and herbs and crushed them in the mortar, careful to not add any of her strange melancholy by accident. She took a deep breath through her nose; the scones were almost ready. She lit a small fire beneath the ceramic teapot. The rain outside began to come down harder.

"I don't know what we're going to do if they can't find Rorin," Lohrna said at last.

Sella closed her eyes. She knew what to add to the tea. Hope.

"You're being such a mouse," Beejee grumbled. "Rorin doesn't exactly sound like he's a super genius…"

Cali's sheet turned to Beejee, it rippled as she laughed. "That's true."

"But he's slippery," Lohrna went on, one fist clenched on the table. She was being surprisingly pessimistic.

Sella felt her jaw tighten. This wasn't Lohrna. At least, not a side of her Sella knew or was accustomed to. Lohrna was the friend who always saw the bright side, even in the darkest times. Sella felt her shoulders sink. It was only now, as she looked at her friend, that she realized how exhausting it must be to always be the happy one. Guilt gnawed at her stomach.

Lohrna continued on, unaware of the dark mood that

descended on Sella, "He's managed to hang out in the woods undetected so far. That's not nothing."

Beejee huffed. "So what? Maybe he's gotten lucky."

Lohrna set her chin in her hand, she looked pensive. "I think I have to tell Benka about… my condition. It'll explain where I was that night, at least."

Sella set down the tea with a thud. Everyone in the room, including the cats, flinched. "Lohrna," she said carefully, "that is only your information to share when you want and with who you want." She pulled mugs from a cabinet, trying to occupy herself with movement after her small outburst. "I don't think it'll make a difference anyway."

"It'll just put the target squarely on Sella's back. If you have an alibi and Sella doesn't, and we have no one else to verify–" Beejee cut himself off, his expression was tired. He looked at Lohrna with half-closed eyes and blinked at her slowly. In the light of the fires above their heads, his pink nose twitched. He was not being cruel, only truthful, and Sella felt that despite all his bluster, he didn't want Lohrna to feel that she *had* to tell anyone about herself either.

Lohrna sighed. "Feels like a no-win situation, to be perfectly honest."

Cali was looking between the two slowly. "We'll figure it out."

"Cali hasn't lost hope." Sella nodded to Lohrna and Beejee. "We shouldn't either. Besides…" She pulled their pastries from the oven and the smell of sweet sugar, honey, and spice perked them all up. "We at least have these. And tonight. We'll figure it all out in the morning." *After plenty of sleep*, she thought to herself.

She served the tea in the little mugs, setting one in front

of each of them, though only she and Lohrna could drink it. The pile of pastries was piled in the center, steaming gently, little flakes of sugar on their surface reflected firelight like faraway stars.

Lohrna grabbed one and stuffed it in her mouth before Sella could warn her that they were still hot. But Lohrna didn't seem to mind. She chewed and rested her chin in her free hand, her gaze falling gently on the ghost at the table. She swallowed and took a long sip of tea, nearly draining the cup.

The fires overhead illuminated her face and wild hair with flickering warm light. Her mouth twitched like she was about to speak, but then she simply finished her tea and reached for another pastry. She held it between her fingers and studied it carefully as Sella poured her a second cup of cinnamon tea. "If not for our sake, Cali, for yours, we'll figure out who did this and bring them to justice," Lohrna said at last.

TWENTY-SIX

Be Back Sooooon

SELLA AWOKE to Lohrna still sleeping on her couch. Both arms were draped over her face and her mouth was open slightly. Sella smiled gently and carefully pulled the thick knit blanket over Lohrna's exposed feet. She crept across the floor to feed Koukie and Beejee as quietly as she could. As she approached her desk, she noticed that in the fog on the window, eerie, dripping letters ran down the glass. Sella froze, studying it with squinted eyes. She let out a small laugh when she read, 'Be Back Soooooon.'

Writing in fog was a classic haunting technique, but in her experience, it was usually much more ominous messages. Cali was getting better.

"Be back soon… Where'd you go?" Sella wondered in a faint whisper. Koukie broke her thoughts. The orange cat pushed at her calf with her head urgently, begging for breakfast. Sella leaned low to scratch the top of her head gently. "Your owner is out," she whispered quietly as she crouched beside the cat. "But I'm sure she'll be back soon."

Sella rose to prepare Koukie's breakfast. When she put

down a bowl of unseasoned fish, Koukie meowed at her chipperly before she began to devour the meal.

Sella left Lohrna to sleep on the couch and took advantage of the fact that, for once, it seemed, she was up before most of the household. She closed the door behind her slowly just as Beejee squeezed his way out with her. "Fancy seeing you awake at dawn," he said snarkily as he wove his way between her legs.

"No breakfast for you?" she asked, descending the narrow stairs to the shop.

"I'll take it by the bay window today, I think."

"Oh, do you?" Sella laughed. "Well then, who am I to deny your request for windowside fish?" She waved her hand and little fires lit above their heads, warming and illuminating the shop.

Outside, a figure approached with an urgency in their step. Sella's heart skipped a beat. She squinted into the dark. The silhouette looked familiar, long antlers, wild curls…

"Aadel?" Sella unlocked the door to the shop as she saw the older woman's face in the window. Aadel looked nervous. She was covered in a fine mist of light rain.

Sella ushered her in. She instinctively locked the door behind her. "What's going on?" she asked, reaching for Aadel's coat as the older woman began to remove it.

Aadel shook her overcoat in the entryway and shuddered before handing it over. "Is Lohrna here?" Aadel ignored Sella's question.

Sella glanced upstairs. "Yes. Did she not tell you she was planning to stay the night?"

"She did not!" Aadel looked up at her with fierce eyes. Her tone was stern, motherly, and it made Sella feel like she was small again, listening to one of Aadel's famous lectures after she and Lohrna had gotten into some kind of mischief. Those talks haunted her into her adulthood. Aadel continued before Sella could think any more of it, "There's a murderer on the loose and she doesn't come home, of course I think the worst!"

Sella barely contained her shrug. She made a good point, but it was also more likely than not that if Lohrna wasn't accounted for, she was with Sella. It had been that way since they met. Still, she empathized with Aadel's worry. She'd be terrified too, if their positions were reversed. "Coffee?" Sella crossed the store to the counter and gestured for Aadel to follow her.

"And!" Once again, Aadel ignored her question. She huffed. "Someone has ransacked Hazen's place!"

Sella stopped. She turned back slowly. "Ransacked?"

Aadel mumbled affirmatively in response. She shook herself one more time and then moved deeper into the store.

Sella subtly grew the overhead fires to warm Aadel. She played low music and a cozy ambient sound. It seemed to ease Aadel and she sank on to her elbows at the counter. Her whole body slumped, but her eyes were alert. "A calming coffee please, dear. I need the energy but not the panic."

Sella nodded and got to work preparing a calming blend, as much as she felt the contradiction. She listened as Aadel described the early morning gossip, of which (so far) only the elders and shopkeepers, who were always up at dawn, were privy to. Sella was amazed, and horrified, at how much could happen in a few hours.

"--And that was after that whole debacle with Benka storming into the tavern. You remember." She finally reached the ending of her tale, and got to the new part that Sella did not know as she slid a cup of coffee across the bar. "Thank you, honey." Aadel took a long sip. Like her daughter, she didn't wait for it to cool, but didn't seem to mind the heat. "We all thought it best to leave Hazen where he was for the rest of the day... and night, if we're being honest. Cirian went to check on him in the very early morning, you know how he worries, and when he passed by the office downstairs, he said the place was in a state!"

Aadel took another long drink. "Oh, this is good. Just what I needed." She let out a long, heavy breath, then continued, "So, then Cirian starts telling anyone who will listen, because Benka's off in the woods hunting some suspect or another, that Hazen's place has been robbed. But it seemed that 'vandalized' was more like it when I showed up."

Sella poured herself her own refill and leaned closer as she drank it all. Beside her, Beejee side-eyed Aadel but said nothing.

"The office was in disarray! Papers everywhere, drawers flung about. It must've made quite the ruckus. I'm shocked Hazen slept through it, even in his condition. But who would do such a thing? They must have been looking for something, probably ran off with whatever it was. Gems, maybe? Wasn't his new bookkeeper in the gem business?" Aadel pushed her empty cup across the counter for Sella to refill.

Sella poured the coffee, but her eyes were fixed on the little fire beneath the metal kettle. It danced happily, red and gold, keeping the coffee warm through the troubling conversation. She knew why someone went through Hazen's office. That much was obvious. But who? She pushed the mug back but her gaze was still far away.

Someone who knew that the letter had made its way to Benka. Someone who knew the letter wouldn't match the quirks in Cali's handwriting. But someone who didn't know any of this until she did. Until Hazen did.

"Sella," Beejee chirped, snapping her from her spiral.

Sella shook her head as if that could clear away the fog and sticky cobwebs that suddenly cluttered her mind. "This is upsetting news. But, at least Lohrna's safe."

Aadel swallowed her mouthful and set the cup down with a clang. "Indeed! That girl is too reckless!"

Sella smiled. 'Girl' would have been an insult in anyone else's mouth. But she supposed they'd always be little girls to Aadel. "I'm looking out for her, Aadel." She gave the older woman's hand a squeeze. "I promise you, I'll do everything I can to keep her safe."

"I know, honey." Aadel placed her free hand over Sella's.

Aadel's hands were small, wearily worn, covered in speckles of dark age spots and fine wrinkles. Sella realized that she never noticed how much Aadel truly aged in the time she was away until that moment. She felt a sudden pain in her chest. Loss. Of time, of watching this happen slowly. Of missing out on her mother's hands changing.

She squeezed Aadel's hand once more and then let go.

GRAY MORNING LIGHT was still glowing from the large circle window in the loft above the shop. Koukie was finishing her breakfast happily by the dying fire while Beejee stared at her food bowl with envy.

"My *mom* came to check up on me? I'm a grown woman!" But Lohrna sounded like an annoyed teen again.

"Well." Sella shrugged. "There's a serial poisoner on the loose, and Hazen's place has been burglarized. I think she's within her rights to check up on you if you don't come home."

Lohrna crossed her arms and pursed her lips. She sat up a little straighter in Sella's bed, and then her eyes suddenly focused, as if she had only now, in that moment, woken up. "Wait, Hazen was robbed? Of what?"

"Your mom said there were papers all over the place. His office, I think, is what was hit the hardest." Sella poured a large cup of coffee and motioned for Lohrna to get up and grab it. "It has to be someone who knows the handwriting won't match. The killer is trying to cover their tracks."

Lohrna rolled her neck from side to side and rose from the bed. She shuffled to the coffee and took a long sip. "What's the daily brew?" she asked.

"Clarity."

"Good work."

"We have to go to the hotel!" Cali's voice boomed so loudly from the corner of the room that even Lohrna turned.

"Did you hear that?" she asked Sella with a raised eyebrow.

"It's Cali," Sella explained. "She says we need to go to the hotel…" She turned to the ghost in the corner. "Why?"

Cali strode across the room triumphantly with her head held high. "Someone knew that I had a– Let's put it generously and say 'less than ideal' ex at home. Someone knew how to brew the potion, which requires ingredients from my homelands, *and* they knew Hazen! It has to be Nicte!"

"Nicte?" Sella asked, more for Lohrna's benefit than her own. It made sense; that man gave her a certain… *off* vibe from the moment she met him. "You're coming around to my line of thinking?"

"Nicte seems so nice, though," Lohrna said. "Are you sure it's not the big boss, Dimas?"

Cali waved her finger, though Lohrna could not see. "No, when we last spoke, it was *Nicte* who was more upset that I had left. *Nicte* felt betrayed that I had left their business. It was *Nicte* and I who never could understand one another. But, he wouldn't know the quirks of my handwriting. He was hardly ever nose in the books, he's more of a wyvern high-view. Plus, he wouldn't be as meticulous as Dimas…" Cali looked at Sella with a ferocity in her gaze. "And, the most compelling part. Get this—"

Sella turned to Lohrna with a gentle hand gesture to wait while Cali continued.

"I was doing some snooping on my own this morning. I went to the market, and figured I'd hear what I could hear if they thought no one was listening. And, the whole town is bustling about Hazen's robbery. There's rumors going around about a letter *and* handwriting being off! No one here can keep a secret. Someone had to have gotten word to Nicte!"

Sella nodded. To Lohrna, she explained, "She thinks someone must've told Nicte about the letter being suspicious."

"Would Hazen tell anyone that?" Lohrna looked

surprised. She took a small sip of her coffee, clearly trying to find an explanation.

"It's possible someone overheard you two talking about it," Beejee cut in. "You two weren't exactly spies, and the shop was unusually crowded. Aadel was there." His eyes flicked to Lohrna for a moment. He went ahead anyway with, "You know she's a gossip."

"That's not wrong." Lohrna gestured with her mug.

Cali came in close, she stood tall to catch Sella's gaze. "Tell her to trust me on this one. I'm certain it wasn't Dimas. It's got to be Nicte. We have to go break into their hotel and find some evidence. Some ingredients of the potion or something!"

"How are we going to break into the hotel?" Sella asked.

Lohrna looked at her with narrowed eyes. "Sella," her tone uncharacteristically arrogant, "we have a literal ghost here. She can go see if there's anything and let us know. Then, we can go to Benka. Publicly, if we have to."

"Great idea!" Cali agreed.

Sella considered their options. If Cali was certain, after all her previous hesitancy, that Nicte was the one who did this, it made sense to try to catch him soon. It was unlikely that they would stay in town much longer, despite Benka's warnings. And he'd already shown himself to be capable of hurting more people to keep his cover. Sella looked at Cali with gravity in her eyes. "Cali, are you sure?"

"Of course!" Cali said. "I can get in and out undetected... Oooo! I've always wanted to go back to the hotel after I first stayed there. It's so cozy!"

"'Cozy' is a word for it." Sella laughed. "She thinks the hotel is cozy," she told Lohrna.

Lohrna, too, laughed, and began to recount the many, many issues the townsfolk had with this particular establishment. Notably, a pixie problem. The owner never did seem to see them coming even though they wreaked havoc reliably every new moon.

The hotel was host to all kinds of characters that sailed in from their small port on their way to bigger and better things. It was narrow, several stories higher than any other building in the town, and displayed a quality about the craftsmanship that made it look utterly foreign.

Statues of two sirens outside sang haunting melodies in a low, primal song whenever storms from the sea blew in. They were universally disliked by everyone in town. The proprietor of the hotel, Penya, once told them when they were children that the sirens were made by an actual siren sculptor deep in the sea. She said they held magic in the stone's inner workings that echoed the siren songs when the wind blew through openings in their stone gills. The song was a warning that storms were approaching from the sea.

"That's true," Sella interjected. "But when I asked my mom about them, she said to not believe everything Penya says. That sometimes things had mundane answers, if you had the right knowledge."

"We never did figure it out though," Lohrna said. "I like the idea of a magic sculptor." Lohrna went on, turning to the corner where Cali stood. She continued ranting about the statues.

"Alright," Sella said at last, interrupting part of Lohrna's tale about the time she and Sella had tried another fateful and unsuccessful spell on the stone sirens. "I think this could work. We just need to figure out how to do it."

"Let's do it right now!" Cali said with a clap.

"We have to be careful," Sella cautioned.

This time, Beejee chimed in, he leaped atop the table to get a better view. "Let's say we do find some evidence… we need to be prepared to get it into Benka's hands immediately. We don't know what they're capable of and putting our necks on the line is dangerous. We're already on Benka's shortlist."

Sella nodded. She was grateful he included her too in the warning even though, if the town rumors were right, it was mostly Lohrna he was after. "Beejee's got a point."

"So, we wait for tonight." Lohrna cupped her coffee close to her chest. "We can figure out the details in the meantime. For now, I think it's worth paying Hazen a visit. If nothing else, we should at least check in on how he's doing after the Garawock poisoning."

"At least?" Beejee scoffed. "We carried him home, put him in bed, gave him a headache cure, *and* all we caught was criticism for it. He owes *us*."

Sella side-eyed him. She could always count on Beejee to advocate for them, even if he was a little unnecessarily harsh about it. "You can stay," She gave behind his ear a little scratch. "But his place was torn up. We should go help him. He's probably having an awful morning."

"I'll keep the shop open on my own then?" Beejee asked sarcastically.

Sella shrugged. "Well, you *can* talk now."

Beejee hissed. "Just close it today. It's not like business will be booming since everyone thinks we're murderers and thieves."

"No one thinks that." Though Lohrna's tone was less

than convincing. "Well, at least no one I've talked to thinks that."

The familiar let out a little huff and trotted away to clean off the bowl that Koukie left behind.

Sella relit the fire so they would be warm and gathered her cloak from the hook by the door. "Ready?" She turned to Lohrna and Cali.

Both nodded.

TWENTY-SEVEN

Clean Up Crew

SELLA HELPED herself to unlock the door with a simple snap of her fingers – a move that, as soon as she did it, immediately filled her with regret. She helped herself into Hazen's tavern on a few occasions when Hazen was away and she watched over his various plants upstairs, but now, she knew it was presumptuous to let herself in… and suspicious. Her eyes darted around the street, but no one seemed to have noticed her small action.

Except for Lohrna, who looked at her with a raised brow. "Really?"

"Habit," Sella tried to explain. She knocked on the door now, harder than she needed to, making a show of it.

Beside her, Cali shook her head. She stepped through the closed door confidently.

"Cali's in," Sella whispered as the ghost's head came back through the door.

"I'm practicing." Cali smiled. "Surprisingly, it's actually challenging to move through stuff. I think it's a mind game, mostly." The door opened through her and she shivered all over. "Ugh, hate that feeling!"

Hazen's broad shoulders took up most of the door frame. "Oh, it's you two," he said. Sella couldn't tell if it was disappointment or relief.

"My mom told us what happened," Lohrna said. "I'm so sorry!"

Hazen rubbed his beard and pressed into his eyes gently. "It's been a bit of a morning. I guess news travels fast here." He stepped aside with a welcoming gesture. "Come on in." Behind him, Cali darted out of the way to make room for them.

"It's a mess in here," she whispered to Sella as the two entered.

And it was. The large hall was torn apart. Papers were strewn about, torn up into tiny pieces on the floor. Chairs, even a few tables, were knocked over. It all seemed a little… unnecessary. Robbing his office would have been one thing, but as Sella's eyes scanned the hall, she was taken aback by the pure chaos of it all. The meanspiritedness of it.

"Any idea who might have done this… or why?" Lohrna asked after she finally lowered her hands from her mouth. She turned to Hazen with a worried expression, but Hazen was difficult to read. He stood among the wreckage so still, Sella wasn't sure he heard her at all.

He finally turned to them, a half smile on his face that shocked Sella. "I heard I was poisoned, too. But Aadel and Cirian said you two got me out of that bind."

Sella's shoulders relaxed.

"It was no problem, Hazen." Lohrna moved through the

debris carefully, avoiding stepping on any remaining intact paper.

"No idea who'd be after me, though." Hazen shrugged. He turned to survey the damage again. "They were after something, though, beside the usual. No Coin missing."

"Hmm." Sella stepped forward slowly. "Has Benka been in to investigate yet?"

"Took him long enough if you ask me," Hazen said. "He meandered in here like he had all the time in the world."

"Oh, Benka's alright." Lohrna picked up a few bits of shredded paper from a nearby table. She turned them over in her hand. "But he does mosey about."

Sella knew that Benka was busy hunting Rorin, but she kept her mouth shut. No need to complicate the morning more than it already was.

Hazen leaned down and began picking up strips of paper. "Anyway," he said with a grunt, like his back couldn't quite take the position. "He was almost no help. Whatever he's thinking, he's keeping it close to his chest."

Sella and Lohrna exchanged glances. Cali spoke their thoughts, "That doesn't sound good for us." She stepped closer to Hazen and bent her body as if to catch his eye. She put a hand on his shoulder and he shivered. "I'm sorry, my friend," she whispered so faintly Sella almost missed it. "You shouldn't have to go through any of this for me."

Sella wished she could stop time, pull Cali aside for just that moment, and remind her that the actions of others, no matter how wicked they might be, were theirs alone. That she didn't cause any of this. But instead, Sella simply started picking up papers as well, sorting through the ones that were less damaged.

The three of them cleaned up for a while. Cali sat on the bar and watched with glazed eyes. Her hair tangled up in a small wind that only existed around her, a sign of her turbulence within. Sella remembered this phenomenon from ghosts she worked to banish in the past. She saw it in Cali a few times now, but this seemed new, stronger. She caught Cali's eye and the ghost flickered for a moment. A small chill blew through Sella and she shuddered.

"Cirian thinks it's the new fellas in town," Hazen said at last. "That they think Cali was in the old business with me discreetly and they were looking for documentation." He chuckled. "But then why not take any Coin if they're after riches?"

Sella paused, she looked over the paper at the top of her pile. It was an invoice for lavender honey from Practical Potions and Honey. One corner of her mouth upturned slightly before she glanced up at them. "Honestly, whoever did this isn't too bright. Stealing things that have monetary value would at least make it look disconnected from the paperwork they were clearly after..." Her eyes glanced at Cali who was now sitting up straighter, the wind around her still. Sella continued, "Did Benka tell you the side effects of poison?"

"Memory loss is one of them," he said simply. "I guess I'm glad to have lost some of it. Saves me some embarrassment."

"No need to be embarrassed," Lohrna said. "People understand that you were poisoned."

Sella set her stack of papers on a free table. She picked

up the chairs beside it and righted them. "Whoever did this, their ship is stuck on a sandbar. They're getting desperate because all the knots they tied are coming loose."

"I have faith we'll catch 'em yet." Hazen looked around at the mostly clean tavern. "For now, it's opening time. The good people need strong drinks if they're going to make it through another day in this town."

Cali chuckled. "Always at service."

Sella smiled and Lohrna spoke up, "We'll help man the bar today. You can rest."

"No, no," Hazen said. "Plenty of rest in the grave. It'll do me good to work. You both have helped me plenty. Come sit, I'll pour you a drink."

Sella laughed. "It's a bit early."

"No such thing." Hazen was already behind the bar. "First one's on me. Come on, what'll it be?"

Lohrna hopped onto a stool excitedly. "A half glass of red wine, for me." She turned back and patted the stool beside her.

Sella rolled her eyes but shuffled forward with her stack of papers. "I'll take the other half."

"Got it." Hazen nodded and poured them each a full glass of blood-red wine.

TWENTY-EIGHT

Ghost Heist

It was late afternoon when Sella and Lohrna stood at the entrance to the hotel, letting the light rain gather in their hair instead of walking in. Around them, a few people passed and gave them a wide gap, eyeing them suspiciously in a way that made Sella's nerves bristle. Her heart began to accelerate by the time a third woman crossed the street instead of walking by them. She wanted to shout that they were trying to save everyone, thank you very much, but she knew it was useless. She bit her bottom lip instead.

"This place has always given me the unnerve." Lohrna squeezed Sella's hand quickly. "But, come on, let's wait inside. I'm getting cold and uncomfortable with everyone thinking we've become statues too."

Sella's jaw unclenched and she stepped forward with her unease clear on her face. She did not give the siren statues a second glance as she passed them. Lohrna followed close behind. The hotel doors shut behind them as the sirens began to sing.

Lohrna shook off her cloak. "Spooky." She laughed, still

shaking herself like she was trying to get their song off her body. She handed Sella her cloak and the witch put both of theirs on a coat rack by the double doors.

The inside of the hotel was warm and bright. The lobby felt expansive, yet homey, with two stories of space in the small area. A great fire filled most of the left wall, contained by a faded red brick fireplace and a high iron guard. On the wall opposite, a small desk hosted the old woman, Penya, who looked to be asleep in her chair.

A few of the patrons were scattered about the length of the fireplace, chatting and sipping from mugs. Sella found an empty velvet couch on the far wall and motioned for Lohrna to follow.

They sat still for a moment, taking it all in. From the high ceiling, rich green vines wove their way down, wrapping around the white beams and descending as if they were reaching for the warmth of the fire. Stacks of old books collected a fine layer of dust in every corner. Little signs hung from each pile with careful lettering reading 'free to good home.'

"You know, now that I look at it again, I think if I wasn't from here," Lohrna whispered, eyes scanning the lobby, "I'd find this all to be very cozy."

Sella's brows rose. She tried looking around again with fresh eyes. It had been years since she'd been in the hotel. It all looked the same to her. But as she looked at the visiting people's faces, she noticed that, actually, everyone looked quite content. The room was warm and comfortably lit. The rain outside could not be heard through the windows or doors. It did all seemed quaint and comfortable. She shrugged. "Yeah, maybe so. I guess it's charming, if you're not used to it."

"You think Cali's alright in there?"

Sella glanced up through all the vines above. She wondered if there was a spell to see through walls, or maybe talk to the plants. She wanted to ask them if they could check in on Cali. She felt utterly unprepared. "She should be back soon."

They waited.

The guests began to filter out one by one until it was only them, and the sleeping host. Sella caught herself staring at Penya.

Penya was old when Sella was a child, and here she was, as if she had not aged a day. She wondered if her memory was just her being a child. Even young adults seemed old to her then. Perhaps, she thought, a lot of her childhood was misremembered, as if she spent it in a dream. She turned to Lohrna, about to ask her if she recalled the owner of the hotel being very old when they were young, when Cali appeared in front of them.

"Good news and bad news," the ghost said.

Sella nudged Lohrna, she pointed to where Cali stood so her friend's eyes could focus on a spot.

"Bad news is, it took me forever to find out which room they were staying in. And that I was wrong about there being evidence of the poison..." She looked a little guilty but went on with a grin growing across her cheeks. "BUT the good news is: in Nicte's drawer, I found a bunch of my crystals, the stuff I brought from home. He must have gone through my place after he murdered me."

Sella relayed the information in whispers to Lohrna. Her friend held her hand over her mouth in shock as she did.

"Sure, they're not particularly valuable, but they were mine," Cali continued.

"Well," Sella said carefully, "Benka has implied theft would be enough cause for him to take someone in under suspicion. This might be the best evidence we can get at this point. You're sure the stones are yours, right? They're not his that he brought with him?"

"I'm certain," Cali said. "I had them on display already at home. One, especially: a bright blue stone with black speckles... It's an imperfection found in the gem's raw form. It's rare to keep them in that state."

Sella thought for a moment. She took a deep inhale, then explained the stone to Lohrna. To Cali, she asked, "So you have a stone that has unique imperfections... but how are we going to prove that you had it and now don't?"

Lohrna snapped her fingers excitedly, a loud sound in the empty lobby. "I know!"

Sella looked at the still-sleeping Penya with wide eyes.

"Oh, sorry," Lohrna whispered. "But, I got it. Everyone in town knows I collect rocks. We could say that I had been to your house before, Cal. That you told me about the raw stone. That would place it as being in your possession prior."

"Plus, Ovina," Cali added. "If she remembers it. She made a comment on it when she dropped off my welcome basket. That's two witnesses."

"Then?" Sella prompted. "How do we convince Benka to search Nicte's room?"

Lohrna thought for a moment, then shrugged. The wide

doors opened and they watched as Nicte and Dimas walked in, a basket of produce hung from Nicte's arm. They were lost in their conversation and walked right by them without a notice.

"I could say I saw Nicte with it when we were talking shop?" Lohrna suggested once the two humans entered the hallway and began to ascend the stairs.

"I feel like this plan puts you at unnecessary risk," Sella whispered. "I don't like it."

"I have to say," Cali told Lohrna, though she could not hear, "I don't care for it either."

"What if we say I did a divination spell?" Sella thought aloud. "That I tried to locate a missing item of yours in hopes of narrowing the suspects down. I could say that spell pointed to Nicte's drawer. It's not an unheard-of kind of magic."

Lohrna tossed a mess of curls behind her shoulder. "Now, that puts *you* at unnecessary risk. That's not something *kitchen* witches are particularly known for."

"A risk, yes," Sella said. "But I think I do think it's a necessary one." She rose from her seat. "I'll go get Benka. Stay with Cali and I'll be back soon."

A Ruckus at the Hotel

SELLA, Benka, and his few men walking down the street together drew enough of a crowd that by the time they arrived back at the hotel, it had become a spectacle. Benka had, somewhat reluctantly, bought into her divination spell story and had agreed to search Nicte's personal items.

Nicte, however, caused the scene to escalate rapidly once he was detained in the hotel lobby. Two men held each of his shoulders to keep him still.

"That *witch!*" he shouted, pointing at Sella with a ferocity and prejudice she hadn't expected. "She's lying! If anyone stole anything from Calisyali, it's Lohrna!"

Sella drew a protective arm in front of Lohrna. But she stayed quiet. Benka would be back from his search soon and they would be vindicated.

"This is ridiculous!" Nicte raved.

Beside him, Dimas pinched the bridge of her nose and closed her eyes tight as though a headache was forming between them. "We'll handle it, Nicte." Dimas' eyes were still sealed. "Calm yourself, you're making a fool out of me."

In fact, the crowd that formed did make it look like he was inciting more riot. People swayed with his every word, some pointed at the two hornless visitors, some at Lohrna.

Sella eyed those who pointed to her friend with a grimace. Her heartbeat quickened.

In the fray, Benka appeared suddenly. He held out a small rucksack for Nicte to examine.

Nicte ripped the bag from Benka's hand and rummaged through it. His brows came together in confusion. Sella thought it looked like an obvious ploy to appear innocent. It wouldn't fool her. "Those aren't mine!" he shouted, still pulling against the men who held his shoulders firm as he dug through the bag. He held up a few stones: gray, speckled, and common. "And… what even are they? They're worthless stones!"

Benka sighed. He took the bag and showed its contents to Sella and Lohrna, who gazed into it with horrified expressions. Inside the sack was a handful of riverbed stones.

Cali screeched, "That's not what I found!" No one but Sella heard, and even to her ears, it sounded like Cali's voice was under water. Far away.

Sella felt her hands heat up. Her cheeks reddened. She advanced on Nicte. "He must have used magic! He's hiding something!"

Benka shook his head slowly, his eyes closed and his head cast to the ground. "That's enough." His voice, loud and clear, stopped Sella in her place.

Sella turned to him with angry eyes, her hands clenched as her pulse pounded in her ears. "Benka! You have to trust us! This… this isn't right. Someone is setting us up! I know those stones weren't like that before."

Ignoring her, Benka turned his attention to Lohrna. The two men let go of Nicte and moved forward swiftly. "This has gone on long enough. I cannot abide you two running amok when I already have what I need to understand what's going on here. Lohrna Longleaf, you are coming with us under suspicion of the murder of Kexyus Calisyali."

Beside her, Lohrna's legs gave out as if she was hit from behind. Her knees hit the ground hard.

"What?!" Sella stepped toward her, hand out to block Lohrna from the approaching men. "Benka, you're mistaken!"

"Move aside," Benka said calmly as his men advanced. One moved around her quickly while the other grabbed at her wrist. Sella yanked it away but he just held her by her shoulder firmly as soon as she was free. She thrashed in his grasp but he held steady.

The man by Lohrna lifted her to her feet. He held her by the elbow and shuffled her closer to the door. Her legs wobbled, unstable beneath her as the man nearly carried her out.

Lohrna looked back at Sella, eyes wide.

"Benka! What are you doing?" Sella continued to struggle against the other man's hold. his fingers only grabbed harder, bruising her collarbone. She felt fire at her fingertips. She imagined the whole place going up in flames. How good it would feel to let it all burn.

"Let the kitchen witch go," Benka said to the man. "She's no danger to us here."

"I'm no danger at all if you just let her go." Sella protested, her fire extinguished as quickly as it had come. She threw her body weight forward and the man released her. She turned back at him with a glare, then pointed at Benka. "You are making a mistake, detective."

Lohrna's eyes pleaded with Sella, they were fearful, urgent. She looked up at the man holding her, "I didn't– I couldn't–" she choked.

"Best to stay quiet," the man said.

Lohrna bit her lip hard, tears pooled at the corners of her round eyes. She turned back to Sella as Benka said, "Take her to the cells."

"No–" Lohrna sobbed, but the man holding her simply escorted her from the hotel. With a slam of the door, Lohrna disappeared from Sella's sight.

Benka turned as Sella lunged forward to grab his arm. The crowd that gathered, their judgmental whispers, none of it mattered. She didn't even care that she could be held for assault as she pulled his sleeve hard. "Stop it!" The sleeve of his shirt ripped between her fingers. "You're making a mistake. You *know* this isn't right!"

Benka glanced over his shoulder at her casually, like he knew that she had no strength in her to move him. His face was impassive, as though Sella wasn't even there at all. "She had means, motive, and opportunity, Sella. I have to go where the evidence – the *real* evidence points."

"Tell that to Aadel." Sella's voice was strong, though her body shook violently. "Lohrna is a good person, Benka. You know this."

Benka sighed but turned to leave, his arm escaping her grasp as though he was made of smoke. "You think you're being set up?" His voice was so quiet, Sella almost missed it. "Then prove it."

Sella remained frozen, as if by a spell. Her hand was still

outstretched, her body ready to fight, but she could not move. She watched Benka leave as the large hotel door opened and he was swallowed in the darkness of the rainy night. The sound of the siren's call echoed in her ears for just a moment, then the door slammed shut again.

Behind her desk, Penya perked up at the sound. She sat up straight and blinked furiously as she looked about the room. "What is all this ruckus?" her ancient voice asked.

And, in that moment, it seemed to Sella that the world suddenly began to come alive again. She heard the sounds of the people around her, all in a frenzy, scurrying about, talking hurriedly to one another. She heard every crack of the old woman's joints as she pushed herself up from her desk. She heard Nicte proclaim that justice was served. She heard the raging sound of the wind, and rain, and siren song outside. She heard all of it. It echoed deep within her shaking bones as she stood there, unable to think of what to do next.

"Sella." Cali's voice cut through the din. Her cold hand grazed Sella's, and a rush of ice went through the witch's body. "Come on, Sella. We need to get out of here."

Sella looked around; her eyes were blurry. From tears, from panic, from anger. "I can't see." She choked and her knees buckled. She caught herself and stumbled forward.

"I'll guide you," Cali whispered. The temperature around them dropped and Sella felt a hand, a real hand, slip into hers, fingers weaving into her own. The ghost pulled her through the hotel lobby and the double doors burst open with a gust of wind, parting for them to make their way through.

Sella heard the gasps of the people behind her, each of them fearful of her power, though none of this was hers.

THIRTY

An Excellent Bookkeeper

"THIS IS RIDICULOUS!" Beejee spat. "They've got the wrong person!"

In the loft above the shop, Sella was furiously stirring a large bowl of cookie mix. "He's an idiot!" She hissed through gritted teeth. Bits of dough flew out from the edges of the wooden bowl. She let out a choking sob and dropped the bowl down with a thud onto the countertop.

"I'll help," Cali said. She reached for a yellow woven dish towel near her. Her hand grasped the towel, but her brows furrowed as she tried to pick it up. It stayed still on the counter. "I can do this," she whispered and reached for it again. But the towel remained fixed to the wood. She tried again. And failed.

"This is all my fault!" Cali screamed and a burst of wind scattered Koukie and Beejee.

Her booming voice shocked Sella out of her own anger. Her brows drew in and she felt herself wrapping her arms across her body. Her heart raced loudly in her chest as she watched as Cali reached for the towel again, but, small as it was, it did not move. The air around them grew cold. The flames above extinguished. Sella shivered and Beejee retreated under the bed. "Why! Can't! I! Do *anything* right! I can't even move this stupid, stupid towel!" Though the window was shut, the wind continued to pick up around them, blowing furiously. Cali sank to her knees and began to cry into her hands.

Sella moved forward, one hand up to shield her from the growing storm forming around Cali. The herbs hanging from the cabinets began to shed their leaves in the violence. Cabinet doors opened and slammed shut.

"It's alright," Sella called through the howling wind. The ghost's form flickered, blinking in and out of the space. Her cries only grew louder. "Cali, listen to me! None of this is your fault, you hear me? None of it!"

The air went suddenly still.

Sella rushed to Cali and fell to her side. She put an arm around Cali's shaking shoulders and found her to be solid, cold, like stone. Cali leaned into Sella's embrace, nuzzling into her shoulder as she cried.

Sella felt her own tears prick at the edges of her eyes. She was afraid that right as Cali needed her, the ghost would dissipate like a mirage in her arms. She pushed her tears from her own eyes with the back of her free hand. It felt silly to be crying now when she, very much alive, was holding on to a ghost. Her other arm squeezed a little tighter.

"It's not alright," Cali breathed. She pulled away from Sella's warmth and looked at her with pained eyes. "I'm dead."

"I know," Sella whispered. There was nothing else to say.

It was a cruel, horrible, tragic fact. Cali was dead, and nothing, no power she possessed, could change that.

Cali went on through her shimmering tears, "I'm dead and my death was meaningless and my life was meaningless and now… Now everyone around me is getting hurt. People I care about are getting hurt." Her voice was shaking as she forced the words from her throat. "I can't even help you right now. And you've risked everything for me."

"I'd do it again," Sella said firmly. She pulled Cali in again until their foreheads nearly touched. "We're going to find a way out of this, okay? We risked all of this because we care about you, Cali."

"It's all meaningless…" Cali's tone was spent. Defeated.

Sella knew that almost nothing she could say would pull her from the dark she found herself in. She tried anyway. "Your life was not meaningless." Sella met her gaze. She smiled, though it hurt her heart to do so. "After all, you were an excellent bookkeeper."

Cali choked out a laugh through her tears. "What? I was an excellent bookkeeper?"

"Oh, thank the tides." Sella breathed a heavy sigh of relief. "I didn't think that would work."

Cali's smile lingered, but another tear fell down her cheek.

Sella leaned in. "Really, Cali. You were only here a short time, but you made a lasting impression on so many. Hazen, Cirian, Ovina, Isra…"

Cali raised a brow. She pushed the tear from her cheek. "The milk delivery lady?" She laughed.

"She's a farmer, technically. The milk delivery is only one aspect of her work. Like how you are so much more than a ghost now, or a bookkeeper, or a traveler then." Sella let out a warm chuckle. "Everyone who knew you adored you. Your life was not meaningless. I'm sorry I only got to know you after it ended. I've been in my own head the year I've been back. I should have noticed you right away."

"You're just being nice."

"No, really, Cali. You have a spark that no one else has and it's evident to anyone who talks about you. I was too busy feeling sorry for myself. I lost out."

Cali laughed again but held a hand over her mouth. "I'm sorry, I shouldn't laugh at that," she whispered. "I would've liked to have known you, too. Not like this – dead… or with so much drama. I was just a number enthusiast; I didn't do much in life. But it would've been nice to see more… and share a cup of coffee with you."

"You crossed the ocean." Beejee trotted over to them at last. "That's better than we ever did. And Koukie won't shut up about how you saved her life."

Sella gave his head a small scratch. "See? And I'm sure there's so much we have left to learn about you. Adventures you've been on, people's lives you changed–"

"Your death might have been meaningless, though," Beejee cut in bluntly.

Sella flicked his nose with her finger.

"I'm not going to lie to her," he hissed.

Cali shrugged and smiled. "I think that means you're warming up to me."

Sella gave her one last squeeze, and she felt Cali's form begin to shift into shadow again. "Listen, I can get my own dish towel, alright? You got me out of the hotel when I couldn't do it alone. That must've taken a lot out of you. Why don't you rest for now?"

"Only if you promise to keep making those delicious-smelling cookies. I can't eat them, but… it smells like home."

Sella nodded, her expression was easy at last. "I'm glad my angry baking is soothing."

Cali closed her eyes. Her form began to fade. "Very," her disembodied voice whispered.

THE COOKIES – infused with nothing, because Sella had worried if she tried, it would only be exhaustion and anger – were cooling on the counter. The room was warm from the fire glowing in the hearth and the flame-fueled oven that had been running throughout the night. Koukie and Beejee were curled up in their respective areas by the fire. They still kept their distance, but both slept soundly – a giveaway that they formed, if not friendship, at least an understanding.

Sella felt an odd twinge of gratitude in her chest. Even if everything was falling apart, some things were still growing.

She sank into her seat at the desk by the window. Her blurry reflection gazed back in the glass and water ran down her image like tears. Her mind drifted to the bees. Lohrna was usually the responsible one who would go out and make sure they were safe in rough weather. She wondered if Seaglass was looking out for them.

Her heart ached dully in her chest. She hoped her friend was able to sleep in the cell all alone in an unfamiliar bed, in a terrifying situation. The full moon was coming soon. Sella needed to do something to free her before then.

"Then prove it." Benka's words echoed in her ears. Was it a challenge, a threat, or something else altogether? She tried to remember his tone, but all she could recall was the utter quiet of his voice. As if he didn't want anyone else to hear…

Sella shook her head. She rubbed her eyes with the palms of her hands. She needed to find something, anything, to bring to Benka by morning. But they were already set up once. Whoever did this, they were both desperate and more calculated than she gave them credit for. It was a dangerous combination. She had no idea where to begin.

"Make some coffee," Cali's voice whispered gently. She appeared beside Sella with a calm smile.

"That was bossy." Sella leaned back in her chair, she let her head hang over the backing.

Cali laughed. "Come on. We're in for a long night, but I have an idea."

"Tell me your idea, then I'll make the coffee." Sella's voice was monotone. She closed her eyes, knowing coffee would be necessary. The walls were closing in too tightly to sleep, but she wanted to play along being stubborn while she could. It felt good, in such a strange and petty way, to have a moment where she could just be snarky for once.

Cali took it in stride. "At the start of all this, you were on Benka's list because of your potions right? You sell some ingredients needed for Cresablatt?"

"Yes, some of the ingredients, but not all." Sella opened her eyes halfway. She stared at the ceiling until Cali leaned down to block her view. Sella went on. "Some of them are common ingredients sold in many potion shops."

"Common in shops, but uncommon in nature?"

"That would be fair to say."

"And what about Garawock?"

"Same, but less complicated set of ingredients."

"Do you see where I'm going with this?"

Sella shook her head. "On second thought, I think I need coffee for my brain to fire rapidly."

"That's why I said to make some!" Cali's voice was jovial, but Sella sensed a hint of frustration.

She sat up, focused her eyes and attention on Cali. "I'm listening."

"Sella, we can go over your books. Write me a list of the ingredients you sell for each poison. I'll cross-check all your sales. See who bought overlapping goods. That'll be compelling enough to at least get Benka's attention. Right?"

Sella's posture straightened. She looked at the floor, then the kitchen, and rose, chair scraping against the old wood floor. "I'm going to make some coffee." Hurrying to the cabinets, she added, "Something extra strong."

"Can't wait to smell it," Cali said, taking Sella's place at the desk. "Alright, bring me your unorganized box of paperwork."

THIRTY-ONE

Like Bees to Flowers

It was dawn when Benka's office and the town's four cells opened. Sella, Cali, and Beejee were already at the door when they heard the faint click of the lock. Sella didn't waste a moment before she threw open the door, nearly hitting Benka's assistant square in the face. He dodged the heavy wooden door with ease, but his expression was furious.

"Do you have an appointment?" he spat. "We've only just opened."

"Is Benka here?" Sella stepped past him and through the threshold. She waved a set of papers clutched in her hand at him. "We need to speak with him immediately."

Cali and Beejee ducked in behind her as the assistant closed the door.

Beejee hissed at him as he passed.

Cali gasped. "Bees go to flowers, you two!"

Sella turned to her with a raised brow. She didn't know the expression but couldn't argue with the logic. Better to be sweet and invite kindness in return. She sighed, lowered her angry waving hands, and took a big step away from the man. She counted silently to three before she spoke again. "Jahra, is Benka in? It really is urgent."

Jahra met her gaze. "Yes, he's in." He stepped through the hall and motioned for her to join.

They followed him. At her heels, Beejee looked up at her and grimaced.

"I know," she whispered.

Benka was sitting behind his desk with his hands folded over his mouth. He looked half asleep still, as if the only thing holding his head up was what little strength he had left in his arms. He glanced slowly at Sella, then his eyes shifted to Beejee, who was already making himself comfortable on the corner of his desk. "Welcome in," he said to the familiar. He looked back to Sella and waited.

"Benka." Sella slammed the papers on his desk, wasting no time. "We have credible suspects and a paper trail to prove it. What happened last night, that was a setup–"

"I know," Benka cut her off. His voice was slow but powerful. It hit Sella like a tidal wave.

She stood there, mouth still open to finish her sentence but no words came out.

"Wait, what?" Beejee spoke for her.

Benka lowered his hands. He grinned at Beejee, then his eyes found Sella. With a small groan, he rose from his seat. "Lohrna, and Rorin, in case you were curious, are in their cells. But the doors are unlocked."

Sella leaned back a little. She squinted her eyes at him suspiciously.

Beside her, Cali leaned in. "I don't understand…"

"Me either," Sella said aloud.

Benka looked at her with equally narrowed eyes, though his wry smile lingered on his lips. "Cali?" he asked as he stuffed his hands in his pockets.

Sella stepped back, and Beejee asked, "Can you see her?"

Benka shook his head. "I cannot." He came around the other side of the desk. "But you're not always subtle, kitchen witch." He looked at Sella carefully, "Why didn't you tell me from the start?"

Sella took another step back, she searched his eyes for any hint, but he gave her nothing. She decided to go with the truth. "I didn't think you'd believe me. Or that anyone would…" Sella paused. She tried to collect her thoughts, but they were racing. "And if they did," she continued, speaking before she could process her own words, "I thought I'd be branded dangerous… I mean, how could you, or anyone, trust what I was saying she told me was truthful? I'm sure people would think I either made it up or… or worse – that I was using her to some sort of advantage."

Benka nodded. "This town, and many like it, can be hard for people who are different, even if they're the ones who help. I'm sure things have been especially hard for you since moving back. No one can seem to get over The Incident…"

Sella hung her head.

Benka changed the subject, seemingly unfazed by the revelation that a ghost was in the room with them. "I'm sure you want to see Lohrna. Come with me, then we'll go over what you found and compare notes."

"Are you alright?" Cali asked Sella as they moved through the hallway again.

Sella didn't answer. She wasn't sure how to. The unbearable crushing feeling that had been consuming her felt like it was loosening its grip. It was as though she had been holding her breath underwater for so long, drowning deeper into the dark with heavy weights fixed to her ankles. But now, now they finally released their hold. She could see the surface. She could almost take a breath... Almost.

They turned into a large room containing four little cots behind four individual cells with thick iron bars.

"Sella!" Lohrna waved from behind one of the cells. "Hi! I hope you weren't too worried about me."

Sella felt like she could collapse. She grabbed at one of the bars to hold herself up. "Lohrna, what in all the ocean? Of course I've been worried about you! I haven't slept at all! I just—"

"Oh, I'm sorry." Her friend opened the door with a loud creak of the metal. She threw her arms around her and sighed into the witch's shoulder. "Benka explained everything when we got here, but it really was dramatic, wasn't it?"

"What is happening?" Sella pushed Lohrna gently off her.

In the other cell, Rorin looked like he was still trying to sleep. He flung an arm over his face dramatically.

"Benka realized we had been set up," Lohrna said quickly. "He went along with it to keep me safe. Buy us some time."

Sella let out a heavy breath. As she inhaled, she smiled at Lohrna. "That feels impossible. But I'm glad you're safe."

Beejee swiped at Lohrna's skirt. "This is outrageous. I am furious with all of you!"

"You were sleeping soundly." Sella laughed. She pushed back tears that formed at the corners of her eyes. She couldn't even tell why she was crying. It was just all too much. "Okay, okay…" She straightened her back and held her head high. "For your protection or not, your name is polluted and we need to purify it. I found something that I think can help us."

"Correction: *I* found it." Cali's tone was chipper as always.

Sella could always count on Cali and Lohrna to lighten a mood.

"Show me what you found." Benka gestured for them to follow back to his office. "I have a few theories of my own forming."

BENKA'S OFFICE felt small with all of them in one room. Cali folded herself up in the corner, making way for everyone to file in.

"Alright." Sella displayed receipts across Benka's desk. She was careful to avoid Cali's corner to not make her squeeze herself any smaller. "We looked for sales that have both ingredients with the poison used on Calisyali and Hazen. Now, these are commonly purchased, but it would be rare to purchase ingredients for both, especially in the relatively short time frame."

"Names?" Benka cut to the point. He shifted the papers across the desk carefully.

"Ovina, Arda, and Isra," Sella said.

Benka's eyes were still fixed on the papers on the desk. He echoed her names, "Ovina, Arda, and Isra. The fisher, the weaver, the farmer…"

Sella waited. It sounded like the start of a fable. Like there was a lesson to learn but she couldn't grasp it.

"The only name that is the same on my list," Benka said, "is Isra."

The room was still. For a moment, no one moved. No one spoke. They let the name hang in the air. Sella was uncertain about any of the names on her list. She knew them all, to some degree or another, and she couldn't imagine any of them committing something so horrible. She didn't think *any* of them was truly capable of murder. But Isra? Isra was skittish, gentle.

Beejee was the first to speak. "Isra? The little farmer girl?"

Cali's hands were clasped over her mouth. "Why is she on Benka's list?" she whispered through her fingers. She leaned in, looking at the papers that she found herself like she didn't believe it at all. Sella felt her heart sink again. "We're friends…"

"Why is Isra on your list?" Sella asked for Cali.

Benka lifted several of Sella's receipts with Isra's name on them. He studied them closely, flipping the papers carefully. "I know it feels like I've been focused on you, Lohrna," he said, still reading, "but I've interviewed most of the town. Especially anyone who ever came in contact with Cali. Isra saw her nearly every day. Her alibi for the night of the murder is so riddled with holes that there is no way it would float. Her farm would be capable of many of the missing ingredients she couldn't buy from you. All I'm missing is a motive."

"Yeah," Cali said. "Me too…"

THIRTY-TWO

Beejee's Spell

LOHRNA HAD, very reluctantly, agreed to stay behind. Isra had proven herself to be desperate enough to hurt anyone close to catching her, and there was no telling what she would truly be capable of if she was pushed to the breaking point.

"But you're going?" Lohrna held Sella's hands in her own. She looked at her with pleading eyes. Though if it was concern for Sella or fear of missing out on the action, Sella couldn't tell.

"Benka may need backup." Sella glanced at the detective who stood at the end of the hallway. His hands were in his pockets and he looked lost in a daydream. Only she could see Cali at his side, looking equally lost. Sella's brows knit. She needed to talk to Cali, and soon.

"He clearly needs it," Beejee added quietly.

Lohrna's eyes followed Sella's and landed on the detective. Her face softened. "Yeah, maybe so," she conceded. She shook Sella's hands and pulled her gaze. This time, her expression was stern. She squeezed Sella firmly and whispered, "Don't use your fire on Isra."

"What?" Sella reeled back as though Lohrna just struck her. "But she hurt Cali. She hurt Hazen—"

"We don't know that for sure yet." Lohrna's grasp on Sella only tightened.

"I can handle it, Lohr." Sella pulled back, slipping from her grasp.

"Listen, I know you're worried about Cali. I am too. But, please, you have to stay in control. Once the fire leaves your hands, you don't know what it will do. *Please* don't use your fire on her."

Beejee hissed at Sella's side. But the witch looked only back at Cali, head heavy. She nodded, but she was busy studying the ghost. The way she stood on uneasy feet. Her confused expression on her face. She wanted to protect her. But she didn't want to hurt anyone either. Finally, she whispered back, "I won't."

"Promise me."

"I promise." Sella lied. She couldn't make that promise, even if she understood why Lohrna had asked.

Sella caught Lohrna pacing worriedly as they shut the door. She wished she could brew her a cup before they left, something with calm and ease and hope. But Benka was insistent, they could not wait for Isra to become more agitated, or to catch on that there was anyone else on her tail. Sella knew he was right, but she was still getting used to the detective being on their side and she couldn't get the taste of distrust off her tongue. She glanced at him with narrowed eyes as they exited the building. Beside her, Beejee and Cali followed.

"We'll try her home first," Benka said, walking so slowly Sella was sure the whole town would know before they crossed the street. "It's outside the town, in the woods."

Sella sighed impatiently. She had to slow her pace for him. He was casually strolling, as though they were going for a leisurely walk on the beach, not chasing a dangerous murderer. She bit her lip, counted her steps... No matter what she did, she was still a few steps ahead, she couldn't help it.

"Benka." She stopped him when they reached the opposite side of the cobblestone street. "Listen, why don't you stay with Lohrna? She's vulnerable, and I don't know if your assistant can do much to help her. If Isra's not home... What if she figured us out, and she's on her way here?"

Benka paused, he looked up at the cloudy sky and put his hands in his pockets.

Sella held back another sigh rising in her chest. She needed to play it calm, but she was desperate to talk to Cali alone. To make sure she was okay. She waited while Benka thought.

"That could be very dangerous for you," Benka said. "We don't know what Isra is capable of."

"All the more reason to stay here." Sella gestured to Benka's building. "Lohrna can't defend herself. I can. I have my magic."

"I thought you were a kitchen witch?" Benka raised a brow at her.

"You know she has enough firepower to stop a mountain troll," Beejee suddenly interjected, backing her up. "And I can cast spells too, if it comes down to it."

Sella looked at him with a small half-grin. She wouldn't

tell Benka that her familiar's spell-casting was rudimentary at best, that any magic Beejee possessed was channeled through her. Or that she had promised Lohrna to not use her fire.

The detective looked at the familiar with a deep stare neither could register. They waited.

"Alright." Benka removed a folded piece of paper from his pocket. "If she's home, give this to her. But don't engage other than that. Leave immediately."

"What's this?" Sella took the paper.

"Summons. To arrive back here without fuss," Benka said simply.

Sella almost laughed. How was she supposed to hand Isra a summons and not engage? She'd have to escort her by the threat of fire, she was sure of it. Still, she stuffed the paper in her cloak. "Look after Lohrna."

"Be careful," Benka countered. "Use your fire, if you must."

Sella felt a stab in her chest. Use her fire. She knew she would if she needed to. But she hated that Lohrna made her promise. Moreover, she hated that her friend was right. Her fire, especially when she was under heightened stress, was too volatile. Too dangerous. She burned her own mother once, badly. Witches healed quickly, but not that time. The scar remained for years.

And though Lohrna never confronted her about it, Sella knew that Lohrna knew… that was the real reason she left. If she did *that* to her own mother, who could say what she would do to a killer?

Benka's eyes scanned Sella's face, but he said nothing. He turned on his heel and Sella watched him silently cross the street. As soon as the door shut, she dashed between two smaller buildings with Beejee and Cali swiftly behind.

"What's with the sprint?" Beejee hissed.

Sella spun on her heel, grabbing Cali's hands as she did. "Are you alright?" she asked, tilting her head low so she could read Cali's green eyes.

Cali was still, eyes wide with shock. "I'm dead." Her image shimmered slightly.

"Are you alright, knowing who is responsible?" Sella prompted, shaking the ghost's hands in her own. Only now did she notice they were solid. She looked down at them and let go before they slipped through her fingers.

Cali stared at her empty hands. She shook her head. "I thought Isra and I were friends," she whispered. "I just don't understand why."

"We'll find out. Together."

Cali's brow furrowed. Her eyes were still avoiding Sella's gaze. "Do you think when she's brought to justice, I'll... move on?"

Sella's stomach sank. She turned away. Beejee looked up at her with sad eyes. "Maybe. If you're at peace. That's why we'll find the answers for you."

"Okay." Cali nodded. But Sella had no idea what that meant. If she was anticipating moving on, or sad, or frightened. Or even just... okay.

Sella gestured for Cali to follow. "Let's go. I know where Isra lives."

THE WOODS WERE QUIET. Light rain began to fall. The gentle tapping on the leaves above sounded like a song to

Sella. Like it was luring them closer toward danger. A siren's song.

She turned back to look at Cali.

The ghost glanced up at her as if she felt Sella's eyes on her. "I like the rain," she said quietly.

Sella and Beejee stopped. They waited for her to go on.

"I don't think I want to leave," Cali's smile grew, almost mischievously. "Now that we're so close to the end… I don't think I actually want an ending. I like the sound of the rain too much."

"Maybe there's rain in the afterlife?" Beejee suggested.

Cali looked at him and laughed. "I like *this* rain. Living rain. I like watching you two navigate through it."

Sella felt a flush cross her cheeks, warming her despite the chill of the air around them. "We'll figure this out. Whatever you decide, we'll figure it out."

"Not much further to go," Beejee cut in. "Come on, ghost girl."

Cali giggled. "Thanks for keeping me on track, little buddy."

Beejee bristled at the term of endearment. But he led the way through the trees with his tail held high.

ISRA'S HOME WAS A FARMSTEAD: An expansive, whitewood house surrounded by tall grass that bent gently in the light rain and a quiet breeze that blew through the surrounding tree branches. It was peaceful, almost comforting, after the long walk… an island after being at sea for too long.

Sella had been here before with her mother, long ago.

She didn't remember why they came, only the feeling of seeing such a big house and meeting such a kind family inside.

Most of Isra's family was gone now, Sella knew. And the house didn't look like salvation anymore. It looked like rot. Sella felt a twinge of pain for the girl deep in her stomach. It must be hard to keep this place running all alone. Isra – at least, the one Sella knew – was sweet and hardworking. She dreamed of living a bigger life.

A part of Sella desperately wanted Isra to explain herself, to prove her and Benka wrong. She didn't want to believe any of it.

The three of them stood at the edge of the woods, watching the house. For a long while, no one said anything.

It was finally Beejee who spoke up. "What's the plan? We're clearly not just hand-delivering a summons."

"No," Sella said. "We're here for answers."

"You want answers, kitchen witch?" the voice boomed like thunder overhead.

The three flinched. Beejee's hair stood on end. He hunched his back, making himself appear larger. Sella set a fire in her hand, and Cali crouched low, looking up at the sky, eyes searching for the voice.

"Isra!" Sella shouted back. The fire in her palm grew. Any trepidation she had before burned away, all that was left was anger. She set her other hand out in front of Cali protectively as her eyes darted from the farmhouse to the tree line. "Come here and look me in the eyes!"

The front door of the house opened slowly. Isra, small frame, little spiral horns, and a wicked smile, stepped through the threshold. She held a knotted wooden stick in her hand.

Sella's eyes were drawn to it. Her fingers twitched. The fire grew. Her mother's wand?

Isra's hand tightened around the wand. Her gaze followed down to her hand.

"She's a witch!" Beejee hissed. His back arched further and his claws extended.

"I am," Isra said. She took a few steps closer to them, her legs swallowed up by swaying grass. "The first witch born into my bloodline that anyone can remember…"

Sella's flame held steady in her hand. "I didn't know."

"Of course not. You left us all here to waste away. And when you came back, you were too self-centered to notice anything but yourself."

Sella took a step toward her, but Cali grabbed at her arm. "Don't," she pleaded.

But Sella took another step, her arm slipped from Cali's grasp. "Is that why you were trying to frame me and Lohrna? Because I left?"

"Again, being so egocentric. Though I have to admit, I did resent you for a long time after your mother passed. I had no one to guide me in my magic; I was completely alone…" Isra shook her head, "No, Lohrna was just convenient. The eccentric stone collector, friends with a kitchen witch. People don't even trust you. Not since–"

"The stupid ocean itself be damned 'Incident!'" Sella's fire burst into a bright light in her hand before settling back into a controllable flame. She nearly laughed at the ridiculousness of it. "That is so stupid!"

"Listen," Isra said, her usual light voice returned. "I didn't want to do this; I had no choice."

"Why would you hurt Cali?" Sella asked. Her voice trembled as she spoke, but she knew she needed to ask. "Why would you kill an innocent person?"

"No one is innocent." Isra lifted the wand, examined it carefully as if it were her instrument of judgment: A scale by which she measured who was worthy of life and who was not. Isra's eyes flicked back to Sella, a deadly expression on her face. "You sold me the ingredients to make the poison."

"Not knowingly," Sella shot back.

"Cali wasn't innocent either." Isra's lips turned down in a scowl. "I learned enough about her and that fool's past with witches… I saw her mark. And you were too blind to notice! She was a stranger here and she was going to bring ruin with her. I had to do what I felt was safest for this town. You certainly weren't."

Sella stopped. The heat in her body grew, the flames in her hands with it. Everything felt hot, dry, oppressive. "You didn't need to do that. Cali is a good person."

"It doesn't matter to you that she had a witch's mark, does it? That means she is a danger to us." Isra held the wand up, pointing it directly at Cali. "I need to correct my mistake. I should have banished her the moment I saw her ghost hanging around you." Isra began to recite a spell, whispered beneath her breath. She drew a sigil in the air. But the symbol and the spell were both unfamiliar to Sella. This was no banishing spell she ever used.

She had no idea where Isra learned this magic. But she didn't have time to think.

Behind her, Cali's scream tore her attention from Isra.

She turned to see the ghost. Wind ripped around her like she was caught in a hurricane. She lifted from the ground, her limbs contorted. Her image flickered and Cali's cries grew louder. Her form began to fade.

At her side, Beejee stood on two legs. Over the wind and the screams, Sella heard his counterspell, trying to ground Cali to the earth. He was buying her time.

Sella turned back to Isra, the fire grew in her hands. Any fear she felt about hurting her, of burning her, was gone. "Let! Her! Go!"

"She doesn't belong here, Sella!" Isra shouted. Her hand was still in the air, letting the magic flow through the wand. "And neither do you! I'm stronger than you!" She turned the wand to Sella and a gash split across Sella's face.

Sella stumbled back. A slicing pain cut across her cheek and the heat of the blood ran down her neck, hotter than the fire in her hand. The pure violence of the action paralyzed her, but only for a moment. Sella held one hand to cheek and with the other, she sent a massive flame hurling toward Isra.

Isra ducked and the hold on Cali broke.

Sella looked back to see Cali collapsed on the ground, nearly transparent. Beejee continued his counterspell at her side.

Sella desperately needed to break her wand... and fast. But getting close enough would be hard. She shot another fireball at Isra while she thought of something to do. "Are you alright, Cali?" she asked, positioning herself between the ghost and the other witch.

Cali's voice was weak; she only gasped in response.

"She's trying to hold on to this world," Beejee said swiftly. "I'm not sure how much longer I can help."

"You're doing great." Sella breathed hard, her hand still clutching her face as blood pooled through the cracks in her fingers. She turned back to Isra. The other witch was advancing on her.

"You're a witch, Sella," Isra called to her. "You cannot allow a ghost to linger here!"

Sella let go of her cheek. The wound had stopped bleeding – it was healing slowly. "I'm a *kitchen* witch!" Fire shot from each finger past Isra, lighting her home behind her aflame.

Isra turned to the house with a gasp, her wand held loosely at her side.

"Beejee!" Sella pointed to Isra and he took off through the grass.

Isra turned back in time only for Beejee to leap out from the tall sea of green with her wand in his jaws. The familiar sprinted back to Sella's side.

"No!" Isra cried. She ran toward them, hand outstretched.

Sella took the wand from Beejee's mouth. She looked back at Isra and snapped it, igniting the broken pieces like kindling.

Isra stopped, her hand still stuck outright. She sank to her knees, her small body nearly swallowed up by the swaying grass. Behind her, her house burned. "That… was your mother's wand…"

"I know," Sella said. She tossed the burning pieces aside to die in the wet grass. "But I won't let you or anyone else use it to hurt people ever again." She turned back to Cali, still crouched on the ground. She wasn't sure if ghosts could linger in pain, but from her own banishing spells, she knew it was never pleasant. Whatever Isra used seemed to be compoundly powerful and all the more painful. She bent down and smiled gently. "Can you stand?" she asked.

Cali looked up at her, color beginning to return to her face as she did. "I think so," she said. "But I don't think I'll be doing any haunting for a while." Her eyes focused and she drew in a quick breath. "Sella! You're hurt!"

Sella touched her cheek; it was still wet and raw. "I'll be fine," she promised. "Witches are fast healers." She pulled Cali up, her form still mostly smoke in her hands. "Let's get you home."

"But first, we have to take care of this one," Beejee hissed at Isra.

"Right." Sella rose to her full stature. She fished the summons from her pocket and held it up for Isra to see. "We have an official summons for you to come with us. So, you know, you *legally* have to."

"Compelling," Beejee said under his breath.

THIRTY-THREE

Not Bad for a Kitchen Witch

"So, being a kitchen witch pays off, then?" Lohrna said, nudging Sella's shoulder.

"No need for wands when the magic is simple," Sella agreed. "Isra will be powerless without my mother's wand. She's no threat now."

"Except for her extensive knowledge of deadly poisons?"

"Right, except for that. But it'll be hard to brew behind bars." Sella laughed. She took a long sip of coffee infused with strength.

The potions shop was calm. Rain was falling loudly outside, but the hum of faint music playing made it feel comforting and safe, as if all the rain was washing away everything terrible that had happened. The small fires overhead lit the space with a warm glow, and the potions on the walls reflected back the fire's red and gold like tiny, glittering mirrors. Sella set her chin in her hand and sighed.

"Cali's resting, then?" Lohrna asked.

Sella nodded. It would probably take time for her to recover. She couldn't say how long. She'd never heard of a banishing spell being interrupted. But, if Cali wanted to stay, Sella knew not even a powerful spell would stop her.

"Your cheek looks better." Lohrna poked Sella's face gently.

Sella winced, she pulled back, laughing. "Yeah, it's still tender, though."

The bell above the door chimed and the two turned to the door from their stools to see Benka shuffle in. "My apologies for not checking in sooner," he said wearily. "The processing paperwork is time-consuming… and I am very tired."

"It's been a long day," Lohrna said. "Coffee?"

"No, thank you." Benka took a few steps into the shop. "I find coffee doesn't quite help what ails me…" He paused, his hands in his pockets, shoulders slumped. "We haven't had this much excitement in our little town in a very, very long time. I still need to tell the ships and hotel guests they're free to go. Much to do."

Sella waited for him to go on. He seemed to be building up to something, but to what, she wasn't quite sure.

"I'm sorry for how things happened today," he said at last. "But it seems like you were able to handle it."

"Not bad for a kitchen witch, huh?" Lohrna grasped Sella's shoulder and gave it a little shake.

"Not bad for a kitchen witch," Benka repeated. He moved the tip of his shoe in a small circle. "All this has shown me… It's my time to retire. I'm not as sharp as I used to be. I'm getting older. I'm tired. And it's so much paper-work." He ended with a chuckle.

Sella blinked. She looked at Benka now with fresh eyes, unclouded by all her previous ideas about who he was and what he was thinking. She looked at him plainly. He was getting old. He always looked tired. But he was sharper than he appeared, and kinder. She wished she had seen that part sooner. "Any idea who will take your place?" Sella asked.

Benka paused. He took his hands from his pockets and handed a folded paper to Sella. "I thought maybe you all would," he said. "It's a letter of recommendation to the council to consult in the detective work going forward, should Marra ever need it. You did well. I thought maybe you could use those skills again."

"Us?" Sella asked, reading the paper with wide eyes.

"I'm in!" Lohrna's excited voice pierced her ears. She was eagerly reading over Sella's shoulder.

"Benka, you can't be serious?" Sella eyed him over the paper. "What about Jahra?"

"Jahra's young. And he likes the paperwork, not the fieldwork," he said slowly. "Hopefully, you'll go another few decades before you even need the credentials. And in case anything does happen, let him handle the paperwork. Just think it over. Consulting can open up a lot of doors for you two. For now, it's time for a well-deserved nap." He turned and left the shop with a ring of the bell.

"Let me guess," Lohrna laughed, "you'll need to sleep on this decision too."

Sella felt a half-smile form. "You know me well," she said.

THIRTY-FOUR

Learn to Swim

"YOU NEVER DID OPEN the rose spell, did you?"

Sella sat across the table from Seaglass. This time, her own mug of steaming tea warmed her hands gently as she comfortably inhaled the calming, earthy aroma. Seaglass still didn't have the recipe quite right, but this was close. It was home, just slightly shattered.

The stained glass reflections were paled, illuminated by the full moon outside. She could hear the waves crashing along the small cliffside from the open window in the kitchen. The fireplace was glowing with warm light, but it cast dark shadows across the room. The features of the Niminé's face looked all the harsher as the darkness and fire-light danced across their features. It just reminded Sella of how opposite it would be to sit across from her mother.

Sella stifled the feeling of guilt at the scene: the wrong-ness of it with the calm she felt. She considered the question she had just been asked; it felt like a riddle. "Not yet," she admitted.

Seaglass tsked and took a long sip of their own tea.

"Your mother always described you as a curious child," the Niminé said at last. "Has this version of you neglected that spark?"

Sella nodded. It stung, but she knew the creature was right. This version of herself, the one sitting there right now, was finally feeling curious again. But it was far too late. "I'll have to find a way to open it myself, won't I? Will I like the spell that's written there?" she asked, knowing as the words left her mouth that Seaglass would not answer in a way she wanted.

The Niminé simply sipped their tea.

"I'm afraid of what I'll find," Sella said quietly. "If it'll help me or hurt me."

A faraway howl outside drew Sella's gaze to the stained glass window. Lohrna. Comfort and guilt filled Sella's heart at once. She made room for both.

Sella turned back to Seaglass. She sighed, then breathed in a deep lungful of steam. Her mind was flooded with questions, but she knew where to start: "Why would my mother give her wand to Isra?"

Seaglass met her gaze with their unblinking silver eyes.

"And why not tell me?" Sella continued. "She could have written… At least let me know that was her plan. That there was another witch here."

"Tria had her reasons," Seaglass said. "But you already know why she didn't tell you, don't you? I do not need to reiterate the past."

"She didn't trust me."

"Trust is not the core of the thing. You know this. Why did she give it away at all...?" The creature trailed off.

Sella waited.

Seaglass went on at last, "The little witch was all alone. After her grandmother's passing, the family blamed Isra's magic. They left her here with shame in their hearts. I suppose she felt she had to hide herself after that. Your mother often spoke about her sadness, the prejudices here failing the girl."

Sella's heart began to beat faster.

"Stillness, Sella," Seaglass warned gently. They raised their mug to signal Sella to drink.

She did and let the warmth of the tea fill her core. She looked at the stained glass window and sighed.

Seaglass went on, "Tria gave her wand to the little one because she thought it was the right thing to do. And that is all any of us can do: What we think is right."

"No matter the damage done." Sella knew this well. Her whole childhood had been spent trying to do the right thing. And yet, a trail of damage followed. And yet, her life was still so full of love and warmth. She just needed to open her eyes to see it.

"We beings who harness magic… This world can feel unsafe for us. Until we know what we are capable of. The little witch was just like any other fearful, powerful thing."

Sella looked away. She knew.

"If Tria had survived her illness," Seaglass said, "I think this would have played out very differently. But then again, you wouldn't have come back home at all, would you?"

Sella shook her head as she stared into her own reflection in the dark liquid. "No, I wouldn't have."

"Playful how fate finds a way to weave the tapestry of timelines together. It is not always our job to question it, no matter how curious we may be. Perhaps, at least this time, accept that you have found yourself here. The current carried you far out to sea. Now you must try to swim, but the direction is up to you," Seaglass said. "I believe you're meant to be where you are, this version of Sella. The seas are calm for now. But, then again, they always are after the storm."

"Swim..." Sella repeated quietly. She wasn't quite sure what Seaglass meant. But she was sure she would in time.

THIRTY-FIVE

Haunting Bees

"BENKA WANTS you to take over his position?"

Cali and Sella sat on the couch in the apartment, watching the fire slowly fade. It was quiet, the smell of freshly baked bread lingered in the air, and Koukie and Beejee were curled up beside each other at the foot of the bed.

"Yes. Kind of. He wants Jahra to head it. We'd be credentialed consultants. But I'm not sure how I feel about it." Sella wanted to say more, but she wasn't sure how. How to explain that this was the most terrifying experience of her life. In all her adventures, and all her wild experiences, nothing came close to the fear of losing those she loved. And yet, it was the most exciting, thrilling thing she had ever done.

Cali cocked her head, watching Sella's racing mind. But her eyes drifted up to the small floating fires overhead and she continued as if she hadn't noticed. "I think it's a good idea. Besides, you have no idea who would take his place if all Jahra's doing is behind the scenes. The new guy could be a real dragon."

"Really could, though." Sella tucked her legs under her and smiled gently. "I don't know, it would give me some sorely needed name-clearing around here."

"I can be *your* ghost consultant. Consultant to the consultant?" Cali smiled back. She leaned a little closer to Sella with one raised brow. "If there's any other mysterious deaths, that is. You can pay me in beekeeping lessons."

"You want to learn to keep bees?"

"Always have," Cali said simply. "I figure I can do it in death, right? If I hone my haunting skills."

"Who knows? Haunting bees could be fun…" Sella trailed off, her gaze focused on the fire in front of them. She wasn't sure she wanted the answer to the big question that had been lingering in her mind since their confrontation with Isra, but she knew she needed to ask. Before she could stop herself, she blurted out, "Does this mean you want to stay? I mean, there are ways I can help you cross over. Gently– not a banishing spell. I'm sure it was awful to have that choice almost taken from you, but… now you get to decide."

A long pause followed, but Sella's eyes remained fixed on the dancing embers: Red, gold, and orange, flickering quietly. Clinging to the wood beneath them.

"I want to stay," Cali said at last. "I like haunting you. I think I'm getting good at it."

Sella felt herself laugh as relief flooded over her. She felt a sting of tears in her eyes. She wiped them away before they fell.

"And I think I could do a lot of good helping out with

Practical Potions Detective Agency," Cali added. "I'm an excellent bookkeeper."

"And we're sure that's the name we're sticking with?" Sella asked.

"I like it. I think Lohrna's a genius marketer." Cali giggled. "But… does this mean you're in?"

The last of the fire began to fade. "Yes, I think I am," Sella said.

THERE WERE two signs hung up in the bay window. The first, Beejee insisted they do not take down, read "Certified Kitchen Witch: Inquire Within for Daily Offerings." While the town was slowly learning that Sella was, in fact, not an accessory to murder, he said it didn't hurt to remind them again that she was a *certified* kitchen witch.

The second, in larger print, read: "Practical Potions and Honey Shop is rebranding as Practical Potions Consultant Agency. Please come back soon."

The End...

For now.

Practical Potions will reopen for more
fantastical mysteries and cozy adventures
in Book Two.

Acknowledgments

I am so incredibly grateful that I have an abundance of people to thank for helping me make this dream a reality. First, I want to say thank you to my husband for always reminding me that things work out despite my excessive worrying. Without your support and off-the-wall ideas, I'd still be swinging wildly from researching excessively to rocking back and forth in a panic. Thank you to my strong, wild daughter. When I look at you, I am motivated to keep pushing so that one day you can stand on my shoulders and see further.

A huge shoutout to my beautiful group of friends, who have loved and supported me throughout this process. Thank you for pushing me, motivating me, and making sure I (at least try to) put myself in the spotlight. You are all such bright lights in my life and I am thankful every day that a series of small choices brought us together. A very special thanks to the one who took my hand and guided me through these woods. All I had to do was summon the courage to reach out into the dark, and you did the rest with a smile and enthusiasm. Facing my fear of being vulnerable and having things still turning out better than I could imagine is a lesson I will carry with me forever.

A million thanks to my big, beautiful family. You guys have been a foundation I could land on when my wild adventures went sideways. Thank you for letting me make "bad" decisions. I promise I needed to make them in order to become who I am today. Sure, I wouldn't have listened to your advice anyway, but it must have been terrifying to watch me run full force into walls over and over again. I got a lot of bloody noses, but that's the only way I learn. Thank you all for always asking if I'm still writing. Don't worry (or do) depending on your feelings about it. I am and will continue to for as long as I can.

A thank you (and I'm sorry) to Carly, my editor. You certainly had your work cut out for you, but you took it in stride. Thank you to my 100 ARC readers for putting up with my typos early on in the game. You all rock and are the reason indie authors survive.

About the Author

Wren Jones lives in the Sonoran Desert with her family and two cats. Like most writers, she has been a storyteller for a long time. After her daughter was born, true crime felt a little too true, and darker fiction felt a little too dark. She started reading cozy mysteries, and after a while, she figured a little dose of fantasy and bi-rep was what she was missing.

She figured what better time to research, write, and launch a novel that she'd been procrastinating on than while working full-time and raising a tiny human? So here we are.

ROSEMARY PALOMA POTION

ADD ICE TO SHAKER
ADD ONE OUNCE TEQUILA
ONE OUNCE GRAPEFRUIT JUICE
A HALF INCH OF LIME JUICE
&
A HALF OUNCE OF ROSEMARY SIMPLE
SYRUP

SHAKE WELL
STRAIN INTO GLASS
TOP WITH CLUB SODA

GARNISH WITH A SPRIG OF ROSEMARY

Recipe by: Sara T. Bond
SaraTBond.com

9 798989 041015